The Misogynist
A Novel

Steve Jackowski

Cover Art by Heidi K. Rojek

ISBN: 978-0-9899729--8-7 (print edition)
ISBN: 978-0-9899729--9-4 (ebook)

DEDICATION

To Richard Hatch

ACKNOWLEDGMENTS

I've dedicated this book to my good friend Richard Hatch. He bears no resemblance to the Richard Hatch character in this novel, aside from his wry wit, intelligence, and committed friendship. He's also read all of my books and for some reason seems to like every one (except he had some understandable reservations about The 15th Juror). I'd also like to thank my first readers – my wife, Karen Noël, and Jo Minola who provide insightful and honest critiques. Last and not least, I'd like to acknowledge Heidi K. Rojek of City Book Review for the cover work she's done on this book and on The 15th Juror.

Steve Jackowski

Other Novels by Steve Jackowski

PREFACE

The Whistleblower

I hate people.

People are the reason this world is such a mess. They're gullible. They believe what they're told. They'll follow charismatic leaders into self-destruction and destruction of others. Give them a political or religious cause and they can justify any action no matter how immoral, no matter how many others suffer from their actions. People lie. They cheat at almost any opportunity. They protect themselves at the expense of those around them.

Tell them a lie and bury it in half-truths or truths taken out of context and you can create true-believers. With the advent of the Internet and Social Media, people with crazy ideas have the means to convince others of their righteousness. Say something sensational, get a following, go viral. More and more will believe you. You can be famous. You can have influence. You can be rich.

And the rich. Don't get me started. I don't mean people who are well off. I mean the truly rich, people who have more money than they could spend in ten lifetimes. They have walled estates around the world, cars whose cost would feed a hundred families for ten years, clothes that cost more than many people's homes. And what do they do with this money? They protect it. They get richer. And they get richer at the expense of others. Their money and the power that comes with it allow them to buy politicians who can convince their constituencies to vote for things that are bad for them but that will benefit their wealthy partners.

The rich get richer and richer, the poor get poorer and poorer as they're promised that there's a way to have the American Dream. And the middle class, they don't even see it coming. They're so damned complacent that they work their jobs, come home and watch television, and repeat. They're getting poorer too and when they lose their homes to failed economies, they join the poor as the rich get richer.

I can't fault the poor. There is too much stacked against them. The few that succeed, never look back. Why would they want to return to desperation when they worked so hard to climb out? Those that don't get out fall into hopelessness, petty crime, drugs, and violence that get propagated to their next generations.

There was a time years ago when the poor had a chance. Stay in school, get an education, go to college, and succeed. Those days are long gone, but the rich keep selling them this ideal and after they give everything they've got and fail to succeed multiple times, despair sets in.

Desperate people do desperate things. They want to believe in some salvation, be it religion, drugs, revolution. Crowds become mobs and mobs destroy without thinking. For God's sake, if people can't even watch a soccer game without rioting and killing fellow spectators, what hope is there?

I went into high tech thinking I could make a difference. I honestly believed that information would set the world free. If even the most downtrodden had access to knowledge and experience from around the world, they could educate themselves. They could recognize that their situation was not normal. They could rise up and demand change. Information seemed like the great equalizer.

I invented technologies that made the Web real. Other technologies made it accessible in the most remote places on earth. Together, we should have made a difference. We patted ourselves on the back when the Berlin Wall fell. Many thought Reagan's arm race with the Soviets brought it down, but those of us in tech knew that without the information about the West that so many received through the Internet, it might never have happened. We enabled communication like it had never existed before. Radio Free Europe? Nice idea, but it didn't have the reach, allure, or the wealth of information we provided via the Web. And it certainly didn't allow anyone to connect to anyone else anywhere, any time.

Yes, we thought the World-Wide-Web meant World-Wide-Change. But commercialism trumped us. It's all about advertising and popularity now. Like it, retweet, vote, give a thumbs up. Hire a social media consultant and flood the web. Distract people with sensational products, games, or videos. Hide the substance. Or, if you're one of the big oppressors out there, capitalize on this propaganda machine that Hitler never dreamed could exist. Think what he did with propaganda. You ain't seen nothing yet.

We have the rich who feel entitled to get richer, we have the complacent middle class, and we have the poor who are lured into making choices against their own interests. We have mobs, extremists, suicide bombers, amoral leaders. We thought information would change all that.

We gave a gift to mankind and they perverted it. If it sounds like the story from the Garden of Eden. Maybe it is.

I'm tired of seeing our technologies perverted to make the rich richer at the expense of others.

Something needs to be done. No, I need to do something.

The Serial Killer

I hate women.

The 'fairer sex' isn't so fair once you get to know them. They're jealous of each other and if it helps them look better among their peers, they will stab other people in the back faster than any of the sleazy businessmen I've met. They use love and sex to lure men in to get what they want and then move on when they have it. Men are such suckers. We believe from an early age that we will find a kind, caring, loving, supportive woman, a life partner. Advertisements promise sex. Movies and novels promise true love. But women are calculating. The Serpent chose one of his own to destroy Paradise.

Like my wife. We married young. She was beautiful and intelligent with a goal of making a real difference in the world. After law school, she worked in legal aid, helping the poor and unprotected. I believed in her and what she did.

But then I got rich. Not just comfortable, not just well off, RICH.

My wife changed. She quit her practice and became a socialite. I never imagined this was possible. She always seemed so grounded. Suddenly, life became about being seen. People needed to know who we were and how wealthy we were. No, not in dollars, but in what we could afford to do or buy. She needed the biggest house with the best view, expensive clothes, and homes in exotic places. We had to throw regular parties for the elite of the San Francisco Bay Area.

I set up charities so that we could 'pay-back', and asked her to manage them, thinking that would bring back some of my 'make-the-world-a-better-place' wife, but these too became vehicles for her social climbing.

When I started giving away our fortune, she filed for divorce. She wanted to make sure she got her half before it became too small to support her new lifestyle. Truth be told, I was glad to see her go.

But I started looking around. Other high tech founders were going through the same fate. Sure, there were many who reveled in their new-found wealth and enthusiastically raced through the social doors their wives opened.

5

But others, those with a conscience, those true believers, often found themselves in my place – stunned at what their wives had become.

I think it's even worse for those who haven't made it yet, who risked it all to be successful in bringing their visions to the world. Their wives hung around for one or two startups, but at some point, they decided that their husbands were losers. And for them too, it was time to move on to greener pastures, leaving in their wakes visionaries who were already suffering after the losses of their technology passions, now emotionally devastated too.

I lost two of these friends to suicide. They could have made a difference but now they're gone. And their wives moved on, their exes' deaths just confirming their decisions.

Yes. I hate women. I'm tired of seeing women destroy the vulnerable. Something needs to be done. No, I need to do something.

CHAPTER 1

"Alone we can do so little, together we can do so much."
- Helen Keller

1

Samantha Louis looked out her second story office window above Haight Street in San Francisco and watched the patient of a lifetime drive away. It was over. They'd just had their last session together. Sam knew it was coming. In her notes and in talking to her collegues about the case, she'd begun to refer to the patient as 'POL' – patient of a lifetime. The POL had made fantastic progress and now seemed to be 'normal' and by any standard, was cured of mental illness – a condition that had threatened relationships and quite frankly, the lives of others. The POL had been dangerous.

Sam should have been proud of her success. It was rare you could point at a psychiatric patient who was actually cured. Most were 'managed' – either through therapy, behavior modification, drugs, or a combination of the three. Far too often it was drugs, but after her years of experience in residency and her work in inpatient facilities, she knew that for many, drugs were the only way to bring some sense of normalcy into their lives.

This wasn't the case with the POL. Yes, some drugs were involved at the outset, but that was just to help manage behavior. As therapy advanced, the drugs were withdrawn. Now the POL had a solid relationship, a good job, and was actually happy. In Sam's opinion, there was zero chance the POL would relapse or would present with other issues. The POL was actually cured.

As much as she tried to convince herself to be proud of her success, Sam couldn't help but feel a sense of loss. This was the case of a lifetime. Her mentor, Dr. Ken Karmere hadn't seen anything like it in his entire thirty-plus year career. What were the chances Sam would ever see a case like this again?

So here she was, thirty-seven years old, almost two years into her private practice, and not making enough money to quit her part-time job at the inpatient facility of San Francisco Community Hospital. At least that paid well.

Med School, fellowships, a long residency, and treatment of the POL had consumed her life. Like many of her counterparts, she had few really close friends. They were all far too focused on getting through their training so that they could make a difference in the world as psychiatrists.

But aside from the POL, who was now gone, her other

patients consisted of a few couples that she counseled and several teens with eating disorders. Nothing exciting and not enough to pay the bills; certainly not enough to repay her student loans.

As for her personal life, Sam didn't even have a pet. She couldn't imagine subjecting an animal to the absences demanded by her psychiatric training. And while she'd had a few relationships with men in Med School, none lasted. Maybe it was her intensity. Maybe, like with a pet, it was her unavailability. She was too often doing night shifts or on Call. Or maybe it was the fact that once her psychiatric training began, she couldn't stop analyzing her dates. It was like the Med-Student Syndrome. Virtually all med students imagine they have every possible illness as they begin studying medicine. She went through it herself in Med School but she got over it. And then, after she entered her psych residency, it seemed like her dates presented with every possible psychiatric disorder. They quickly sensed that she was in analyst mode or she herself would become paranoid about what she thought she saw in them. Certainly, this wasn't the path towards a successful long term relationship.

But, it was hard to complain about the wonderful apartment she'd found just a few blocks from her office and only a few hundred yards from Golden Gate Park.

Housing was a challenge in San Francisco, but luckily, the elderly owner of the house wasn't interested in the ridiculous rents others were charging nearby. In exchange for checking in regularly and an occasional dinner together, her landlord made Sam feel more like a granddaughter than a tenant.

Sam stepped into the small shared bathroom outside her office and examined herself in the mirror. She was still attractive. There were a few strands of gray starting to show if you looked closely, but her blond hair concealed them well. Small lines were beginning to show on her face. Worry lines? Still, nothing too bad. And since she'd finished her residency four years ago, her more flexible schedule had permitted her to take yoga classes three days a week and Pilates two days a week, with a couple of jogging sessions in the park added in. She'd dropped most of the weight she'd put on during Med School and residency.

Looking at herself objectively, Sam decided that it was time to work on the personal side of her life. It had been put off far too long. She needed to find some group activities. She could make friends. Maybe she could even meet someone.

Sam returned to her desk to review her notes before her next patients arrived. She couldn't help seeing the irony that she was providing couples therapy but had never had a long term relationship herself. That would have to change.

2

George Gray printed the two emails, put on his black horn-rimmed glasses, and stood up and stretched his lanky, six foot four inch frame. The eight by eight work spaces were really too small for him. Maybe one day he'd move up to a real office. Sadly, the chances of that happening any time soon were miniscule. Still, he was grateful for the freedom he had in his job. It was a far cry from when he'd started at the New York Sentinel almost two years before. Now he could choose many of his stories and most of them were printed. Back then, he went months before any of his stories were accepted. Now he had credibility, and he was sure that with these two emails, he'd be onto something that would hold his interest and that of the Sentinel readers for some time to come.

George walked past the other cubicles on the 11th floor of 555 Montgomery Street in San Francisco to the corner office occupied by Morris Levinberg, George's boss at the New York Sentinel. Morris was heads down, reading glasses hanging precariously from the end of his nose, a red marker in his hand.

"No, No, No!" Morris grumbled, clearly not pleased with what he was reading.

Morris was in his mid-fifties, with a sweaty balding pate and wiry gray hairs poking out over his ears. While frumpy wasn't a term that was generally applied to men, it was the first word that came to mind when George looked at Morris and his middle-aged paunch, five o'clock shadow in the middle of the day, and disheveled clothes. It was amazing what physical appearances could hide and how easy it was for people to judge others by their bodies. But one look at Morris' face with its oversized beak and eagle-like eyes, and you could sense the keen intelligence that had won him a Pulitzer and made him a bestselling author.

George let Morris finish the page he was reading, then knocked on the open door.

Morris looked up. "George! To what do I owe the honor of a visit from one of our most talented young reporters?"

"God, I sure wish I was talented. I work my butt off and most of my work still never sees the light of day.

"But I'm not here to complain. I have a dilemma and need your advice. When I got in this morning, I had two somewhat strange emails in my Inbox. I tried to track down the authors, but the email addresses and the paths the emails seem to lead nowhere."

"Learning some tricks from Janey?" Morris asked.

"Yeah. My high-tech guru wife showed me how to follow email paths through multiple servers. I've been getting pretty good at tracking down 'anonymous' emails. But these two definitely led nowhere."

"Are they from the same sender?"

"I can't tell. The sender names are just a scramble of letters. Here. Take a look at the first one."

Morris took the email and began reading.

From: sqprw93uy4nk <sqprw93uy4nk@sqprw93uy4nk.com>
Date: September 29, 20XX 05:31 AM PDT
To: George Gray <GeorgeGray@nysentinel.com>
Subject: Exposing Unethical Zillionaires

George,

I read your article on Michael James, someone I greatly admired, and appreciated your even-handed, honest reporting of the situation he found himself in. It's tragic that we lose people like Michael while unscrupulous high tech moguls screw people and make millions or billions doing it.

I've managed to collect some very interesting information on several of these scumbags, information which would ruin them personally if it were exposed to the public and to law enforcement.

I'm not some crackpot. I only want to see justice done.

Of course I expect you to verify any information I give you, but assuming you do determine that I'm providing factual information, I would like you to publish articles which will expose the crimes these people have committed. If you can't verify the information I provide, I expect you to tell me to take a flying leap.

I'm untraceable by email and replying to this one won't work, so if you're interested in the next step, tweet "sqprw93uy4nk, I'm interested".

sqprw93uy4nk

"What do you think? Should I pursue it? Is this something the paper would approve?"

Morris thought carefully. "George, I don't see any reason not to. See what he or she has to say. As the email says, if it's bullshit, all we lose is the time you take to verify the claims. If not, we might have a great story."

George thought back to his last 'great story'. He and Janey were driving up the coast on their way to a brief honeymoon in the City when they saw a gray Audi go soaring off the cliff. The driver was killed. Starting work at the Sentinel the following Monday, George was asked to do a story on a successful Silicon Valley entrepreneur. By some weird coincidence, they were the same person. He and Janey had watched Michael James commit suicide. His months of chasing the story had left him frustrated. Initially thinking Michael James was a scumbag like sqprw – whatever described, he found out he was wrong. He searched for why someone like Michael James would kill himself. It seemed to be about a divorce, but at the end of the day, he didn't really understand why this gifted, apparently ethical man, had died.

"Since your fan brought up Michael James, I have to ask, any progress on that novel you're writing based on the Michael James story?" Morris asked.

"No Morris. I keep coming back to the facts which didn't lead to answers. The story haunts me and though I can write about it, I can't get past the unknowns."

"George, take it from a fiction writer. If you base a novel on facts, you need to give the facts some time and distance. They need to become a bit hazy. Then, as ludicrous as it may sound, you just need to make shit up. Remember, it's fiction!

"But back to the reason you came in, what about the second email?"

George handed the next email to Morris.

From:x63qxr8k4mu5<x63qxr8k4mu5@ x63qxr8k4mu5.com>
Date: September 29, 20XX 06:41 AM PDT
To: George Gray <GeorgeGray@nysentinel.com>
Subject: A woman will die

George,

The former wife of a Silicon Valley entrepreneur will die this week. I will tell you why after she's dead.

Don't bother trying to trace this email. It's untraceable. I will contact you.

x63qxr8k4mu5

Morris looked up at George. "This probably is from a crackpot. But we need to hand it over to legal. They can decide if they want to give it to the police. If you get more like this, forward them to legal immediately and cc me."

"But do you think they're from the same person?"

Morris laid the two emails side by side and examined them closely. After about a minute, he circled the From name, the email address, and the signature, then the word 'untraceable' in both.

"Well, we have the word 'untraceable' and I see that each of the senders' names has twelve characters. The tones are different but I've seen some very disturbed people change their tones dramatically in seconds. And, we have two emails on the same day, just a bit over an hour apart, both sent to you. It may be just coincidence, and as we discussed before, unlike many of my police buddies, I do believe in coincidence. But just to be safe, forward the first one to legal too."

George thanked Morris and left his office, more than a little worried about what he was about to get himself into.

3

Mark Johansen made his way slowly up the stairs past the bakery on his way to his first outpatient session with Doctor Samantha Louis since his psychotic break several weeks before.

God, it smelled good. Lately he'd had challenges controlling his eating and coming here certainly wasn't going to help. Maybe it was the medication.

It had been a rough year since Janice left him. He'd been depressed. He'd started drinking. Then it was the cocaine. It seemed to help elevate his mood. When using, he felt like he was almost back to his normal self, the charismatic CEO of Johatchen Software.

But as he now recognized, what he thought were brilliant new presentations were just rants. What he believed to be his renewed enthusiasm for his work was perceived by his team as mania. When he thought he was bringing them closer, he was driving them away. And then Janice appeared.

At first, it seemed normal. He'd see a woman on the street and would mistake her for Janice. Then she showed up at work. At least he thought she was there. Every day he'd see her in the break room sipping coffee. But it wasn't her and what was really scary was that it wasn't anyone else either. No one saw her. He tried to pass off his questions about the woman at the table as just a joke, but unbeknownst to him at the time, his overly intelligent team saw through him.

He did his best to ignore her appearances, but then she started following him around. She'd show up everywhere. He'd be sitting on the toilet and when he looked up, she'd be there looming over him, shaking her head in disgust.

She showed up in meetings. Just when he thought he'd gained some sense of normalcy, she'd show up and give him a dirty, disapproving look. He'd stop in mid-sentence and would stare, hoping she'd go away. His team recognized the gaps.

But it really got bad when she started talking to him.

She wasn't talking to him; she was lecturing him. And it didn't stop. He became paranoid, looking around corners, and behind plants and large objects to make sure she wasn't there plotting to leap out at inappropriate times. But she did. He'd cover his ears, but nothing he tried could drown out her criticism. He'd stop mid-sentence and run out of a meeting for no apparent reason.

She berated him at night and he couldn't sleep. He'd then show up to the office disheveled and exhausted, no longer the smartly dressed, cheerful CEO with a kind word of encouragement for everyone. He took sleeping pills, but that only made it worse. He knew he was on a downhill spiral, with cocaine to pick him up and alcohol and pills to help him sleep and avoid Janice, but he couldn't stop himself. This went on for months.

And then disaster struck. He was in a meeting, barely holding his own when Janice walked in. He knew she wasn't real, but he couldn't ignore her.

"You ridiculous excuse for a man," she began.

Mark ignored her. He'd heard it before.

"It was bad enough you were never around, always working, but for what? These people don't care about you. Look at them. They don't respect you. They don't care about your ideas. They just want your money."

"Janice get out of here!" Mark had shouted to the dismay of his team.

But Janice just smiled menacingly. "And Richard there. Your 'partner'. He was just along for the ride. He capitalized on your genius and now that you've lost it, he's planning to kick you out."

Mark looked over at the astonished face of Richard Hatch, his best friend from college and his cofounder of three startups. They'd been through some really rough times together and each had always supported the other, even through failures of their first companies and relationships.

"I trust Richard completely!" Mark stated calmly as others in the room realized he was having a conversation with someone who wasn't there.

"Hah!" Janice chided. "He's no friend. I know he's planning to get rid of you because he told me so himself last night as he was fucking me senseless. He's a real man. He knows what he wants and he's not afraid to take it. Why do you think I left you?"

Mark didn't even think. He picked up his water bottle and threw it at Janice, missing her and hitting a young female intern squarely between the eyes. Seeing Janice laugh at him, he looked over at Richard who was wide-eyed with fear. Richard was guilty. Mark could see it in his face. He'd been fucking Janice for years. Richard was the reason she'd left him. Richard and Janice were trying to drive him crazy so they could take control of the company.

With uncontrollable anger, Mark raced behind Richard and pulled his chair backwards, spilling him to the ground.

"How could you?" he screamed, seizing a stunned Richard by the shoulders and slamming him over and over to the ground. "Lying to me, fucking my wife and stealing my company. I'll kill you both!"

Others in the room reacted quickly. Four of them pulled a frantically struggling Mark off of Richard and tried to calm him down, but Mark was completely hysterical.

For Mark, aside from the gales of laughter coming from Janice, the rest was a blur until he woke up in a private room at San Francisco Community Hospital strapped to a bed.

Seeing him awake, a nurse stepped into the room.

"Hello Mr. Johansen. My name is Ann. I'm one of the nurses here. How do you feel?"

"Other than a wicked headache and no recollection of how I got here, I feel okay. Actually, I feel pretty good. I assume I'm in a psych ward?"

"Yes. You're in at the Psychiatric Institute in San Francisco Community Hospital. You've been more or less out of it for two days. We had to both physically and chemically restrain you. But from what I can see, you look stable now. I'll talk to Dr. Louis and we should be able to remove those restraints. I'll be right back.

Mark waited patiently. He wasn't sure why but his head seemed clearer than it had in a long time. He looked around room and was disappointed to see Janice sitting in a visitor's chair thumbing through a magazine. She seemed to be ignoring him.

About twenty minutes later, Ann returned followed by an attractive female doctor who was reading a chart.

She put the chart down and introduced herself.

"Hi Mark, I'm Dr. Samantha Louis. Do you know why you're here?"

"Well, I remember Janice, my ex, chiding me in a meeting and just losing control. Did I hurt anyone?"

"No, you did attack your business partner, but he wasn't injured, and I understand you threw a water bottle at one of your employees, but from what I've heard, she was more startled than anything else. But given the violence you exhibited that day, you were brought here to prevent you from hurting others, and from hurting yourself. It's been two days. How do you feel?"

"Aside from the headache, and some confusion about what's happened, I feel surprisingly clearheaded. Unfortunately, I still see Janice. I know she's not real, but she's sitting right over there glaring at me."

"That's okay. Do your best to ignore her. I'll ask Ann to remove the restraints. You can get a shower and put on some clothes – your friend Richard brought you some basics - and Ann will show you around. She has some forms for you to fill out, including visitor authorizations. Your presence here is confidential and you can choose who visits and who can call you."

"Can you exclude Janice for me?" Mark asked jokingly.

"Well, as I said, you get to choose, and for now, it looks like you chose to let Janice stay. We can talk about that more during our upcoming sessions. In the meantime, try to take this time to decompress a bit."

And that's what he did. Janice was still there, but somehow, in this environment, Mark was largely able to ignore her. His sessions with Dr. Louis, who he now called Sam, were informative and day by day, Mark was feeling more and more like his old self. Richard came by daily and Mark began to reconnect with his best friend.

During one of Richard's visits a few days later, Sam came into the room.

Introductions were made and Sam turned to Richard.

"Richard, Mark suffers from late-onset schizophrenia. While this may sound shocking, we're seeing some great successes, even some cures with proper treatment. Since you're Mark's best friend and because ongoing social support is critically important to treatment of the disease, I have something to show you that should help you both understand what's going on. As technologists, I'm sure you'll find this as fascinating as I do."

Doctor Louis led them to a softly lit room with what appeared to be a dentist's chair. A huge machine and an associated helmet-like device loomed overhead. She sat down in front of a keyboard and a huge monitor and touched a few keys. The room filled with a low humming sound.

"Mark and Richard, meet MEG – our magnetoencephalography machine. Mark, please have a seat in our place of honor. Richard, you can pull the visitor's chair up next to him.

"Okay. What we're going to look at is the activity in Mark's brain. Mark, is Janice here?"

"Yes, she is, but for once, she's not talking. She looks curious."

"Great. I'm going to lower this gigantic helmet-like thing onto your head and we're going to get a 3-D image of your brain."

She carefully positioned the helmet, went back to her keyboard and quickly hit a few more keys. "Watch!"

Sure enough, an almost too-real representation of a brain appeared on the screen. Areas of the brain seemed to light up randomly.

"Okay, lift your right arm."

Even before Mark moved, an area on the lower center left of the brain lit up, then an area near the back.

"The first lighted area is associated with speech recognition, the next with movement.

"Now Mark, say something to Janice that will make her respond."

But before he could say anything, Janice interrupted. "Tell this know-it-all bitch that I'm not a trained seal that will bark on command."

The speech recognition area lit up again.

"What did she say," Doctor Louis asked.

"She said to tell you that she's not a trained seal that will bark on command."

"Don't forget to tell her I called her a know-it-all bitch," Janice ordered.

Mark ignored her but from the screen, it was clear he'd heard something.

"You really do hear her talking to you, don't you?" Richard asked, completely fascinated. "What did she say this time?"

"Nothing worth repeating," Mark replied.

Doctor Louis hit a few buttons and then came over to remove the helmet.

"So, as you can see, you really do hear her. It's not just 'imagined' in the classic sense. Your brain has created her and as far as your brain is concerned, she's real.

"As I mentioned, you have late onset schizophrenia with

hallucinations and paranoia as your main symptoms. The actions that brought you here were not indicative of a tendency towards violence. From what we've talked about, anyone with so little sleep, suffering from the effects of cocaine and alcohol might have behaved similarly. Contrary to popular mythology, people who suffer from schizophrenia are rarely violent, except against themselves. They have a much higher suicide rate than the general population. That's why I'm glad Richard is here. As we continue treatment, you need all the support you can get."

"Okay, so what is the treatment? Can I be cured?"

"Mark, I'm going to be brutally honest because it's important that we all acknowledge what we're dealing with. A minority of people suffering with schizophrenia never see any improvement. These are usually people who were diagnosed relatively young – in their teens or twenties. A much larger percentage manage their symptoms through a combination of drugs and psychotherapy. They can usually lead normal, productive lives. Another very small percentage is actually cured. Usually these are either late-onset patients or, based on some new ground-breaking work, patients whose condition is in large part a result of trauma, usually childhood trauma."

"So there's a chance he could be cured?" Richard asked hopefully.

"I wouldn't expect that. More likely Mark's condition will be managed.

"Mark, I've started you on a very light dose of an antipsychotic. We'll be going with an 'atypical' antipsychotic since they tend to have fewer side effects. If that doesn't work, we can increase the dosage or switch to a typical one. Also, if you're game, I'd like to start you on a course of ongoing and eventually outpatient psychotherapy. This will help you manage your symptoms and hopefully your life, and if, indeed, yours turns out to be one of the cases where trauma is the root cause of the problem, we might, and I say might, see a really good outcome. But for now you should set your expectations that this is something that will be with you for the rest of your life.

"I know. It sounds really scary. But if I told you that you had high cholesterol and needed to manage that for the rest of your life with a combination of drugs initially and lifestyle changes, you could do that, right?"

"I would hope so," Mark replied nervously.

"Well you're an intelligent man and you have one of the biggest challenges of the condition in hand – you already recognize that the Janice you see and hear isn't real. Now you just need to learn to live as normally as possible in spite of her.

"Not a chance!" Janice promised. "You made my life hell for years so now it's my turn to return the favor."

"Shut up, Janice!"

"Mark, we'll talk about managing Janice in our therapy sessions. The antipsychotic should reduce the frequency of her appearances, but it will likely take a few weeks to really have that beneficial effect."

"God, I could really use some relief from her."

"As I said, not a chance," Janice replied smugly.

This time Mark ignored her.

"What about work?" Richard asked.

"One part of controlling schizophrenia is to reduce stress. From what I understand, work is not terribly stressful for you Mark. So my thoughts are that after several more therapy sessions and once the medication kicks in, if it looks like you can control your behavior and avoid drugs and alcohol, I would think that in a month or so you could return to work.

"In the meantime, remember that cocaine worsens symptoms. Janice will appear more often if you use it. Exercise is critical. It will help you. If you have a sport, get back to it. If not, find something interesting and physically challenging. Something that will engage your mind and body and that can leave you physically exhausted. That should help you sleep too.

"Given what I've seen so far, you should be able to get back to a normal life if you can stay with the management program. It may sound easy, but it won't be. There may be some relapses, but we can work through them.

"Suffering from schizophrenia sounds bad. But it's not like you have terminal cancer. You can control the outcome. In that respect, you're luckier than a lot of people."

And so, here he was, out of the hospital and about to do his first outpatient session with Doctor Samantha Louis. Mark was hopeful. He was also more frightened than he'd ever been in his life and he had no idea why.

4

Ashima James pulled her plugin Toyota Prius into her Pacific Heights garage in San Francisco. She felt lucky to have been able to buy this house, and guilty too. Part of the money came from the divorce settlement with Michael. But the big surprise was that in spite of the divorce and the fact that she'd ruined his life, Michael had left her as beneficiary of a large insurance policy.

Now she had this very expensive house. It was paid for and with the separate apartment for the downstairs tenants, it generated a good income too.

Michael was dead, but Ashima's life went on. If possible, it was better than it had been before. She was independent, teaching at a private school not far away, and was active in local women's groups. She even had time to pursue ballet, something she'd given up after leaving the university where she'd briefly majored in Dance.

Her daughters Brittany and Francine were grown and now had their own lives. They called individually or together at least once a week and she received countless text messages. What more could a mother want?

Francine was happily doing environmental research in Oregon while Brittany was living on the East Coast, struggling to keep a job in Washington DC. But Ashima was worried about Brittany.

Brittany had had issues since she was a little girl. Finding her baby brother's body was a horrible experience which left her paranoid. Until she was a teenager, if she saw a mushroom growing in a field, she'd panic, sure it would find a way to kill her because some child had told her that mushrooms were poisonous and could kill you.

Being molested by a baby sitter a few years later just exacerbated her psychological and ultimately social problems, and although it looked like Michael, who'd been her stepfather since soon after her seventh birthday, had helped her get her life under control and become successful, ultimately, the underlying damage resurfaced. Brittany demanded that Ashima divorce Michael and focus on her instead of Michael.

For a brief period after the divorce, as Ashima spent more time with her, Brittany seemed better. But Ashima would later learn that even during this 'calm' period, Brittany had gone out of her way to destroy several people's lives – costing a professor his job after claims of sexual harassment, sending an innocent young man to jail for stalking her. Then, with Michaels's suicide, Brittany lost all semblance of control. She became hysterical and even violent. She was hospitalized for a while but with medication, when she took it consistently, she seemed to function almost normally. Unfortunately, Brittany frequently stopped taking her meds and inevitably fell back into paranoia, lashing out at colleagues and friends, attacking them verbally or in writing with no sane justification, and after losing another job, she'd end up hospitalized again.

Each time, Ashima hoped that the cycle would end. She did her best to help, but Brittany wanted her independence and there was only so much Ashima could do from nearly three thousand miles away. Yes, Ashima worried about Brittany. But Brittany was old enough to lead her own life. That's what she'd chosen to do and Ashima could only make herself available.

Still, aside from Brittany, Ashima had no worries. In spite of all the bad things she'd done in her life – neglecting her daughter, causing Michael's death, and some things she didn't want to admit, her life was perfect. She was very lucky indeed.

Ashima made her way up the stairs and was pleased to see a Unixpres package on her doorstep. She had tracked the package since she placed her order for custom dance shoes a few weeks before, and it was here today as promised, just in time for her dance class tonight. Her other shoes were worn out and provided no support. These had been custom designed for her based on measurements and impressions that she'd sent in to the company. She couldn't wait to try them on.

Closing the door behind her, she took off her coat and shoes and used one of her keys to cut the tape holding the package together. She didn't even get to see the shoes before the explosion killed her instantly, blowing out several windows and destroying the front entrance to her beautiful Victorian home.

5

"Mr. Gray?" Joyce, the receptionist called as George pushed through the glass doors the New York Sentinel's offices. "These two policemen are here to see to you."

"George Gray?" the stocky older one asked, setting down his coffee and extending his hand. "I'm Detective Mike McKensey and this is Detective Bob Simpson. Can we have a few minutes?"

George didn't even blink. Although he'd been with the Sentinel less than two years, talking with the police had become almost routine. He'd started doing crime reporting not long after he began working. He hated to admit it, but he found the investigations intriguing. Most were solved quickly by the police, but some of the more complex ones actually relied on information reporters could provide.

"The Golden Gate conference room is empty," Joyce offered.

"Thanks Joyce. Detectives, please follow me."

Once seated in the spacious conference room with floor to ceiling windows that looked out across the City towards the Transamerica Pyramid, George asked what he could do for them.

"Well," Detective McKensey began. "We're looking into the murder of Ashima James. We-"

"Ashima is dead?!" George exclaimed. "What happened?"

"You knew her?" Detective Simpson asked, clearly surprised.

"Absolutely. I interviewed her for a story a bit over a year ago. What happened, and why are you here if you didn't know that I knew Ashima James?"

"Actually," Detective McKensey began. "We were following up on an email you received which threatened to kill the wife of an entrepreneur. Ashima James was killed by a package bomb last night as she arrived home."

"Good God!" George exclaimed, clearly shaken. Was he responsible for Ashima's death? Of course he was. If he'd never written that story, Ashima James would be alive. But no. He couldn't go there now. He was a professional and the police needed his help. He needed to hold it together in front of the detectives. He needed to step back, to be objective, to control his emotions.

George closed his eyes, visualized himself running through the redwoods near a creek in the Santa Cruz Mountains, took a deep breath, and turned his attention back to the detectives.

"Sorry, you really caught me off guard. What can I do to help?"

"Mr. Gray, we believe the suspect will contact you again. From the email, she or he, and I believe strongly that this is a man, wants to use you as forum for his agenda.   We want to work with you.   Your help will be essential in catching him. We've already spoken with Mr. Levinberg and he's assured us that the paper will cooperate in the investigation."

"Please call me George. Of course, I'll do whatever I can.

"Okay. We're Mike and Bob. Have you checked your email this morning George?"

"I worked from home this morning and most of the way to the City on Caltrain. I didn't have anything unusual when I shut down my laptop at the station.   Let's go to my cubicle and take a look."

The two detectives followed George through a maze of cubicles filled with reporters busily at work either on the phone peppering people with questions or typing furiously. George stepped into his cubicle in the middle of the chaos.

"Have a seat if you want. You can grab another chair from Johan's cubicle across the way. Sorry - it's kind of tight in here."

George pulled a laptop from his backpack, placed it in the docking station and powered it up.   "It'll take me a minute to log on."

The two detectives scanned George's space,   noting the miniature basketball rim, a framed desk photo of a gorgeous redhead with stunning green eyes, and a picture of George crossing the finish line of that year's Race through the Redwoods with a digital clock showing 40:32.

As George paused, waiting for his system to load, Detective Mike McKenzie commented, "If I remember correctly, that's a damn good time for the Race through the Redwoods. I did it a few years ago and I think my time was just under fifty minutes. You must have finished up there."

George smiled sheepishly. "I love to run and I especially love trail running. That race is a bit demanding with the single track, steep hills, roots, and ruts, and of course, the crowd. But yeah, I got lucky. No falls, no twisted ankles, and I didn't have to wait much to get past others on the trail. I finished 11th overall and 3rd in my age group which isn't too bad considering I work sixty to eighty hours a week.

"So you run too?"

"Yeah, I run. Running has been my primary stress reliever for years. I usually ran trails in Land's End or in some of the parks in Marin, but my wife, who now does Ironman Triathlons, got me into Triathlons a few years ago so I now mix my running with swimming and biking. You should try it.

"I could probably handle the bike, but I'd never survive the swim. I can swim, but it's not something that I do well, unless dog paddling counts."

Looking back at his screen, George continued.

"Mail is up and yeah, it looks like he emailed me again though I don't know if you're aware that there may be two different people emailing me with similar encrypted email addresses. I guess legal sent you the one from the murderer, but there's another guy or woman, who says he or she wants to expose corrupt Silicon Valley moguls. My gut tells me they're not the same person and my boss Morris agrees that I should check out the stories once he or she sends me something to investigate. I suspect legal might have a problem with you guys seeing those but I really have no way to know before opening them which person might have sent them. Even this one. But with the subject 'one down', I suspect it's the guy you're looking for. I'll open it. But if it's the other guy, I think you need to leave it to me. Is that okay?"

"Give us a minute."

Mike and Bob walked down the hall, out of earshot. They returned a good ten minutes later. Mike took the lead.

"We called our Captain and he talked to your lawyer. We're agreed. We're to disregard anything you believe is not from the perp unless you ask us to take a look at it. Are we good?"

"Sounds right to me. Let me open this one."

George opened the email and called them over. "Yeah, it's from him. Take a look.

The two detectives leaned over George's shoulder and began reading.

From: d67jki7r3pj5 < d67jki7r3pj5@d67jki7r3pj5.com)
Date: October 3, 20XX 08:43 AM PDT
To: George Gray <GeorgeGray@nysentinel.com>

Subject: One down

George ol' Buddy,

I really appreciated your article on Michael James so I thought I'd kick off my bitch cleansing by eliminating Ashima James. Don't feel bad. She got what she deserved. While I didn't know Michael James personally, I recognize the brilliance of his work. The world needs geniuses like him and needs to be rid of women who would prevent them from fighting the good fight to make the world a much better place. This woman killed a genius as sure as if she'd put a gun to his head. Of course our justice system would never stop someone like her, so I had to. The world is a better place without her.

She was an easy target. My next will be a bit more difficult, and it will take me a few weeks to line everything up, but don't worry. I'll give you some clues a few days before so you can help the police try to stop me. But you really shouldn't. My targets don't deserve to live and continue to ruin lives.

It's going to be fun working with you George. Try to enjoy the ride. It won't last forever.

d67jki7r3pj5

"Bob, why don't you give Sameer a call and get him down here," then turning to George, "George, I'm sorry, but I'm going to ask Sameer Bodepudi, one of our best techs, to take a look at your system and this email in particular to see if he can spot something useful. As promised, Sameer will disregard anything that doesn't concern this case and he'll keep that confidential – he won't even tell us about it.

"While we wait for him to get here, why don't you fill me in on Michael James. Although our perp says he didn't know him, you never know. We'd like to pick up on anything you have, notes, thoughts, and of course, your article to see if it gives us any leads."

Bob, who was still on his cellphone nodded at Mike.

"Can we go back to that conference room? We're going to want to take some notes."

"Sure. I'll ask Joyce to bring in some coffee."

Just then another email popped up with a similar From address. The subject read 'Our First Target'.

"Should I open it?"

"Yeah, We'll head to the conference room. Come get us if it's the same guy."

George opened the mail.

From: g87olh6t9wi8 <g87olh6t9wi8@g87olh6t9wi8.com)
Date: October 3, 20XX 09:32 AM PDT
To: George Gray <GeorgeGray@nysentinel.com>
Subject: Our first Target

Hello George,

Thanks for the tweet. You should find our first target quite interesting. I suspect you'll be able to write a number of stories not just about our Bad Guy, but about the practices he's used and their impacts on unsuspecting people. You will definitely be able to make a big difference in the lives of many of the exploited people in our world.

Our Bad Guy is Ryan Hamilton, CEO of lotsofjobs.com. You may be familiar with the site. As a job seeker, you pay a small fee, and enter detailed information about yourself, your likes, dislikes, and your experiences, both personal and professional. lotsofjobs.com not only generates a perfect resume for you, it also matches you with employers and creates associated cover letters guaranteed to get you in the door of at least one – or you get your membership fee back.

The site does not discriminate. It finds all kinds of jobs from high level professional to blue collar positions. It can find jobs overseas and it can find jobs for people who want to come to this country. It even finds jobs for illegal immigrants - somehow that has found its way under the radar of the immigration authorities.

The Artificial Intelligence (AI) engine that Hamilton created is a brilliant piece of work and he earned millions from it. But for some reason, that wasn't enough for him. You see, George, the AI engine categorizes people. It's up to the designer to decide which categories candidates can fall into, what to look for in prospects. For example, you could create a category of people with few personal connections who are interested in working outside the country. Or, people from outside the country who are desperate to get in. Or, young runaways willing to work in a different city.

If you were unscrupulous, what could you do with people like that? Does human trafficking come to mind? As it turns out, Hamilton has made more money from human trafficking than he has through the legitimate side of lotsofjobs.com. And it's all kinds of trafficking. Obviously, there's sex trafficking where teenagers and young people are sold to buyers here and overseas and young people in other countries who come to the US expecting a legitimate job and then get coerced into the sex trade. But Hamilton also makes quite a bit of money from indentured servitude and slavery where people are 'sold' as workers to foreign governments or are brought into the US to work as servants for the rich. In the latter case, one of lotsofjobs.com's affiliates arranges temporary visas and travel, but lets the visas expire. At that point, the 'employee' is illegal. They work in slavish conditions with no recourse to the authorities. Yes. Hamilton is a piece of work.

To get you started, I've attached information about four of his victims, who, until now, have been afraid to come forward. Marta and Eva Macdonald escaped from a sex worker service here in San Francisco a few months ago. Jimmy Abrams is a mechanical engineer who managed to evade his captors in Saudi Arabia, and Roberto Rodriguez is currently employed as a tutor for Maxim and Amanda Rivas. They work at the Salvadoran Consulate and paid to have Roberto brought in to tutor their children. He's now a slave.

If you're still skeptical that all of this is tied to lotsofjobs.com, the second attachment includes a thread from lotsofjobs.com and a fictitious profile I created which fell into one of the trafficking categories. That profile is of an 18-year old teenager, 'Michelle', who has been offered a position in Croatia. The hiring firm is a front for a sex worker service.

And finally, the third attachment includes a list of offshore accounts owned by Ryan Hamilton (or one of his shell companies), and includes payments to those accounts made from countless unsavory sources (including for Marta and Eva, Jimmy, Roberto, and "Michelle's" future employer).

I suggest you review the documentation I've included, and that you contact the victims. When you're convinced, bring in the authorities and break the stories.

George, you're on your way to making a big difference in the world. I'll be back to you again soon to hopefully advance us further in cleaning up the Internet.

g87olh6t9wi8

George forwarded the email to Morris asking for a meeting to follow up later in the day, then he made his way back to the conference room where the detectives were waiting.

"So?" Mike asked.

"It's interesting. I still find it a strange coincidence that I received an email from this guy who wants to expose Silicon Valley corruption right after I received an email from the guy who killed Ashima James. Same thing last time they contacted me. Even more coincidental is that they both mentioned Michael James. Then again, that story kind of made my career, such as it is."

"I don't believe in coincidences," Bob Simpson began. "Maybe we should take a look at this other situation too."

"I'm not ready to let you do that yet. With this second email, I'm a bit more sure that we're looking at two different people. The tone of this email is completely different.

"It's funny. My boss, Morris Levinberg, says that most of the police he knows don't believe in coincidences, but that years of doing this job have taught him that coincidences happen more often than we think."

Mike smiled. "Yeah, I started out like my younger partner here, convinced I saw leads everywhere. The human brain, and especially detectives' brains, loves to look for patterns. But like the constellations, sometimes a pattern of stars is just our brains looking to make connections out of something random. I learned that the hard way.

"Anyway, did you get a good lead from this other guy?"

"We'll see. He claims that one of the major players in the Silicon Valley is making a fortune from human trafficking. You guys will probably want to get involved in this too."

"Actually, it won't be us," Mike corrected. "We're just homicide investigators. But I'm sure some of our colleagues will be working with you on this if it pans out. Or maybe it will be the FBI. Either way, you'll likely be seeing a lot of the San Francisco Police department in the coming weeks."

Over the next hour, George led the two detectives through his year-old investigation of Michael and Ashima James. Nothing jumped out as an obvious lead, but the two detectives promised to use the information to try to identify possible suspects and to keep George informed of their progress.

Late in the day, Morris dropped by.

"Let's go for a walk," he suggested.

These walks had become part of their routine. Many managers have daily or weekly meetings with their employees. Others take them to lunch to get offsite to discuss events and problems in a different environment with a different perspective. While Morris did both, it seemed to George that their most productive discussions took place on walks around downtown San Francisco. And, if Morris was to be believed, this was his only form of exercise.

They exited the elevator and walked past the security desk, stepping out into the Financial District of the City. Although he'd worked here since beginning his career, George still found it hard to believe that the majority of the men on the street were wearing suits and the women wore either suits or business-appropriate outfits. It was a far cry from the Silicon Valley where casual was a step up for most people working there. While Janey always dressed nicely, she often went to work in jeans and running shoes. Most of her cohorts, especially the engineers, wore t-shirts, shorts, and sandals to work. But here, it was different. Maybe that was part of what he loved about working in the City even if he had to commute ninety minutes on the train most mornings and evenings.

George and Morris made their way to Market Street and turned towards the Embarcadero. At the end of the street was the Hyatt Regency Hotel and across the Embarcadero on the edge of the Bay, the landmark Ferry Building with its giant clock tower and four twenty-two foot diameter clocks. Since its renovation over ten years before, the Ferry Building had become a tourist attraction with its huge marketplace and spectacular views, in addition to housing the ferry terminal and a number of business offices. In the background, countless sailboats bounced across the white capped waters of the Bay towards Yerba Buena Island and the Bay Bridge.

After five minutes of companionable silence, Morris kicked off the discussion.

"I've read the email and documentation you forwarded me from your source, and I've discussed it with legal and with Sterling Rockwell. We'd like you to proceed, but we want you to be very careful."

"Sterling Rockwell? George interrupted, surprised that Morris had brought this to the attention of the Sentinel's Publisher and CEO.

"Yeah. He and I have been discussing doing a series on trafficking. It's a problem that lies just beneath the surface of our society, and too many people are just not aware of it. Most understand that sex trafficking exists, but very few think it happens here. Virtually no one is aware of other, less sensational types of trafficking like your engineer who was sold to an oil conglomerate. We've wanted to raise public awareness to help stop trafficking, but until now haven't had a story big enough to capture the public's attention. If your informant is right, this is a big one."

They continued in silence for a few minutes longer as they turned onto the Embarcadero, which runs along the Bay from ATT Park, almost to Fisherman's Wharf.

"So how would you like me to proceed?" George asked, intrigued.

"What we'd like you to do is to verify everything that your

informant has given you. Meet with the victims. Promise them confidentiality until Hamilton is arrested. Go through the lotsofjobs.com thread he gave you and verify the links to the accounts. Keep us in the loop. If everything checks out, we'll bring in the SFPD Special Victims Unit and turn over what we have. They will likely bring in the FBI to tie ownership of the accounts to Hamilton. Once an arrest is imminent, we can break the story and then start our series on trafficking.

"Obviously, it will take a while for the SFPD and the FBI to do their work, so once we hand it over, I'd like you to get started on the series so we're ready to go when we break the story of the arrest.

"Each story should explore one aspect of trafficking and how it's happening right in front of us. Our goal is to open people's eyes so they can start to spot it and report it. I'd like to keep this just between you and me until we're ready to publish. When we do, we're thinking of an article a week for several weeks. We'll also set up social media accounts as a modern hotline. With luck, by then, the SFPD and FBI will be working with us and we can funnel vetted reports to them."

They turned up Washington Street to head back to the office, both lost in thought.

"George, have you given any further thought as to whether you're dealing with one or two people? Both have mentioned Michael James…"

"You know, Morris, I'm not sure. There's definitely a part of me that thinks that these two informants are the same person. Thus far, their emails have always arrived within minutes of each other. And yet, their styles are different and their objectives are different. Actually, I'm hoping they're different people. But as far as Michael James is concerned, the whole case haunts me. And it's worse now that Ashima James is dead. I feel responsible."

"Yeah, I had a feeling you would. I've been through it countless times in my career. You can't write anything in any way controversial without risking some damage. All we can do is to do our best to seek out the truth and hope we do more good than harm."

George's eyes filled with tears. He didn't want to say anything more knowing he'd lose it.

For his part, Morris saw George's distress. "Talk to Janey.

She'll help you put this in perspective. Martine has done that for me over the years."

At that point they were well down Montgomery Street nearing the office. They took the elevator up in silence and Morris squeezed George's shoulder as they parted company.

6

After spending the afternoon going through the documentation and setting up meetings for the next day, George packed up and made his way to the Caltrain station. Ninety minutes later he walked up the steps to his Mountain View apartment and opened the door.

'Honey, I'm home!" he shouted, unable to avoid repeating what had started as a joke when he got home from his first day of work at the Sentinel.

For her part, the woman whose braided red hair almost reached her waist, leaped up from her computer, raced to George, and jumped into his arms wrapping her legs around him.

"Take me to bed or lose me forever!" she joked, replaying for the nth time what had become a welcome home ritual.

After almost two years of marriage, the magic was still there. Sure, there were nights where one or both would have to work late, where they both got home too tired to do much else than order takeout and fall into bed exhausted, but somehow, there seemed to be more times like this one.

"Bed may have to wait a bit. I'm starving and have a lot to talk about. I think you're going to be more than intrigued."

"I suspected you'd deny me tonight, so aside from the salmon, dinner is ready. Go change and I'll have it on the table in seven minutes."

"You know I never deny you. Take it as a brief postponement. I'll be right back!"

George dragged himself to the bedroom, exhausted by the day's events but simultaneously intrigued by the possibilities and guilty about his involvement in Ashima James' death. It would do him good to talk to Janey. It always did.

Janey was the most intelligent woman he'd ever met. He still wasn't sure why she'd married him but he was glad she had. They were a great fit. She worked as a software designer for a Silicon Valley startup which seemed to be well on its way to major success, and a good payoff on Janey's stock options.

Maybe he'd just never met anyone super-intelligent before, mistaking the top people in his university classes for geniuses. But their single-mindedness was totally different than what he now knew. Those people seemed brilliant at what they did, but not so much at other subjects. Janey, on the other hand, was brilliant at everything. And at the same time, she was gifted in social situations, reading and understanding people with a facility that was truly astonishing. And she never got mad.

He'd asked her about that once and she claimed that if you really tried to understand a situation, you couldn't be angry – at least you couldn't be emotionally out of control. You could see motivations and mistakes on all sides. And while they had agreed that there really are evil people in the world, and you could recognize the injustice and do your best to fight it, anger rarely helped any situation. George tried his best to follow her example, but he just didn't have her patience.

They'd also talked about his comparatively low intelligence, and Janey had explained that in her view, there was much more to a person than intelligence. She gave examples of people she'd dated who were extremely intelligent but who were ultimately not people she wanted to be around. She said she admired George for his ethics, his sense of right and wrong, his gentleness, and ability to put people at ease. She also told him he was the best lover she'd ever had and was more fun to be with than anyone else. Somehow George had quit worrying about the intelligence difference. They were just good together. No. They were magic together.

"Is there anything I can do to help?" he asked as he made his way into their small dining area.

"No George. The wine is poured. Have a sip and tell me about your day."

George looked over at his gorgeous wife. She was happy. They were happy. Could he separate his home life from his work? It hadn't worked well so far but Janey had done her best to help him put difficult situations in perspective.

Should he start easy or just dive into his responsibility for Ashima James' death?

"When I got to the office, there were two police detectives waiting for me," he began. "They told me Ashima James had been murdered by the person who emailed me a few weeks ago saying he would be killing women who ruined entrepreneurs' lives. The guy emailed me again today and said that he liked my story on Michael James so much that he decided to start his quote bitch cleansing unquote, with Ashima James."

And then George lost it. He'd done a good job of holding it together in front of the detectives and among his coworkers, but now, he was home. Janey was here. She would listen.

Janey came over and took George in her arms. She didn't say that it wasn't his fault. She just held him and let him cry.

When the worst was over, she walked him over to the table, guiding him into his chair. She kissed the top of his head and said she'd be right back.

Two minutes later she returned with dinner in hand placing a plate filled with grilled salmon, garlic-dill mashed potatoes, and green beans in front of George. She set her own plate down and sat across from George.

"Eat. I guarantee you'll feel better. Take a couple of bites then tell me what you're feeling."

George did as he was told. The hot food seemed to settle his stomach and as he followed it with a sip of wine, he could feel himself relaxing.

"It's my fault," he began. "If I hadn't written that article, Ashima James would still be alive."

"That's probably true. I know that situation haunts you. You still don't understand how that family could have driven Michael James to suicide. But knowing what you knew at the time, could you really not have written the story? You already second-guess every significant story you write, afraid it will hurt someone innocent. But to avoid something like this, you'd have to give up writing. I don't think you're ready to do that."

George nodded and continued to eat in silence.

After a few minutes of contemplative silence, George excused himself from the table. When he returned, he handed Janey a copy of the email the killer had sent him. She read it thoughtfully.

"What an interesting character! He's confident, but knows he'll eventually get caught. He's on a mission, but for him, it's a game. He sees you as his voice to the world but also as a partner and someone who will help him get caught. I don't sense any ill-will towards you whatever you decide to do.

"So, what are you going to do?"

George thought about his situation. Could he really accept that his reporting has this kind of collateral damage? How many crazies would take work he hoped would help people and turn it into justification for violence?

"I don't know. I can see that I'm a bit depressed about this, but I don't want people to be hurt or killed because of me. I know it sounds extreme, but maybe I should give this up and try something else."

"Well, you must be depressed. You've wanted to be a reporter and writer your whole life."

"If you write anything that gets published, whether it's an article for the paper, a blog, a novel, an email, anything that could be widely read, you lose control of how it's going to be interpreted. There are always crazy people willing to use anything to justify their insane actions. You really can't take this as your fault. This guy was intent on settling some sort of score against women. You certainly couldn't have stopped that. Though by working with the police to help catch him, you may save some people.

"Hey, do you remember what Morris made you do when you thought about taking on the Michael James story?"

"Yeah, he made me watch Citizen Kane. What's your point?"

"Well, I have another movie for you to watch if you haven't seen it. Do you know *Run Lola Run* by Tom Twyker?"

"No. What's it about?"

"It's the film that made Tom Twyker famous in the US. It's about a young woman who gets a call from her panicked boyfriend who finds himself in a life or death situation. She tells him she can save him, puts down the phone and starts to run. Her boyfriend dies."

"What, you give away the ending?"

"Actually, no. The film restarts with the same call, and she runs to save him again, but this time there are some differences. I guarantee you'll find it fascinating.

"Finish up your dinner while I look for it on Netflix and On-Demand. Worst case, we can go rent it somewhere."

George did as he was told, then cleared the table and did a quick wash of the dishes.

"Did you find it?" he called.

"Yeah. It was available on both. I've got it loaded and paused. Come snuggle with me."

George joined Janey on the sofa and pulled a soft blanket over the two of them.

"Thanks Janey. Just being here with you makes things better. A little escapism may be just what I need."

But it wasn't escapism at all. The frenetic music just made George more tense. Still, Janey was right. It was fascinating.

Lola would run and along her path she'd encounter people. Sometimes they'd be delayed or would stop or have to hurry and the filmmaker would do a rapid-fire collage of their lives from that point forward. Depending just on a few seconds of delay in the different running scenarios, George saw people's lives change dramatically, from ending up in a hospital to lying on the beach after winning the lottery (a few seconds delay resulted in purchase of the winning ticket). An auto accident was avoided when the driver waited for Lola to pass. Even the death of her boyfriend, hinged on just a few seconds of difference in timing. Clearly the point was that the tiniest things can have dramatic, unforeseen impacts. Chains of events cannot be predicted.

George got the point. Maybe letting a pedestrian cross in front of him against the light resulted in that person's death later on. There was no way of knowing his impact on people around him. All he could do was the best he could do. And as Janey said, maybe he could help save some lives.

"Ready for bed?" Janey asked, not pressing him for a decision or for his thoughts on the film.

"Not yet. It's nice here under the blanket with you. Plus, I need to tell you about the other big thing that happened today.

"The other emailer, the one who proposed exposés, contacted me shortly after the one about Ashima James. The tone was different, but it still bothers me that the two emails arrived so close together like the last time.

"Anyway, this guy – I think it's a guy – says that Ryan Hamilton, CEO of lotsofjobs.com uses his AI algorithm to find people he can traffic. He sent me bios and introductions to two women who were sold into sexual slavery, an engineer sold to an oil conglomerate, and an immigrant who is now a domestic slave for some consulate people in the City. He gave me links to offshore accounts and to transactions linking Hamilton to the victims and the accounts.

"Morris and Sterling Rockwell want me to do a series on human trafficking. It should only take me a couple of days to meet with the victims and to verify the information, then we'll turn it over to the police while I get started on the series."

"George, this is exciting. If ever there were a question about whether your writing could make a difference, this should answer that. You could help countless people. I'm so proud of you! I'm envious. All I do is design and write software."

"And help me with my work. You kept me on track with the Michael James story when I was about to go completely astray. I have a feeling you'll be helping me with these two stories. I couldn't do what I do without you."

George kissed Janey as he picked her up and carried her to bed.

7

It seemed awfully early as Sam pulled her car into the lot on the north end of Lake Merced. There was frost on the ground and steam was rising from the lake's surface – it was hard to see the water, but she could just make out a few brave souls gliding silently, effortlessly, across the placid lake. It looked like a meditative sport, one where technique and strength combined to deliver a sense of harmony between mind, body, and nature. At this point in her life, this was much more appealing than biking, running, swimming, or cross fit – activities that many of her compatriots at the hospital had taken up. It was more - elegant. And it was different.

She made her way to the somewhat decrepit-looking wooden building perched, or perhaps teetering, on the side of the lake and checked her watch. She was a bit early. The class was to start at 7 and it was only 6:40. She walked most of the way around the building, then made her way back to the bulletin board which graced the wall next to a closed and locked sliding door. She had read most of the notices promoting upcoming rowing events as well as several ads offering sculls for sale when a familiar voice interrupted her reverie.

"Doctor Louis, Sam! Are you taking this class too?

Sam turned to see a smiling Mark Johansen standing next to a tall, slender man of about the same age.

"Ah, this is Jack Trageser. He's a fellow entrepreneur. Maybe you're heard of his latest startup, Balanced News?"

"Yes, someone at the hospital mentioned it. If I understand the concept, it's a search and news site that goes against the grain of customizing news to the habits of the user. It tries to present a balanced set of results instead. Is that it?"

Jack was striking, His dark hair contrasted with his stunning blue eyes. His air of self-confidence was not imposing. In fact, he seemed very comfortable with himself and with those around him. Yes, very attractive, indeed.

"Yep. That's it," Jack replied, taking in all of Sam objectively. "And you must be the miracle-working Doctor Samantha Louis. Thank you for returning Mark to us."

"Well, he's the one doing the work. What brings you two out here on a dreary Saturday morning?"

"Well, you said I should get some exercise, something that

41

would wear me out, and Jack suggested rowing. He's been doing it for quite a while and actually teaches here on weekends. It's his class today. This doesn't present any conflict issues does it? I mean us being in the same class?"

Sam thought about the issue. She should probably leave. That's what she'd been taught in her professional ethics training. It was dangerous and potentially a breach of confidentiality to have relationships of any kind with a patient outside of the office. Still, Mark didn't seem to have a problem with her being here, so the confidentiality issue seemed moot. She couldn't see how just being in a class together would create a problem.   And then there was Jack. Maybe just this one time. She'd be careful.

"I'm not supposed to have interaction with patients outside the office but since it's a class, maybe I could make one exception for today.   However, I really do need to keep our relationship strictly on a professional basis."

"I hope that doesn't apply to me," Jack replied jokingly.

"I'm not sure yet. Let's see how today goes."

"I like her, Mark. Encouraging but cautious."

Then seeing a group of people approaching, Jack excused himself, "I see our other class members have arrived. I need to get things ready. See you guys in a few minutes.

Jack pulled out a set of keys, unlocked, then slid open the large wooden door and went inside. A young man and a young woman from the approaching group followed him while the rest approached Mark and Sam. Introductions were made.

Five minutes later, Jack invited the six students inside. He gave each standard liability forms, reviewed their clothing, and introduced Steve, the coxswain and Mary the bowman. Jack would be the stroke.

The lesson began with verbal introductions and then followed with each person getting individualized instruction on a standard rowing machine. Jack explained that they wanted to avoid back and shoulder problems by getting proper body movement in place before stepping into the boat. Sam had previously done rowing workouts in gyms and as it turned out, Mary only made minor corrections in her technique.

Sam looked over at Mark who was being coached by Steve. He seemed to be struggling a bit and Sam couldn't help feeling a bit guilty, suspecting that the medication was affecting Mark's coordination. But her worries proved groundless as within a few minutes, Mark was deemed ready for the boat.

The boat in question was an odd-looking wooden craft that probably hadn't been in the water in decades. Jack, Steve, and Mary helped each of the students take their places one-at-a-time in the boat, showing them the shoes and how to handle the large oars. Each practiced for a few minutes before the next took his or her seat. Jack, Mary and Steve took their positions.

Jack explained that when Steve gave the order, they would all stroke together following his lead and matching his rhythm. The process was tedious and it was a good half hour before the crew had any semblance of consistency. Both Sam and Mark were surprised at how tired they were, and they hadn't even gotten into the water yet.

It was even worse when they got into the water with a real boat. Somehow, Sam hadn't expected that the boat would feel unstable. That improved a bit once they started moving, but moving was a challenge

Inside, coordinating their strokes had been easy. With the water resisting, it was much harder to work together. For the first twenty minutes, they stopped constantly.

It did get better though as each person adjusted the strength of their strokes to match Jack's, and as they really learned to focus on Mary for the proper rhythm and direction.

By the end of the hour, they were moving smoothly through the water, making turns at the ends of the lake, and following commands uniformly. They were a team.

"Great job!" Jack praised as the exhausted team exited the boat. "Change into your dry clothes and let's get together for a debrief. Restrooms and changing areas are inside, men's to the left, women's to the right.

Ten minutes later they all gathered together and Jack began, "Congratulations to all of you! You've just learned something that only a fraction of the population can do. Rowing is a unique sport. It can be competitive or it can be pure recreation. It can also be solitary and contemplative. Some of us practice all aspects. Personally, although I still compete from time to time with the club here, I must admit to loving to row alone or with one other person.

"Here in the Bay Area, we're really lucky. We can row all year long and have choices of placid lakes, the San Francisco Bay, and even the ocean. If this class piqued your interest, I'd suggest taking additional lessons from the club. We have reduced rates for members and ultimately, you can just reserve boats at no charge.

"A few of you have expressed interest in rowing alone. I strongly suggest taking lessons with a group initially, then moving to just you and an instructor, then graduating to a single person boat. Also, if you want to row the Bay or the ocean, it's best not to do so alone until you're very confident with your skills and your water knowledge. Mother Nature can throw you some big surprises when you least expect them.

"Anyway, if you want to continue, let one of us know and we can help set you up with a program. Thanks for coming out this morning, and again, congratulations!"

As the male students approached Jack and Steve, Sam went up to Mary.

"So, what's it like to be a woman in this sport?"

"It's probably not what you'd expect. Most people have heard about men's crew teams and international competitions. But not many know that the NCAA only sponsors women's teams. I actually went to college on a rowing scholarship. Women's participation in the sport is growing rapidly. Not just in school, but at the recreational level. Our club has several great women's teams at all levels as well as a few coed ones. And while every sport has its macho component, there's not as much of that outside collegiate competition. With the recent push towards fitness, I think even more women are participating for recreation and fitness."

"Well, I'm not a terribly competitive person. I think I'm one of those women looking for fitness but also to meet people. I've spent what seems like decades in medical school and residency, and I need to get out more. At the same time, I'm no longer in my twenties, so the bar scene is not something I'm interested in."

Sam wasn't sure why she was confessing this to a complete stranger, but Mary didn't seem to notice.

"Yeah, I gotcha. On that front, I think that rowing is a great place to meet very fit men. Most are working professionals, and while you have to watch out for the married ones, the single men seem grateful to find someone who they can share a sport with.

"Did I hear that someone is looking for a single rower?"

Sam and Mary looked up to see a grinning Jack approaching.

"Give it up Jack," Mary replied. "Can't you let two girls have a conversation without trying to be the center of attention?"

Looking from Mary to Sam, Jack's expression changed. "You're right. I'm sorry. I can be a jerk sometimes. Please forgive me."

"You're forgiven. Now get lost."

As Jack slinked away, Sam asked, "Is there a story here?"

"Yes and no. We did have a thing for a couple of years. We split up amicably and are actually very good friends. That's why I can be so blunt with him. But every once in a while, little things he does piss me off. Sorry about that. He's clearly interested in you and Jack is one of those guys who goes after what he wants and usually get it."

"You're saying he's as successful with women as he is in business?

"Don't get me wrong. Jack is a great guy. And he's not a player. But I think he could use a bit more subtlety. Unfortunately, that's not in his nature. And if you do decide to see him, be aware that like in rowing, Jack is used to setting the pace. Try to find your own pace and rhythm, not his. Otherwise, the ride gets too crazy and you can lose yourself."

"Ah, I'm not thinking about getting involved with Jack."

"Okay," Mary agreed, a bit facetiously.

"Mary, can you help set me up with a program? I had a great time today and I think it's something I'd like to do."

"Sure. If you join the club, you get fifty percent off lessons and as Jack mentioned, you can get boats for free. I'd suggest taking a group class each week for the next few weeks. Then you can decide how you want to proceed. If you like, after next week's class, we can set up a time and I can take you out, just the two of us. That will give you a completely different experience. How's that sound?"

"That sounds perfect."

Sam joined the club and signed up for a lesson the following weekend.

A few days later, as she began her weekly session with Mark, she brought up the weekend.

"Mark, before we get started, I think it's important to discuss what happened Saturday."

"I thought it went really well. I had a great time, didn't you?"

"Actually, yes I did. However, ethical rules and treatment rules dictate that I can't have any interaction with patients outside the office. I discussed this with Doctor Karmere at the hospital. He's always been a great mentor for me and he made it clear that I had crossed the line on Saturday. He said that I should have left and rescheduled."

"But I don't have any problem with you being there. You've saved my life. And as we've discussed in our sessions, it's important for me to be able to admit to myself and to others that I have this problem."

"That's true. But it goes well beyond just the confidentiality. You need to see me in a very specific role – your psychiatrist. In that role, I can help you and we can work together professionally. Unfortunately, when you see me involved in other activities or with other people, you begin to think of me differently and that will affect how we can work together in the office."

"Okay. I think I can sort of see where you're coming from. I really don't think we'd have any problems, but if this is what we need to do, well, as they say, you're the Doctor.

"So, where do we go from here?"

"Well, Mark, I'd like to continue rowing. So if you're going to continue as well, we need to make sure that we're not taking classes together. I'd rather not talk to the instructors about this – again, a confidentiality thing, so perhaps you could check schedules or work with Jack to make sure we're not there at the same time."

"That sounds complicated. I mean, there are only so many classes. Plus, once the classes are done, how do we avoid each other if we're just showing up to row or if one of us is already rowing and the other shows up?"

"You're right. This is harder than I thought it would be. I think I need to pick another sport or find another club."

"I wouldn't want you to give up rowing on my account. I'm actually not that into it anyway. Maybe I should give it up."

And now Sam understood what Ken Karmere had reiterated. Just this one incident had complicated her relationship with Mark. If she quit, he'd feel bad. If he quit, he might resent her or she might resent him. This was not good.

"Mark, you can see that this has already complicated our working relationship. I should have done the ethical thing on Saturday and left. I knew it, so this hiccup is my fault. As the doctor, I'll make the decision. I'll either find another club or another sport to pursue. I really apologize for making this so complicated."

"Okay. I'll go with your decision. There's still a big part of me that thinks it wouldn't be a problem to see you outside the office, ah, casually. But I understand."

"It's settled then. Let's move on. Tell me about your week."

And amazingly, their session got back on track. Using the Socratic Method, Sam challenged Mark to take new perspectives on some of his beliefs. At times it was difficult, but per the plan that Sam had laid out, therapy was moving forward.

8

Brittany stormed into the Investigations Bureau of the San Francisco Police Department.

"I want to see Mike McKensey now!" she shouted.

Melissa, who had manned the front desk of Investigations for over ten years, examined the young woman who was clearly upset.

"Do you have an appointment?"

"I don't need a fucking appointment! My mother, Ashima James, was murdered two weeks ago and from what I can see, that asshole McKensey hasn't done shit to find out who killed my mother."

"Ms. James, may I remind you that this is a government office. You need to calm down or I'll ask an officer to have you removed."

"I don't need some god-damned glorified secretary to tell me to calm down. I'm a citizen who pays taxes and you work for me. Now get me McKensey before I come across that desk and rip your throat out!"

Melissa nodded at a concerned police officer who came up and took Brittany by the arm. Brittany took a swing at him but he deftly ducked.

"Ma'am, you have just assaulted a police officer. If you don't calm down, I'll have to arrest you."

"Fuck you, asshole! You assaulted me. I know my rights. I'm going to sue you and this whole fucking department for police brutality."

The officer glanced at Melissa who nodded in assent. Clearly this one needed to be restrained. The guard pushed Brittany against the wall, pulled her right arm behind her back while attaching a handcuff, then did the same with the left. Brittany screamed and continued her litany of non-stop epithets. After a few minutes, she went suddenly quiet and seemed to relax.

As she was being led away, Mike McKensey approached.

"Ms. Spangler, if you can calm down, my partner and I can give you an update on the investigation."

Seeing her nod as she tried to hide her tears, Mike continued, "Have a seat. I'll find a conference room and will be right back. Shawn, you can remove the cuffs."

As he walked away, Mike wondered about Brittany Spangler.

Although they had a lead via the emails that George Gray had received, they'd still checked into the whereabouts and backgrounds of the people closest to Ashima James.

Brittany had a pretty extensive sheet which included numerous arrests for assault, property damage, drug possession, and harassment, as well as quite a few hospitalizations. From what he could understand, she'd been diagnosed with Borderline Personality Disorder. He didn't know a lot about psychological disorders, but this one appeared to be one of the worst. Brittany was also highly educated and very intelligent. And according to those he'd talked to about her record, she could be quite devious, often using charm and vulnerability to divert attention from issues at hand. Although not at the top of their list, Brittany was certainly a suspect.

Mike stopped at Bob Simpson's desk.

"How do you want to play this?" Bob asked.

"I think we need to update her on where we are, tell her about the lead, and see how she reacts. Then we can push her on why she lied to us. Hopefully, she won't get violent."

Five minutes later Brittany, Bob, and Mike were seated in a conference room with a view towards the Bay. Mike and Bob sipped from their mugs of coffee while Brittany took great gulps from the bottle of water that Mike had brought her.

"I'm sorry about my behavior at reception," Brittany began. "But it's really frustrating. My mom is dead. Murdered. And you haven't caught the killer. Do you have any leads?"

"First Ms. Spangler, we need you to understand that investigations of this sort are very sensitive."

Seeing her about to react, Mike raised his hand. "What I mean by that is that information about the investigation that gets into the wrong hands can help the suspect and make our job more difficult.

"In general while we try to keep family members up to date, we don't give too much detail. It could put the investigation at risk. Plus, as you probably know from movies and books, most often, the killer is a member of the family."

Brittany's eyes went wide with shock. "You don't think that one of our family did this do you?" Then with sudden understanding, "You don't think that I killed my mom, do you?"

"At this point, we haven't ruled anyone out. But we do have a question. Why did you lie to us about your whereabouts at the time of your Mother's death?"

Brittany looked stunned. "Ah - " she began. Then she looked down at her hands, clearly deciding what she wanted to say. "Do I need a lawyer?"

"We can't advise you against getting a lawyer. However, at this point, we don't think you're a strong suspect. We're just trying to gather all the facts and part of our process is to look for inconsistencies. Can you tell us why you said you were in Washington when in fact you were in San Francisco?'

Brittany thought carefully. It almost looked like she was having a silent argument with herself. Mike and Bob weren't sure whether she would get angry, get up and walk away, or respond to the question.

After a long silence, her agitation calmed. She looked directly at Mike and responded, "I can see how this looks. The truth is, I wasn't supposed to be here. My mom and the rest of our family thought I was in DC. But I met this guy on the Internet and he invited me out here. I didn't want anyone to know because of what happened before. I got into trouble once in a similar situation and had promised not to do this again. I'm sorry I lied to you, but I didn't kill my mom. I loved her. She gave up everything for me."

And Brittany began to cry softly.

Bob walked over to a nearby credenza, opened it and removed a box of tissues which he handed to Brittany.

"Ms. Spangler," Bob began, sympathetically, "Is there anything more you want to tell us about your relationship with your Mother or that might have come to mind since we last met? Can you think of anyone who'd want to harm your Mother?"

Brittany thought carefully. "No. I've racked my brain and I can't think of anyone who'd want to harm her. She taught little kids, was active in her church and women's groups, and took dance classes. I really don't see who could have had anything against her."

She paused suddenly. "Unless it has something to do with Michael – my former stepfather was Michael James. He – ah – he killed himself. It was my fault, but I think people blame my mom. She left him because I asked her to and he killed himself because he lost his family and because I damaged his reputation. Oh God! If someone took revenge on my mom because of Michael, then it's my fault. I killed my mom!

And she burst into tears again; this time unable to hold back deep sobs. Bob got up to get her another bottle of water and when he returned, they waited for Brittany's tears to pass.

She wiped her eyes, blew her nose and sipped some water. She sat up straight, smoothed her clothes, and apologized, "I'm sorry. It just hit me. I seem to screw up so many things these days. I don't want to be the one responsible for my mom's death. Can we start over? Can you tell me about the investigation?"

Mike looked at Bob who nodded. "Ms. Spangler, can you agree to keep what we tell you confidential? This means you don't tell family or friends, no postings on social media, no contacting the press. As I mentioned, leaking this information could jeopardize our investigation."

"Yes. I promise to keep what you tell me to myself. But I really want to know."

"Okay. We have a good lead. A person claiming responsibility contacted a member of the press via email and said that she or he had killed your Mother because of what she had done to Michael James. So your idea may have been correct."

"Was it George Gray? The reporter, I mean?"

This time it was Mike and Bob who were surprised.

"How do you know George Gray?"

"I met him when he was doing a story on Michael's death. It seemed logical that if Michael was the reason, the killer would contact George."

"We can't confirm that, but I can assure you that we are in contact with the reporter and our best cybercrime investigators are tracking emails," Mike responded, kicking himself for revealing more than he wanted to.

"Emails, plural?"

"We really can't tell you more at this point. We will do our best to keep you up to date. You have our cards. If you have questions, or ideas, don't hesitate to contact us by phone or email. And please, if you do come back, be nicer to Melissa. She holds this place together."

"I promise. I am sorry. Sometimes I don't control myself very well."

Mike and Bob walked Brittany out and when the door had closed, Bob asked, "What do you think? Did we just hear a confession?"

"I'm not sure about the confession, but what we saw was

probably a very good act. From my research on Borderline Personality Disorder, most don't feel guilty or sorry about anything. We need to keep an eye on her. And I need to give George Gray a call to let him know who's coming to visit."

CHAPTER 2

"More than 150 years after Lincoln's Emancipation Proclamation, slavery is illegal almost everywhere. But it is still not abolished - not even here, in the land of the free. On the contrary, there is a cancer of violence, a modern-day slavery growing in America by the day, in the very places where we live and work. It's called human trafficking."

- Josh Hawley

1

George picked up his ringing desk phone knowing what was coming. It had only been fifteen minutes since he'd gotten off the call with Mike McKensey. He was sure Brittany Spangler was here to see him. He'd decided not to duck.

"Hi Mr. Gray. There's a Brittany Spangler here to see you. She says she doesn't have an appointment but claims that you'd certainly like to speak to her. The Golden Gate conference room is available if you need it."

"Thanks Joyce. I'll be right out."

George took a few minutes to review his notes. Mike McKensey had done a lot of work for him by summarizing Brittany's life over the past year. She'd been unable to hold a job, had been arrested and hospitalized several times, and had been diagnosed with Borderline Personality Disorder.

This sounded like a far cry from the young woman he'd met when he'd investigated the Michael James story. That Brittany seemed to have her life all planned out. She was intelligent, attractive, and already moving forward with a mission to end child slavery and violence against women in Haiti. What had happened? Then again, he probably knew what had happened. Brittany had finally realized that she'd destroyed Michael James and was now overcome with remorse.

But as he approached reception, he was surprised. This was not the out-of-control woman that McKensey had described. Brittany looked calm and confident. Very much the same young woman he'd met before.

Seeing him approach, Brittany stood up held out her right hand and smiled. "Mr. Gray, it's great to see you again!"

George took her hand and noticed her cool firm grip. "Ms. Spangler, good to see you too. And please call me George."

"And of course, you should call me Brittany."

As he led her to the conference room, George asked, "Can I get you anything? Coffee, a soda, water?"

"No thanks. I'm good."

Brittany took a seat at the end of the table and George sat to her right.

"Now, what can I do for you Brittany?"

"I understand you've been contacted by my mother's killer. I'd like to help find out who did it. My mother and I were in constant contact; I knew most of her friends and I have a lot of time on my hands right now so I can chase any leads you have. I'm also pretty good with computers and networking so I might be able to help chase down the person who emailed you."

George decided not to act surprised that Brittany knew he'd been contacted by the killer. She was smart enough to know that Mike McKensey would have called him after their conversation.

"Well, first, why don't you catch me up a bit on what's been going on with you since we last met. Weren't you working against child slavery in Haiti? Are you still associated with the same group?"

Brittany looked at George sincerely.

"Actually, no. It's been a rough year for me. I think I've been struggling to come to terms with the fact that I caused Michael's death. I was in denial for a long time. I felt neglected by my mom, so I pushed her to leave him, exaggerating things that happened between me and him. Looking back at it now, I find it hard to believe that I hated him only a year ago. I realize that I loved him more than my biological father for many years and I'm not sure why I turned so completely against him so suddenly. He begged my mom for family counseling but I refused and told her that if she went, I'd never speak to her again. At some point, family and friends began to see through my claims and my world came crashing down. To be quite frank, I've been unstable since, getting into trouble and having psychological problems which haven't been resolved."

"Aren't you living in Washington?"

"I was. The NGO I was working for there fired me right before my mom was killed. I was actually here in the City that day. I'd come to visit someone I met on Facebook. That didn't work out – I should have known better. And then with my mom, I completely lost it. As I've learned, people with my condition don't do well with sudden upheavals in their lives. I was hospitalized for a few days. The good news is that I met a fantastic psychiatrist. I've been through so many over the years, and especially this year, but Sam is different. She really seems to understand what's wrong with me and has introduced me to a therapy I'd never heard of before. It's called Schema Focused Therapy. Do you know anything about it?"

"Ah, no, I don't. Sam is a she?"

"Yes. Samantha Louis. She splits her time between inpatient

work at San Francisco Community and her own private practice. And her office is right above an amazing bakery in the Haight.

"Anyway, Sam is helping me reframe how I act and how I see myself and what has happened to me in the past. I really feel like she's helping me actually change for the better. Part of that is finding something that is important to me and going after it. In the past, I did a lot of things, tried a lot of things, but never could stick with anything – I just got bored. I'm hoping that if I can help with the investigation, I'll have a purpose. I've moved into my mom's house in Pacific Heights. The damage was repaired pretty quickly. My sister Francine has agreed that I can stay there for the foreseeable future. As her big sister, I convinced her that I could stay on top of the investigation so that she could continue her life."

George looked at Brittany who smiled back at him expectantly. This was definitely not the woman that Mike McKensey had described. So what was going on? Was she just a great actress? Was this part of her condition? His earlier quick Internet search on Borderline Personality Disorder described one of the symptoms as radical changes in moods. And even radical changes in feelings about people. It also warned those dealing with people who suffered from the Disorder to choose their words carefully. These people were experts at seeking negative meaning in the most innocuous statements, then turning against the person who spoke.

Where should he go with this? He didn't need the help. Janey could work on the computer side if he needed resources beyond Miguel, head if IT here at the Sentinel. And quite frankly, he didn't trust Brittany even if she did claim good intentions. He decided to punt.

"Brittany, at this point, I'm not sure how we could use you. While we often call on outside sources for information, the Sentinel doesn't usually let us use outside people for investigation." Then taking two business cards from his notebook, George continued. "Here's my card. If you write your number on the second one, I promise I'll call you tomorrow. I need to talk to some people here to see if there's any way to make this work."

Brittany studied George's face trying to discern whether this was a stalling tactic, a way to get rid of her, or if he was being honest. His open smile didn't reveal any ulterior motives so

Brittany smiled in return, scribbled her phone number on the back of one of the cards, and stood up.

"Thanks for listening to me. I hope we can meet again and that you can tell me more about your progress in finding my mom's killer.

George walked her to the reception area, shook her hand warmly and they parted ways.

Back in his office, George wrote up a quick email summarizing his conversation with Brittany and sent it to Morris and Mike McKensey.

2

Brittany returned home. The repairs were almost complete. Francine had initiated the work while Brittany was in Community Hospital. By the time she was out of the hospital, they'd replaced the windows, framed and replaced the front door, and installed new flooring in the entry way. A week later, the sheetrock was done and it only needed paint and decorations to be back to normal, or at least the new normal.

She really loved her mom's house, especially the upstairs with its views of the City. She'd envied her mom. After Michael's death, her mom had gone through a rough patch, but she certainly came out of it quickly. Then when Michael's money came to her, she moved on without looking back and had built an idyllic life in San Francisco.

Sure Brittany had asked her to leave Michael. But Brittany now realized that she had been unreasonable. Yes, she was jealous of her mom's relationship with Michael. And yes, she had demanded that her mom leave Michael. But once Michael died, shouldn't her mom have suffered more? Brittany certainly did. But her mom just moved on, happy in her new life while Brittany endured an endless Hell built on guilt.

Yes. Ashima James was a piece of work. Brittany realized that now. Her mom had stolen Brittany's biological father from her own best friend, seducing him after the couple had a fight. Then, years later when her new best friend bragged about her amazing entrepreneurial husband, her mom went after him too, capitalizing on rough spots in Michael's former marriage. And when Michael had assured his fortune, she decided to divorce him on Brittany's claims, guaranteeing herself an even better future.

Looking back at her childhood, Brittany knew that her mom was largely absent. It was Michael who took her and Francine to school. Michael who helped them with their homework, went to parent-teacher conferences. Michael who took them to after-school activities. Michael who took them to doctors' appointments, to friends' houses for parties or sleepovers and Michael who did almost everything around the house. Ashima James had her career. She didn't have time for her children.

As she thought about it more, she realized that it really wasn't long after she and Francine had left for their respective

Universities that Ashima had left Michael James. She had used Michael to raise her children then dumped him when the job was done knowing she would be assured of a solid financial future after the divorce.

Michael had loved her mom unconditionally and was destroyed when the family that he had raised turned against him.

Maybe her mom got exactly what she deserved. Maybe the killer did the world a service.

And now, Brittany had this wonderful house and enough money to live on for the rest of her life.

3

Mark Johansen and Richard Hatch were celebrating Mark's first day back to work by wolfing down pintxos at Txepetxa, the hot new tapas bar in Los Gatos.

"I can't believe how good these tapas are," Mark began, eyeing the Rioja on the tray of a passing waiter. "God, I wish I could split a bottle of that Rioja with you. I love Spanish wines."

"Yeah, but this Mosto is surprisingly good. I remember drinking it in the Basque region of Spain. Who would have thought that filtered grape juice with a slice of orange and an olive would be so good."

"It's okay but that Rioja…"

"Mark, I know it's hard, but as Dr. Louis explained, you really can't mix alcohol with the antipsychotic. Like the cocaine, it will bring Janice back. She's gone, right?"

"No, not completely. I see her less often, still hear her, and almost always feel like she's watching me. But we're working on it. I think I'm managing better. That's what a lot of this CBT - Cognitive Behavioral Therapy - is about, looking at different ways of reacting to things that I think I experience. And yes, I know about the alcohol. And the last thing I want is to have Janice come back or to relapse, but you can't blame a guy for missing an excellent wine pairing. Maybe someday…"

"I'd just try to put that out of your mind altogether. I'm sure there are a lot of things you've had to give up in life. I can name some things from college if you need reminding, but you've done just fine without them. Alcohol can be the same. Just start looking at people who drink as addicts who dull their senses and aren't as smart as they could be."

"Sometimes a guy can use to have his senses dulled a bit."

"You know I'm here to help. I won't be drinking either and if I can do it, so can you. Enough on that subject for now. How'd you feel about your first day back?"

"I must admit to being nervous. Between you and Sam, I now pretty much remember my performance at that last meeting, and I can see my downward spiral that was obvious to everyone but me. Today, I was afraid that no one would take me seriously anymore. But I was surprised to find everyone welcoming. I even had some great architecture discussions with the team. They seem to be welcoming me back almost as if nothing has happened."

"Mark, you're the founder of the company. The vast majority of the senior employees and many of the junior ones came on because your career, your leadership, and your management style inspired them. They know you went through a rough patch with the divorce. We all tried to be supportive through the process and a lot of us wish we'd done a better job. Several of us wondered if putting a contract out on Janice would help.

"We've all been hoping you'd get back to the Mark we all love and admire. It doesn't take much to recognize that guy, and everyone saw him today."

Richard raised his glass of Mosto. "To you Buddy. Welcome back!"

"Right back at you Richard. I couldn't have done it without you. Now if I can just stay on track."

"Well, as Dr. Louis said, if you practice good behavior, it will become part of you and you won't have to work at it so much. You've done much harder things in your life and we've both gotten up from some bad falls. I think once you know you can be successful, you can do it again. We can do it again."

"Speaking of bad falls, how's it going with Mindy? I guess your divorce is final now, too. I'm sorry I was so out of it. I should have been there for you."

"No. Mine was different. Mindy and I had been growing apart for years. I wasn't starry-eyed in love with her like you still were with Janice. I knew she was fooling around with her yoga instructor. I thought it was just a phase she was going through. But I was blown away when she announced that she was leaving me for him. How typical is that? Years ago it was men who had midlife crises and left their faithful wives for younger women. Now it seems to have flipped. Middle-aged women are leaving their husbands who've worked their asses off to be successful. They take half or more of what we've worked so hard for and off they go to have a good time. Well, good riddance. I'm done with that for good. I'll never get married again."

"God, you're in bad shape too. I've never heard you so cynical."

"Nah, don't worry about me. I'm really fine.

"Hey, this is supposed to be a celebration. Let's grab a couple more of those pintxos. I can't stop eating the mini croissant sandwiches, filled with that spicy salted cod.

"And tell me about your sessions with Dr. Louis. What's this new CBT technique she's using – if it's not confidential?"

"No, it's not confidential. As Sam explained it to me, behavior, feelings, and thoughts all affect each other. My beliefs result in specific consequences, both emotional and behavioral. CBT seeks to help me look at why many of my thoughts and beliefs are not based in reality. If I change them, then my feelings change and my behavior changes as well. If my behavior changes, then so will my thoughts and feelings. Ultimately, I should be able to manage on a daily basis, even if my schizophrenia never goes away.

"I saw a bumper sticker the other day, and while it's an oversimplification, it said 'Don't believe everything you think'. Obviously with my hallucinations, and my paranoid behavior, this is true for me. But not believing everything you think or feel is hard. We're working on that."

4

George had spent the last three days chasing the leads about Ryan Hamilton. So far the evidence was pretty damning. InfoEuro's account balances didn't match up with their sales. Money seemed to be coming in from another source. When George followed up on the names of the 'suppliers', he discovered shell companies that were run by individual 'procurers' – people in Eastern Europe with a knack for finding virtually anything, legal or not.

George met with the two young women who had escaped from their 'owners' and they gave him details on their stories. He had never imagined how vulnerable people could be. A part of him had thought that trafficking victims were primarily kids with personal problems or people on the fringes of society. The interviews had proven him wrong.

Each of these victims was intelligent and motivated to get ahead in life. Hamilton was a predator who had found a way to take what appeared to be a legitimate, positive tool for those looking to advance, and instead, to use it to trick people into situations from which they had no hope of escape. It was modern slavery. Instead of going to Africa to rip families from their homes, he perverted the Internet, using its extensive reach to find his slaves.

George began what would become continuing research on human trafficking. His first search turned up polarisproject.org which also sponsored the human trafficking hotline. And George was blown away.

He thought he knew about human trafficking, or at least sex trafficking. He knew that minors were at risk. He knew that young people, and especially young women and girls in Europe and Asia were victims. He knew that organized crime profited hugely from these exploited people. He also remembered the backpage.com scandal that had only recently been prosecuted.

Backpage.com was formerly the second largest classified ad website on the internet. Over the years, although they appeared to work with authorities on stopping ads which resulted in human trafficking, in the end, the CEO and several others were indicted on conspiracy and money laundering charges stemming out of the trafficking that occurred on the site. George had gone back through the articles on Backpage to see how it had evolved (or perhaps devolved) and found quite a few similarities to the subterfuge lotsofjobs.com used to recruit victims.

But it was the Polaris Project that really opened his eyes to the extent of trafficking, not just in or from third world countries, but here in the US.

The project had examined tens of thousands of cases of documented trafficking and sorted them into twenty-five categories. Sure, a few were familiar to George: Illicit Massage Parlors, Brothels, Outdoor Solicitation, Strip Clubs, Escort Services, Pornography, Sex Hotlines, but the others were shocking. The Polaris Project identified huge numbers of trafficking cases in what we think of as normal, day-to-day services:

- Recreational Facilities
- Health Care
- Forestry and Logging
- Carnivals
- Factories and Manufacturing
- Commercial Cleaning Services
- Arts and Entertainment
- Landscaping
- Hotels and Hospitality
- Construction
- Health and Beauty Services
- Agriculture
- Peddling and Begging
- Restaurants and Food Service
- Travelling Sales Crews
- Domestic Work

In each of these categories, the Project explained the nature of the work, how victims were recruited, and who profited. Human trafficking was everywhere around us. We just didn't see it and didn't know how to recognize it. George hoped to change that, revealing the extent of trafficking to all of the Sentinel's readers.

With interviews and preliminary research done, George started outlining his first article on Ryan Hamilton using the information that the informant had provided. He decided to include the parallels with Backpage. Lotsofjobs wasn't an isolated case of exploitation.

Next, George laid out a plan for the series of follow-on pieces. The first would begin with sex trafficking. That would get people's attention, particularly as he emphasized unexplored vulnerabilities.

He'd then continue with subsequent articles following the Polaris Project's categories, focusing on how to recognize trafficking and its victims in each area.

George attached his plan to an email and sent it to Morris, asking for a meeting the next day to discuss how to proceed. He took a deep breath and dove into the first draft of the exposé on lotsofjobs.com. He lost track of time.

His phone rang.

"George, did you lose track of time?" Janey asked. "It's almost eight o'clock."

"Janey, I'm so sorry. It's the trafficking. I got a bit carried away."

He glanced at his watch and continued.

"If I race out now, I should be able to catch the eight thirty train. That should get me home before ten."

"It's okay George. Did you at least eat something?"

Thinking back on his day, George realized that he hadn't even had lunch.

"Now that you mention it, I'm starving."

"Well, if you're starving, pick something up at the Caltrain station if you have time, and I'll order a pizza. I can't wait to hear what you've learned!"

George shut down his laptop, and raced to the Caltrain station. He made the 8:30 train and by the time he arrived in Mountain View, he was nearly done with his first draft, except for the details of Hamilton's impending arrest. He'd review the draft with Janey. This time he was on to something that would really benefit a lot of people and, for a change, shouldn't have collateral damage. He was even more excited than he was on his first day at the Sentinel.

5

Checking his email before leaving for work, George was only slightly surprised that he'd received a message from Morris timestamped five thirteen am. Hamilton had been arrested at his home in the wee hours of the morning and lotsofjobs.com had been shut down. George tried to access the site and indeed, there was a Department of Justice intercept banner stating that lotsofjobs.com and affiliated websites had been seized as part of a Federal investigation by several agencies. It appeared that the Justice Department moved surgically in situations like this one.

Morris' email also included details of the arrest, including the fact that it had taken place at just after four am. Along with the arrest, searches of Hamilton's homes, his offices, and computers were underway and related information, bank accounts, and investments were being seized as evidence.

Morris' email was surprisingly detailed and for all intents and purposes, he had written the rest of George's story. In fact, George was only half way to the office when he completed the cut, paste, and edits, and then uploaded the article to the Sentinel server. He sent a copy directly to Morris and dozed for the rest of the ride to the City.

Arriving at the office, Joyce let him know that Morris wanted to see him as soon as he got in. George made his way to his cubicle, dropped his laptop into the docking station, booted it and raced over to see Morris.

Motioning George to the somewhat ratty couch in his office, Morris came around his desk, closed the office door and pulled a chair to face George.

"George, Sterling Rockwell asked me to thank you for the excellent work you've done on this story. If you were a rising star before, now corporate has a good sense of what you can do."

George found himself at a loss for words. Morris just smiled.

"Not so great at accepting compliments, huh?" Morris joked.

"No. It's not that. It's just that the last several days have been a whirlwind. I'm glad everyone is pleased, but really, this is all due to the informant, whoever he or she is."

"Well, he or she chose you and you've done a superb job of turning a lead into a great story. This is one of the biggest exposés the Sentinel has seen in a long time. And, as we've discussed, this is just the beginning."

"Yeah, I'm looking forward to continuing to pursue this. I'm not sure if you could tell from my proposal, but trafficking goes much deeper and hits much closer to home than I ever imagined. So, what did you think of my proposal?"

"I've discussed it with the Sterling and the editorial staff and we'd like you to do an in-depth article once a week for the foreseeable future. We're still debating the order, but since you spoke to sex trafficking in the article on Hamilton, we'll likely save that for later. For next week, we'd like you to get started on indentured servitude and slavery in the tech sector. We'd like you to show people that even highly educated workers can get trapped by these scams. It may not be as sensational as the sex trafficking, but we think it will be a real eye-opener, with particular impact in the Silicon Valley and the Bay Area. We'll get back to you weekly with what we think should be next."

"I hadn't really thought of it that way, but it's an excellent idea. People need to know that it's closer than they think. You're right. This is a better way to kick it off."

"George, for now, this should be your primary focus. We need to figure out what we're going to do with the Ashima James story, particularly if there are really more murders."

"Morris, I know you've warned me before about taking on too much, but I can't let that one go. I feel responsible and I need to be part of helping catch the killer. Please don't take me off the story."

Morris thought about it silently for a moment, looking intently at George who felt like he was being examined by a psychiatrist.

"Okay. I'll tell you what George. I really think this is going to get too big for you. So, if you're not willing to give up on the murders, we need to get you some help. I'll be back to you later today after I decide who will be working with you. You'll take the lead, and I'll be watching closely for a while to make sure you can delegate some of the work, but that's my decision. Either choose one or accept some help."

George asked himself whether he could work with someone else on a story. He wasn't sure that he could. Thus far, he'd pretty much been on his own. Every story was his. Could he share? Even more challenging was could he lead someone else?

For now, he'd agree. And then he'd talk to Janey about how

this could work. She led multiple teams of engineers at her company and claimed that some of them were better engineers than she was. That was hard to believe. But somehow, she made it work. He'd met her team on several occasions and they loved and respected Janey. They really were a team. Maybe George could learn to lead a team too.

"Okay. I'll do my best. I'm not sure how good I'll be at leading someone else, but I'll try. And I'll be back to you for advice."

"Of course, George! That's what I'm here for. And one last thing. What your informant gave us was huge. If he does this again, you're going to be buried. Delegation and working with a team is something you need to do. I guarantee it will be great for your career."

George left his office with his head spinning, both excited at the dramatic change his work was taking and terrified.

6

Sam looked out her window as Brittany drove away. Her practice was definitely picking up. How could she have imagined that finishing up with her last patient would be a big letdown? Sure, it may have been the case of a lifetime, but with Mark Johansen and now Brittany, her practice certainly hadn't become a parade of adolescent eating disorders.

With Mark, they were about to move into another phase of therapy. The CBT was working, helping Mark manage his behavior, and he was tolerating the medication well. Now maybe, just maybe, they could get to the root of his problem. More and more, Sam sensed that Mark had been subject to some childhood trauma. As to whether or not it was the cause of his schizophrenia, that was another story. But it was certainly worth pursuing.

As for Brittany Spangler, Borderline Personality Disorder or BPD was always a challenge. In fact in Sam's opinion, it was the biggest challenge in psychiatry today. Like schizophrenia, a family history of the disorder tended to increase the odds of suffering from it, so it could be genetic, but then again, it could be a question of environment, or a genetic predisposition. Childhood trauma seemed to increase the chances too. These days, that could be said about most psychiatric problems.

But beyond understanding the cause, treatment of BPD was difficult, particularly for very intelligent patients like Brittany. Most BPD patients were master deceivers. And though the Schema-focused Therapy appeared to have started well, it was quite possible that Brittany was just trying to manipulate Sam. Time would tell.

Just as Sam was finishing up her notes on her session with Brittany, her office phone rang.

"This is Doctor Louis. How can I help you?"

"Hi Doctor Louis – ah, Sam. This is Jack Trageser. You took my rowing class a few weeks ago."

"Hi Jack. How are you?"

"I'm doing well. I understand that you've continued your lessons and from what Mary tells me, you've made great progress. She said you'd been rowing with her and that you're a natural."

"I doubt that I'm a natural, but so far I'm finding I really do enjoy it," Sam replied, in nervous anticipation of what would come next.

"Well, I was wondering if you'd like to get together sometime. I'd like to get to know you. Maybe we could take a double out on the lake?" But sensing some hesitation on the other end of the line, "Or maybe lunch?"

"Lunch would be nice. When did you have in mind?"

"Are you by chance free today?"

Sam was free for lunch today but she remembered Mary's advice about not letting Jack set the pace.

"Actually, I'm booked today. Let me check my calendar. Um, how about Thursday? There's a nice bistro not far from my office called Mario's. One o'clock?"

"Ah, sure," Jack responded, clearly a bit surprised.

"Great! See you then."

"Thanks Sam, I'm looking forward to it."

Sam hung up, pleased with how she'd handled Jack. During the hours she'd spent with Mary rowing, the conversation had turned to Jack Trageser more than once. And it had been Sam who brought him up.

Mary was clearly amused. She shared some details of their relationship and from what Sam could see, although they had a lot of fun together, it was ultimately clear to both Jack and Mary that they weren't really meant for each other. They'd had what Sam thought of as a very rare amicable split and were still good friends.

After getting to know her over the course of their lessons, Mary encouraged Sam to pursue Jack. And while Sam couldn't see herself actually initiating contact, she knew Jack would call. Mary had mentioned that Jack had asked about her and had asked Mary if Sam might be willing to go out with him. Mary had cautioned Jack, suggesting he go slow. And now, Sam was about to have her first serious date in a very long time.

7

Sam had made twelve-thirty reservations at Mario's and showed up on time. This gave her half an hour before Jack would arrive. Sam wanted to be the first there to help avoid the awkwardness of meeting Jack at the front and getting seated together. She'd described her guest to the host and was seated at her favorite table in a quiet part of the restaurant with her back to the wall. As she took her seat, she had to admit that this was about control.

Sam had pulled her hair back into a low pony tail and had dressed conservatively. Attractive, but not sexy was the goal. Slacks, a collared shirt, flats, and minimal makeup did the trick. With luck, she'd come off as the friendly girl next door.

And, as she always did with her patients, she had a plan. She would control the conversation while making an assessment of Jack Trageser. That was the plan. Then again, this wasn't a psych session. This was a date. What was wrong with her?

The waiter came by and she ordered an Afghan iced tea with cardamom and cream, then sat patiently, eyeing her surroundings to make sure that no patients were nearby – a professional habit.

At five to one, the host brought Jack to the table. She stood up and offered her hand before he could make a move for a hug or a quick kiss on the cheek. If he was disappointed, he didn't show it.

"I'm really glad you agreed to meet me," he began.

"It's nice to be here. I haven't been out on a – to lunch in quite a while.

Mistake number one.

"How's your time look for lunch? Do you have to be back in your office soon?

"No, not really. My next appointment is at two-thirty, so we should be able to enjoy a leisurely lunch."

Jack took a deep breath and relaxed.

"What's good here?" he asked.

"Well, as you can see, it's a Mediterranean Bistro. Much of the food is from the Middle East, but there are also some Greek and Italian dishes. The salads and sandwiches are great as are most of the entrees. But I have to say that the pumpkin Borani is amazing. Maybe we could start with that.

"Since lunch is my primary meal, I'm going to order the

Moroccan Stuffed Chicken."

"I think I'll do the same. Wine?"

"I don't think so. I have patients this afternoon. Feel free to have some if you like."

"No. I'll pass. I have client meetings this afternoon too. You know, not that long ago, wine at lunch was the thing in the Silicon Valley. I found that I worked a bit slower in the afternoons. I've been much clearer and more focused since that period passed."

"So you've been in high tech for a while?"

"Yeah, I started out at Cisco in its relatively early days, made out pretty well on stock options, then left with a few others to do my first startup. It went reasonably well – I learned a lot. But at the end of the day, the investors made out and the founders didn't. Making it in the Valley isn't as easy as the media hype makes it out to be. Still, with my latest startup, I think I've finally done it right."

Jack looked up as the waiter approached. He asked if they were ready, focusing on Jack, but Sam jumped in.

"We'll start with the pumpkin Borani, and will both have the Moroccan Stuffed Chicken. Jack, what would you like to drink?"

"I'll have whatever she's having. It looks good."

"Afghan iced tea it is," replied the waiter. I'll be back with that in a few minutes followed by the Borani. Thank you!"

"So tell me about your startup. Balanced News?"

"Yes. Balanced News. Well, I like to think of myself as one of many who helped develop the Internet. We had a common idea that the Internet would be the great leveler. I mean that everyone is created equal on the Internet and with unlimited access to unlimited information, the world would become a better place. It's hard to repress people if they're well-informed.

"And for quite a while, it went that way. Most of us are in tech for the technology. We love to create and we love to work together to change the world through our inventions.

"Mark, Richard, and I, along with several others who started out in Silicon Valley had religion. We really believed we could be a force for change.

"Unfortunately, over the past few years, that purpose has been perverted. Now we have people manipulating the Net for their own personal and often insidious purposes.

"Even one of our own group, a guy named Marcus Jameson,

decided that money and power were more important. He got caught up in his own success. I can't come up with a less over-used phrase, but he really went over to the dark side.

"He runs a company called Unbreakable Systems and uses his position and power to influence people to give him even more power and influence.

"But it's not just the rich and powerful.

"You've probably seen how social networks help you propagate your own points of view, and how even the most reputable news sites tend to tailor the news you see to stories you've looked at before. This creates more polarization. To some degree, we're all responsible for this, as we tend to appreciate things that reinforce our beliefs.

"Our great social experiment in the Internet is now creating more divisiveness among us when its original purpose was to bring diverse people together. I'm hoping Balanced News can help."

"So how does it work?" Sam asked, cutting into a slice of the spiced baked pumpkin topped in a creamy garlic-mint yogurt sauce that the waiter had just delivered. "Yum, by the way."

Jack took a forkful from a slice he served himself and nodded appreciatively. "This is really good!

"Well, I'll try not to go get into the technical weeds, but we do three things. First, we validate sources. We have a sophisticated algorithm that identifies news stories, blogs, and even personal posts on a variety of social media sites, and establishes a credibility rating based on the credibility of the original source and of the people who have forwarded it. Second, we don't tailor what's delivered to you. Indeed, if you have a predisposition to a particular type of news, sports, or other interest, we balance what you receive. You can choose to ignore it, but if you do, you might find a little bit more of opposing views in your feeds. And finally, we have a forum moderator. This is a piece of AI software – artificial intelligence – that ensures that people are respectful to each other, even when they strongly disagree. If someone responded 'Fuck You, you know-nothing asshole' to a comment, before it gets posted, our AI moderator would respond asking that the profanity be eliminated and if the disagreement could be put in a better way. It won't let a nasty post get through."

"And this works?"

"We seem to be doing surprisingly well. I admit that even though this was my idea, I was a bit skeptical. But we've had some great feedback. Several hardcore liberals and conservatives have sent us thank-you letters, emails, and site comments telling us they're learning things they never knew, that they're starting to see other perspectives, and that even if they disagree, they're beginning to have discussions with people they would never have given the time of day."

Lunch arrived and the two ate in comfortable silence for a few bites.

"It sounds impressive."

"Well, we'll see. More than one of my brilliant ideas has fizzled in the Valley. I'm hoping it will make a difference, but I have a feeling that it's too little too late. Plus, those guys who have perverted the Net need to be stopped. I wish I could find a way to do that.

"But enough about me. How do you like being a psychiatrist?"

Sam thought a minute before responding.

"I really like it. I must admit that after med school, internship, residency, and then my psych residency, I was pretty burned out. I'd spent too much time doing things I didn't want to do, following ridiculous orders, and being submitted to long hours and what seemed like hazing from the Attendings and senior residents.

"When I started working at Community, it was hard. We see a lot of homeless and very low-income people with major psychological disorders. They need to be on medication. They need therapy. But as psychiatrists, we're discouraged from doing therapy, and for our indigent patients, it's almost impossible to keep them on meds or to get them to change their lifestyles when they don't have a consistent place to sleep, regular meals, or stability in the rest of their lives."

"Sounds tough. Why do you do it?"

"Well, I have to believe that something is better than nothing. Plus, I seem to keep stumbling into interesting cases. And now, with my private practice starting to pick up, it's more and more up to me to decide on my mix of patients and whether I want to do therapy or not. I'm beginning to feel like I do make a difference."

"That's all we can ask for."

8

At 7am sharp on Saturday morning, Sam knocked on the door of Mary's small house in Daly City. It was one of those rare fall days where there was no fog in Daly City. In fact, with the warm winds blowing from inland, there was no fog on the coast at all and it promised to be an unusually warm day for this often chilly residential area on the cliffs overlooking the ocean just south of San Francisco.

"Want some coffee before we go?" Mary asked after she opened the door.

"No, I'm all set. Actually, I'm pretty excited about my first time on the Bay. It looks like a perfect day for it."

"Yep, we lucked out. It should be an excellent day for rowing, though I must admit that I prefer quiet foggy mornings."

They jumped into Mary's van and began the ten-minute drive down to Oyster Point in South San Francisco. The plan was to row to Coyote Point and back, a sixteen-mile round trip.

After getting the double scull set up and Sam comfortably seated aboard, Mary took the boat out. Once they were a hundred yards out, Sam joined in the rowing, following Mary's lead, getting into comfortable rhythm.

"How do you feel?" Mary asked.

"I'm settling in. I'm still a bit nervous. This is pretty different from the lake. But I'm concentrating on my stroke and watching you."

"Don't worry. Before we get to Coyote Point, you'll be enjoying the scenery. It all becomes natural, almost unconscious.

"Part of what I love about open water like this is that you don't have to think about boundaries. You can just keep going.

"Speaking of boundaries, how'd it go with Jack?"

"We had a nice lunch."

Sensing some reluctance, Mary pressed a bit, "Ah come on. You can tell me. Spill!"

"I guess I'm a bit reluctant to talk about it on two counts. First, this is all new to me. I really haven't dated or had any kind of romantic relationship in quite a while. And second, Jack is your ex."

"Hey, you know that Jack and I are good friends now. There's no reason to worry about me. I'm very happy with how things are between me and him. Ultimately, I'd like to see Jack with the right person. It just wasn't me."

"I guess I sort of admitted I'm interested in him. So tell me, what happened between you two? You're both successful, dynamic, physically active people. You seem like a perfect fit."

"At the beginning, I thought so too. And when it was just the two of us, hiking, rowing, running, or doing other physical things together, it was perfect. That's probably why we're still great friends."

"So where did it go wrong?"

"I don't know if I can say it went wrong, exactly. I guess the main thing was that he's a bit of a showoff. You don't see it much when he's alone with you, but in a crowd, at a party, or sometimes, just among friends, he needs to be the center of attention. And as I said before, as much as he hides it in his deference, he really wants control. That's my job!" she laughed.

"And I guess there's one more thing. I'm not sure I ever saw the real Jack. I don't know if it's all a show or if it's just that there's a part of him that he keeps hidden. Ultimately, as I think about it now, I realize that what I thought of as that missing spark, was more likely a lack of true intimacy. We had lots of fun, but for a life-long partner, you need intimacy and we never got there. Maybe you'll have better luck."

They rowed silently, enjoying the meditative rhythm of their strokes each lost in thought. As they approached Coyote Point, Mary eased up.

"How are you feeling, Sam? We've been rowing for over an hour. Are you tired? Should we take a break here at the Marina?"

"You know, Mary, I haven't felt this good in forever. My body is in sync. You were right, I've relaxed into it and I love being on the Bay. I'm sure I'll be exhausted, a complete waste of space when we get back, but let's keep going. I'll buy you lunch.

"And thanks for talking about Jack. I am interested. I'm also a bit intrigued. But don't worry. I'll try to take the lead. And I'll watch out. I'm going to go very slowly."

9

Mark stopped at the bakery to buy two pain au chocolates (or was it pains au chocolate), before making his way upstairs for his session with Sam. What was that battle raging in France? In the north, they called these pain au chocolate and in the south of France, it was chocolatine. He had a French friend on Facebook who posted a picture of two baguettes with a chocolate bar in between saying that this was pain au chocolate. The subsequent picture showed the regular pastry with the 'chocolatine' label. The post had over 100,000 Likes and thousands of comments arguing the merits of each position. It must be nice to live in a country where you could have a heated debate over the name of a pastry.

Mark made his way upstairs, chocolatines in hand. Just as he started to take a seat in her reception area, Sam's office door opened and Sam greeted Mark warmly.

"You're a bad influence on me, Mark. I have a hard enough time staying away from the bakery downstairs without you bringing it with you."

"I know you like these chocolatines as my French friend calls them and for me, I can relax a bit more at the beginning of our sessions sharing a snack with you. This session may be more difficult than most."

"Well, we'll get to that shortly. I have hot water ready. Did you want some tea?"

"Yes. Please."

"Okay," Sam began, taking a seat across from Mark's rocking recliner. "Tell me what's going on. Why don't you start with the medication. Having any more side effects?"

"Ah, that's part of what I wanted to talk to you about. I'm not sure if they're side effects or something else. I've been having weird dreams and I'm getting what is probably just paranoia about Richard."

"Well, let's spend the session on the dreams and on your feelings about Richard. However, I also want to check in on your journal. Are you keeping up with it?

"Pretty much."

"Let's try to make that a solid yes next time. Mark, the journal is very important. You can look back through it and see how you've been doing. You'll see progress, be better able to spot potential problems, and it may help you get a better handle on what you're perceiving versus reality. I honestly think this could be one of the most important tools for managing your problems. And if there is any chance of a cure, the journal may be the critical piece."

"Sorry. I'll be better."

"Before we talk about the dreams, and potential issues with Richard, I just want to check in on Janice. How are you doing with her?"

"Well, she's pretty much gone. I don't see her anymore. I do hear her from time to time, but before I can react, I remember what we've worked on, and I make myself realize that it's not real. I think I'm managing really well and actually making progress. I feel like I'm starting to get some control over my life."

"Excellent!" Okay. Tell me about the dreams."

"The one that bothers me the most seems to be recurring with only slight variations. I wake up in the middle of the night and look around the room. It's usually lit by moonlight coming in through the skylights above the bed. It is my room. It seems to be correct in every detail, even where I left my book on the nightstand. If I change that placement the next night, it's represented in my dream.

"Anyway, I look down towards my feet, and they're huge. They seem to be getting bigger and bigger. As I turn back towards the room, everything is getting bigger, and I'm getting smaller and smaller. I look at my hands and arms, and they're tiny. But my feet keep getting bigger. I try to get up out of bed, but I'm paralyzed. Even if I could move, it would be too far to reach the floor. I do my best to control my panic. I tell myself it's just a dream and that I'm going to wake up but I'm stranded for what seems like hours.

"Eventually, I do wake up. I repeat the ritual of looking around the room, but this time, everything is normal. I think what's most scary about this is that I really can't tell the difference between being asleep and awake. The room is so real."

Sam nodded understandingly. "You know, I can remember having almost an identical dream when I was a kid. In most cases these dreams come from a feeling of helplessness. The world is too big for us and we don't have control over its effects on us. The timing on this dream is interesting, as is the fact that it's recurring. I suspect our therapy sessions are starting to have a deeper impact. As we discussed, sometimes things get a bit worse before they get better.

"So tell me about Richard."

"You know that Richard is my best friend. We've been friends forever and we've been through some really rough times together. I've always trusted him completely – well, except for my psychotic episode.

"Anyway, lately, I'm getting a strange feeling about him. I can't put my finger on anything concrete, but it just seems like something is going on that he's not telling me about. Like I said, I'm probably just being paranoid."

"It's possible that you're being paranoid. But just as we've talked about you not believing everything you see, hear, or think, you can't not believe everything either. You need to get to the point where you trust your deductive powers, and then your instincts.

"You know, it's quite possible that Richard is keeping something from you or is a bit resentful after your return. After all, the company was pretty much all his while you were out. I'm not saying you have anything to worry about. I'm just suggesting that what you're sensing may be accurate, but your condition might be magnifying its significance.

"Look at it objectively, and if it seems appropriate, have a talk with him. He's certainly been there for you. And, he's been really supportive of your efforts to get back into the company. I think you should keep the door open with him. Talk to him."

"That makes sense. Thanks!"

"Well, we don't have a lot of time left today. I want to take our remaining time to continue with free association. I went through your answers from last time and they gave me some ideas. I created a set of words so we can do some word association. Let's give it a try and next time, I think we're going to do a bit deeper dive."

10

Detectives Mike McKensey and Bob Simpson had just left their status meeting with their boss, Lieutenant Jim Connors. Connors wasn't pleased.

After weeks of investigation, they had no leads and Connors was pushing for them to move on.

"I can't believe we're at a dead end," Bob began. "Nothing. We've got nothing."

"Yeah, and I don't like Ashima's daughter Brittany for the murder. I know she has a lot to gain, but when I talked to May about it, she suggested I take a look at how many bombings had been done by women. I searched, and if you rule out terrorist suicide bombings, I couldn't find any – zero!"

"I sometimes forget that your wife works homicide for Marin County. I gotta admit that I never thought it would work – you two. Most cop relationships with regular people fail miserably so I couldn't imagine two cops married to each other."

"But you know Bob, I think that's why it works. First, we're older than most. We've each been through those bad marriages where our spouses could never understand our hours, the risks we take, the depression, or the stress."

"Yeah, sure. Now you've got twice as much!"

"No. Really. We each understand what the other is going through. And when we talk about our cases, the other can not only listen and understand, they can give new perspectives. Like with Brittany. She looked good for it, and maybe she still is, but May's right. Women just don't seem to use bombs to kill people."

"Yeah, but Brittany is a piece of work. You remember what George said about how she behaved when she got to his office after meeting with us? Instead of the emotional wreck we saw, he saw a cool, calm, focused Brittany. I still like her for this. She's smart. Too smart."

"You may be right, Bob. But she voluntarily turned over her laptop and phone to us and the techs found no emails or visits to bomb-making sites."

"Like I said, she's smart, and we don't know how smart. She told George that she could help out on the computer side. Maybe she's a hacker that's good enough to hide her tracks from our techs."

"Maybe. It just doesn't feel right to me. The tone of the emails is male. Plus, I have a gut feeling that the guy who gave George the trafficking lead is the murderer. Brittany couldn't get the detailed information that guy has given George. I may believe in coincidences but having those emails go to George back to back is no coincidence. We've got to keep looking."

"Yeah, but will Connors let us spend more time on this without another lead? I know I like Brittany, but we've got bupkis. We can't hold her; we can't get a warrant to search further; and we can't get resources to tail her. We're stuck. Sometimes I hate this job!"

CHAPTER 3

"My goal is to see that mental illness is treated like cancer."
- Jane Pauley

1

With all the attention his articles on the trafficking case were receiving, George had been getting into the office much earlier than usual. He wanted to be responsive to the countless email and social media postings asking about trafficking. The more people knew, the sooner human trafficking would end.

So it came as no surprise that George was sitting at his desk when the first email came in. It was just like the last time except that George was receiving it in real time.

From: tf7u93ig8vpk4<tf7u93ig8vpk4@tf7u93ig8vpk4.com>
Date: November 13, 20XX 07:59 AM PDT
To: George Gray <GeorgeGray@nysentinel.com>
Subject: Exposing Unethical Zillionaires

Hello George,

I'm pleased to see how successful we were in bringing down Ryan Hamilton and his perverted use of the Net for human trafficking. With your articles and social media postings on the subject, I think we've made a real dent in trafficking and have dramatically increased the public's awareness of how insidious trafficking is and how it can exist in plain sight.

As you might imagine in receiving this email, I've got another one for you. Boris Yanofski, the founder of NoConspiricies.com needs to be stopped. I know. A lot of people think his site is just trash that appeals to conspiracy theorists everywhere. That is certainly true. However, it has enabled him to amass a fortune and to wield un-justified political influence while further enriching himself. Unfortunately, there is no law against this in the US (unlike in Europe where there are laws that protect citizens from this type of malicious disinformation). But there is a law against murder.

If you open the attached file using my name as the password key, you will see proof that Yanofski murdered his wife.

Since you don't know how I got this, I believe it can legally be used as evidence. While this alone won't bring down Yanofski's empire, his wife's family will likely shut it down once he's convicted. Have fun!

tf7u93ig8vpk4

George didn't know who Yanofski was and he didn't remember anything about an internet mogul committing murder. Surely that must have made some news.

He used Janey's special software to scan the attachment for viruses and finding none, opened the zip file. In it was a document that described the murder, and a video.

According to the document, Yanofski, his best friend and future business partner Mikhail Papapovich, and Yanofski's wife Sandra were hiking on the Pacific Crest Trail in the Sierra Nevada. Just above a cliff with a drop of thousands of feet, Yanofski asked Papapovich to take a video of him and Sandra against the spectacular backdrop. The shocking video showed the couple posing and then Yanofski pushing his wife over the edge.

Although the family suspected foul play, with just the two witnesses who claimed this was a hiking accident, that's what the inquest concluded. Yanofski inherited his wife's fortune which he used to launch NoConspiracies.com.

George spent the next hour scouring the Net for information about Yanofski, his wife, and NoConspiricies.com. He was about to leave his office to present what he'd found to Morris when he heard another email come in. His intuition told him to take a look, and indeed, just over an hour after the previous message, here was one from the murderer.

From: rtuf8n6pgm52h<rtuf8n6pgm52h@rtuf8n6pgm52h.com>
Date: November 13, 20XX 09:01 AM PDT
To: George Gray <GeorgeGray@nysentinel.com>
Subject: Kaboom!

George ol' Buddy,

It's that time again. Another bitch is about to bite the dust. Or should I say be blown to dust. A hint for the cops: same MO as last time. But I doubt they can do anything with less than 48 hours remaining.

rtuf8n6pgm52h

George forwarded the emails to Morris and wound his way through the mostly empty cubicles to Morris' corner office. As usual, Morris was hard at work. He didn't look up so George knocked softly on the door frame just as Morris' computer indicated incoming email.

"I assume that's from you?"

"Yeah, it looks like round 2 is on. Both for the Internet corruption and for the murder. That one came in less than an hour after the first. It's getting harder to believe this is a coincidence."

Opening the second message first, Morris suggested they call Mike McKensey. He picked up on the first ring.

"McKensey."

"Mike, it's Morris and George at the Sentinel. We've got another email from the murderer. It's short."

After hearing the contents, Mike responded, "Shit! I'm not sure what we can do about this. It's a credible threat, but I don't see how we can stop the Postal Service, UPS, and every other carrier from delivering packages for 48 hours. I guess we can alert them and they can increase their scanning. Maybe we'll get lucky, but I think the chances are thin.

After a pause, Mike continued. "You know George, all we have to go on from the last murder was that you knew the victim and she had screwed her husband in some way. It's a longshot, but maybe you know this one too. Maybe our perp is targeting people you know. What do you think?"

"I guess it's possible," George replied pensively. "I'll put together a list of all the tech wives I can think of who might have left their husbands and I'll get it to you ASAP."

"Okay. In the meantime, I'll have our tech come over to get a look at the email. It probably won't go anywhere, but you never know. Even the smartest make mistakes sometimes."

"Ah, there is one more thing you should know," Morris interjected nodding towards George.

"Yeah. About an hour before that email came in, I got another one from the guy that exposed Ryan Hamilton's trafficking. The last time, the two emails that came in didn't seem related, but once again, we've had both the offer to expose an Internet bad guy, and notification of an impending murder not far behind."

"Sorry to interrupt, George, but before we dive in deeper or I forget, given my advancing senility, I just wanted to say that I followed your stories on Hamilton, and you did a fantastic job. I'm not the only one who thinks so. Our Special Victims Unit couldn't be more pleased. Not only did you help take down a real scumbag, they're getting more leads on trafficking than they ever have. You've given victims and witnesses the courage to come forward. Anyway, go on."

"Thanks Mike, I'm responding to emails and posts every day. I do feel like I've helped raise awareness of something that lives beneath the surface of our everyday lives. But now, it looks like we're on to something else.

"Like the last time, I got two emails. The tones are different, but the formats of the emails are the same. This one claims to have proof that Boris Yanofski murdered his wife. There's a video attached showing him pushing her off a cliff."

"I'll be right over," Mike replied, clearly excited. "We investigated Sandra Yanofski's death but couldn't come up with any evidence. The family was convinced that Yanofski murdered his wife to get her fortune, but we had to drop our investigation for lack of evidence. I can't wait to see what you've got!"

"Hold on Mike," Morris interrupted gravely. "We haven't

even verified that what we have is valid. I don't think we're ready to turn it over to you."

"Morris and George, I'm sorry to pull this on you since we've been working so well together, but you are in possession of material evidence relevant to a murder investigation –"

"Which to my understanding is closed," Morris argued.

'Sorry guys. I'll see you in fifteen. And George, email me that list." And he hung up.

"Morris looked at George and shook his head. "He's right. We have to turn it over."

"Well, do you think he'll give us an exclusive on the story?"

"I don't see how he can do that George. He'll have his techs verify the video is original, then he'll go to the DA. He'll probably ask us not to publish anything until the DA decides to charge Yanofski. Then again, there's no reason you can't have a story ready to go. Get Mike that list of tech wives that you know and then get to work on the Yanofski story. At least we can be the first to press."

George paused for a second in thought.

"You know Morris, when we did the story about Ashima James' murder, we didn't mention the email tips or the reasons given for the murder. Although we talked with Mike about not scaring the public with the possibilities of other murders, maybe we should put something out now. I mean, we have a real credible threat."

"I don't know George," Morris lamented. "Yeah, it may be credible, but how do we get the information out without creating some kind of panic. I'm sure the package delivery companies would be at our throats. Hm. Tell you what. Why don't you see if you can draft something short in the next hour or so. I'll run it by legal and we can discuss it with Mike when he gets here."

"Will do, Chief!"

"And don't call me Chief!"

2

It was after eight when George finally got home. Janey had dinner on the table ten minutes later.

"So tell me about it, George. You sounded excited on the phone, but worried too."

"I am worried," George replied taking a large gulp of wine before downing a forkful of the vegetarian lasagna that Janey had made. "It's a repeat. I get an email about Boris Yanofski. Then, less than an hour later, one from the murderer cavalierly stating that his next victim will die within forty-eight hours.

"I suggested writing a story about the impending murder and while I drafted something that might have warned people, legal didn't sign off on it and Mike McKensey shot it down from his side. We're not doing anything to prevent the next murder other than trying to warn some wives of technologists to be careful. Well, I guess the police have asked the major delivery companies to do extra scanning of packages being delivered today and tomorrow.

"I feel so impotent. I can't do anything to stop the murders and so I'm complicit. If I weren't there would these women still be killed?"

"George, I know what you're feeling. You have one of the toughest jobs. You do great things exposing corruption like with the trafficking, then you get caught up in something over which you have no control. You just have to stand by and watch it happen. That's a terrible place to be."

"Yeah. Just when I'm feeling like I've made a real difference, I get hit with this murder. And this Yanofski thing. You know, with all the violence we see in movies, TV, and video games, you'd think you'd become jaded about it. But that video. Oh yeah, the informant sent me a video. It shows Yanofski pushing his wife off a cliff. I was blown away.

"I've been asking myself why it hit me so hard. And while the cold-bloodedness of it was bad, at some point I realized that he wanted to film it. He probably has watched it over and over. What kind of person could do something like that?

"You know, I spent the whole day doing research on this guy and how he works. What's weird is that he doesn't seem to have a specific political agenda. He inflames the left as much as the right. He either finds or creates conspiracy theories and targets susceptible people to believe them and to propagate them.

"The recipients think they're getting real news from family and friends – sources that they trust. And the reach of the stories expands and expands.

"From what I can see, he just wants to stir things up. At the same time, he's making hundreds of millions of dollars in advertising. He even runs crowdfunding campaigns which supposedly will combat the evil that these conspiracies reveal. And it's growing. The more people turn against each other, the more he can capitalize on his stories."

"Yanofski is a piece of work. This guy is using the money he inherited from his wife to turn us all against each other. Someone on his staff is a genius at manipulating social media. And people just eat it up.

"According to Mike McKensey, after verifying that the video was not doctored, they picked up Mikhail Papapovich, Yanofski's best friend, the one who took the video. They showed it to him and he flipped. They arrested Yanofski. All this in one day, if you can believe it.

"So yeah, my informant seems to be a good guy. First the Ryan Hamilton and trafficking, now this. He really seems to be a good guy."

George paused and looked thoughtfully at Janey.

"I'll tell you though, Janey, even if he's a good guy, my gut is telling me that he is the murderer. It's just too coincidental that the two emails come in so close together. I have a feeling that if we can find my good guy informant, we'll find the murderer too."

"Well George, I didn't want to say anything before, but I've been working on something that might help. I'll get a copy of the latest emails from your laptop and input them into my bot. With a bit more testing, I can turn it loose and may come up with an answer."

"A bot? I know what a bot is, but how is that going to help?"

"Well, as I mentioned before, this person or these people have been remarkably clever in hiding their tracks. They generate names, create temporary DNS entries so that mail servers don't mark them as spammers, and then remove the DNS entries before they can be traced. They are also using some clever encryption code that I haven't seen before, and I've seen most everything out there.

"At first I thought it might be part of the pirated NSA

software everyone has heard about, but I went through all of that code and none of it does what this does. So, I'm in the process of creating a bot that will search the Net for the program that generates these names."

"You can do that?"

"Yes. Such power exists," Janey joked, referring to their favorite old-time science fiction movie, The Day the Earth Stood Still."

"Is it legal?"

"Not the right question. But, I still have a ways to go. I didn't have enough information before and as I said, these new emails will likely help. Then I have lots of testing to do. So far, that's taking longer than I'd hoped. And once I do get it working, it's going to take at least several days to do everything I have in mind. I have to hide my bots and propagate them invisibly. Then we cross our fingers that the person or people aren't smarter than I am. Then again, I often find that really smart people get overconfident. I'm hoping to exploit that.

"Enough about my little project for now. Just trust that your loving wife has your back. I'll do whatever I can to help."

They finished dinner and most of the bottle of wine, did the dishes and spent the rest of the evening trying to forget that there were murderers among us.

3

Sam greeted Mark warmly, but frowned at the small bag of pastries he carried.

"I thought we talked about this. I really can't afford to indulge with every patient. I'll turn into a blimp!"

"Ah come on. I'm sure that I'm the only patient that brings you pastries, and once a week isn't so bad."

Sam served tea, and bit into the warm pain au chocolate, or chocolatine as Mark now insisted they be called, and began what was becoming a familiar routine. As they consumed the tea and pastries, she checked in on medication status and how the week had gone.

Sam had decided to continue to allow more informality into their therapist-patient relationship. To proceed with the next steps, Mark needed to trust her, to have confidence in where she was taking him. It would be difficult for Mark. His nightmares would increase and the new stress of the work he was about to embark on could trigger more positive symptoms – hallucinations, voices, and perhaps worse.

But if she was there for him, just maybe he could avoid losing the control he'd developed in the weeks of work they'd done. Just maybe he could avoid falling into his former drug and alcohol habits – a new downward spiral.

It was going to be a challenge for Sam as well. While she'd trained in Psychodynamic Therapy techniques, this was the first time she'd applied them in such a serious case. But so far, it was working.

"Mark, we talked about the Psychodynamic Therapy we've started. At this point, it has probably seemed pretty innocuous, particularly the free associations we've been doing. But after our last session, I have some ideas about some of the sources of your problems. As we discussed when we first met, late-onset schizophrenia is not the most common form we see.

"Most psychiatrists believe that schizophrenia is caused by chemical imbalances in the brain and that these imbalances are the result of genetics. The bad genes are a waiting time bomb where drugs, alcohol, the environment, or just time, can trigger the disease. Once it's started, all we can do is manage it. We can adjust the brain chemistry, and use therapy to help patients regain some control over their lives. These psychiatrists believe that schizophrenia is incurable.

"However, there are a few outlying psychiatrists who now believe that while the majority of cases are genetic and incurable, a small percentage may be the result of childhood trauma. The argument against this is that we can see that the brain is acting differently physiologically, thus it can't be just a psychological problem.

"But, on the other side, there have been success cases with therapy. The theory, and it's only a theory at this point, is that childhood trauma actually causes behavioral changes that result in changes to the brain chemistry. That's why the drugs work in these cases too. But they've gone a step further.

"I didn't want to give you false hope at the beginning, and I'm hoping you'll be patient with what we're about to start, because the chances of a cure are still small.

"Most psychological research has shown that as babies we have to learn to experience the world. We have to learn to interpret sights and sounds to create our reality. Many also believe that this is the case with emotions – that fear, envy, anger, and others have to be learned and interpreted. And we have to learn how to react and to protect ourselves. We develop patterns. These patterns become expressed in how we move, how we think, and how we react. Our bodies adapt and so do our brains.

"Bottom line – it's possible that if we get to the root of what caused patterned thinking, feeling, and reacting, and their associated behaviors, we can change them. In the case of trauma victims, we can slowly reverse the damage and retrain the brain to be, for lack of a better non-technical word, normal."

Mark looked at Sam and tried to think. He racked his brain. He tried to remember. They passed a few moments in silence.

"Gee Sam, this all sounds great. There's just one problem. I didn't experience any major, life-changing childhood trauma. I had a pretty normal childhood, I think."

"Mark, as I said, therapy is difficult. I could be wrong about this, but after carefully studying our last sessions, I believe that you did experience some significant trauma in your childhood. And if I'm right, the therapy is going to be challenging. It will be the hardest work you've ever done. You're going to have to work really hard to maintain the control you've developed and to stay clean no matter how bad things seem to be getting.

"I can't promise a cure, but there is a possibility, and I think you're up to the challenge of giving it a shot."

Mark thought about it. He still didn't see how his childhood could be the cause of his condition, but if Sam thought so, he had to trust her. She'd helped him get this far. Maybe he could get his whole life back. He'd been through some pretty difficult challenges in his life. Why not one more?

"Okay. I'm in. Where do we start?"

"Mark, tell me about your family."

"There isn't much to tell. My dad was a great guy, super intelligent, and always joking around. He worked for military intelligence for many years and was away a lot while I was growing up. And then, he died suddenly while I was away at college. My mother was quiet. I did sometimes wonder how they ended up together. She worked to support me and never remarried after my dad died. Unfortunately, she died of cancer a year or so before Janice and I separated."

"Then let's start at the beginning. Tell me about your earliest memories of your mother."

"My mother?"

4

Julia Lewis took a sip of her champagne and looked out over the crowd that had gathered at the Palace of the Legion of Honor with its spectacular views of San Francisco.

It appeared that most everyone she had invited was there and most had brought guests. This was her big charity event of the year. Last year she'd raised over half a million dollars for humane animal farming. This year, they were going to try to help stop the needless slaughter of kangaroos in Australia.

Although protected in most of the national parks, the Australian government had authorized the 'culling' of over a million kangaroos this year and in their trade negotiations, the government was pushing kangaroo meat to partner countries. The number of kangaroos was dropping fast. Extinction was a real possibility and the environmentalists were decrying the fact that the longer-term impacts on Australian lands were unimaginable.

Several months before, Julia had watched a documentary on the subject and then heard an interview with the filmmakers on NPR. Apparently, they had just started out trying to document the life of kangaroos throughout Australia, following several families. They were shocked when their families were ruthlessly slaughtered, the young defenseless joeys left to starve or to be killed by predators. And so, the filmmakers changed their focus. They researched the environmental impacts, the governmental plans, and as expected, they filmed horrible scenes of gruesome massacres of hundreds of kangaroos. Julia decided to take this on as her cause this year. She knew the pictures and videos would tear at her guests' heartstrings and that their purses would open wide. Given the pace so far, she would certainly beat last year's take. With the silent auction still to come, who knows, maybe she'd break a million dollars.

As she gazed out across the City's lights, she couldn't help but reflect on how she got here. She'd married young, too young. The children came along before she could finish her graduate studies in marketing communications and she'd spent the next twenty years being a mom. Shuttling the kids to after-school events, to music, dance, and gymnastic lessons, she didn't have time to miss her independent life. But as the kids became more self-sufficient and moved away to college, and her workaholic husband was increasingly absent, Julia made up her mind to make a change. Her husband Marshall had just left his prestigious high-paying job at Xerox Research Park to launch a startup. He'd started dipping into their substantial savings to fund the company and Julia knew that if she let this continue, he'd burn through it all in pursuit of a dream that only he could understand.

She planned carefully. Using the social contacts she'd made through Marshall's business associates, she lined up a product management position with a well-known high tech firm. They even offered to pay for her MBA.

She told Marshall that now that the kids were on their own, she needed to build her own career. He happily agreed, already worried that his wife had too much time on her hands as he dove headlong into his new company.

And once the job was secure and she had a decent income, she filed for divorce. He never saw it coming. Of course, he was devastated. In his pain, he didn't fight for his half of their wealth. Instead, because he ardently believed in his new venture, Julia had no problem arguing that Marshall's startup was worth as much as the rest of their properties and savings. He wanted his company and certainly didn't need her as a partner, so he caved. She took it all.

At first, the girls supported their mother's quest for independence. Their father had always worked too much and their mother was clearly a distant second to his passion for new technologies.

But then, as they saw the impact of the divorce on their father and as they discovered what their mother had done to him financially, they turned against her and tried to save Marshall from the abyss that he was about to fall into. To no avail.

Just as Julia had known all along, Marshall's company failed. He started drinking and eventually drank himself to death.

Her daughters hadn't spoken to her since.

That was a disappointment, but it wasn't devastating. After giving up the best years of her life to raise them, Julia needed to take care of herself.

By anyone's measure, she was a success. She had climbed the ranks in her company and now made mid-six figures as their Executive VP of Marketing. Socially, anyone who was anyone in San Francisco and the Silicon Valley knew and respected her marketing skills. And they all came to her fundraisers which boosted their esteem of her while cementing her reputation as one of the elite.

On the romance side, she was glad to be single. She'd never marry again. She'd never play second-fiddle to a man again. Instead, with her money and not-so-bad looks at fifty-one, she bedded pretty much whoever she wanted. She tried to stay away from married men, but sometimes the temptation was too great. She loved to make the power elite beg for more.

Yes. She had it all.

As the moon rose above the East Bay hills, she turned to go back inside. A clumsy waiter carrying a tray of champagne-filled glasses bumped into her, causing her to spill her drink but he somehow balanced the tray of glasses without spilling a drop.

"Watch where you're going!"

"I'm terribly sorry, Ms. Lewis. Here's a fresh chilled glass."

Julia looked at the not-so-young man offering to replace her now empty glass. He looked contrite. He also looked a bit familiar, but she wasn't sure where she could have seen him before. Maybe she'd just noticed him earlier that evening.

She set her glass on the tray and as charmingly as she could, admonished him with, "Please be more careful."

As she made her way back inside, Marie, her partner in crime, was calling the crowd together to announce the results of the silent auction. Julia needed to join her. But for some reason, she kept thinking about the waiter. About her age, he had gorgeous gray-green eyes, was well-built, and well, who knows? Maybe they'd hook up later. Many of the people working the fundraiser were volunteering their time. For all she knew, he could be a billionaire.

Julia gulped the glass of champagne as she joined Marie on the podium in front of the crowd. You could almost feel the anticipation. This was fun! Julia loved to watch them hanging on her every word. And then, she felt a pain run down her left arm. She found she was sweating profusely and a wave of nausea overtook her. She couldn't breathe. She clutched her arm and fell to the floor.

As she lay there, she couldn't help thinking that she shouldn't have ignored her doctor's advice. She couldn't believe that she was a candidate for a heart attack and so she'd refused to change her lifestyle or take the medication that she'd been prescribed. But most people survived a first heart attack, right?

She looked up and saw Laney Sampson, her doctor, bending over her.

"You'll be fine," Laney assured her as she began CPR.

5

Forty-eight hours passed and the murder hadn't happened. At least nothing had been reported, and if rtuf-whatever was to be believed, there would be another explosion. That wouldn't have gone unnoticed.

George started to hope. Maybe something happened to rtuf. Maybe he or she had a change of heart. But as soon as he thought it, George knew that couldn't be the case. Rtuf was just screwing with them. The forty-eight hours was just a distraction. George was sure that Mike and much of the police force were doing whatever they could to protect possible victims. But a part of him knew. Rtuf was going to murder someone, probably very soon.

New email came in and after ignoring it for a few minutes, George decided to go through it. The email about trafficking was slowing down, but it wasn't gone yet. And at least he felt useful directing victims and those suspicious of trafficking to the right places to get help.

Scanning the list of emails, he saw it. A part of him wasn't surprised. He double-clicked and read the message:

From: fu6o03qplkmr2< fu6o03qplkmr2@fu6o03qplkmr2.com>
Date: November 16, 20XX 07:01 AM PDT
To: George Gray <GeorgeGray@nysentinel.com>
Subject: Kaboom!

George ol' Buddy,

It's done. Sorry for the misdirection. I can't make it too easy for you and the cops, can I? I hope you all didn't go to too much trouble chasing packages or women that you know. That would have been a waste of time.

I was much more subtle this time. Her name was Julia Lewis. You've probably heard about her husband, Marshall Lewis. He worked at Xerox Research Park years ago and was really the father of everything we think of as user interfaces. Others made billions off of his ideas. He might have done pretty well himself if his wife hadn't declared him a workaholic failure and left him, taking pretty much everything they had. He drank himself to death and we lost one of the truly great geniuses of our age. Don't cry for her George. We don't need women who derail the technologies that will save mankind. At least she won't do it again.

I'll be in touch before I rid us of another viper.

fu6o03qplkmr2

George forwarded the email to Morris and to Mike McKensey and raced to Morris' office.

"He killed a woman named Julia Lewis, wife of someone named Marshall Lewis. Have you ever heard of him?

Morris typed the name into a search engine. "Yeah. I vaguely remember a story we did about him a few years back. Yeah, here it is. It was in the History of the Silicon Valley series."

Morris' phone rang. "Levinberg. Yeah Mike. Yeah Mike. Sure. See you in fifteen."

George looked at Morris expectantly.

"As soon as he got your email, he and Bob Simpson made a few calls and found Julia Lewis – or her body. From what he could gather, she collapsed at a charity event last night and was rushed to Community Hospital where she was declared DOA from an apparent heart attack.

"Your buddy timed it perfectly. Another hour or two and she would be in Colma."

George thought about Colma and its weird history. Located a few miles south of San Francisco, Colma was a city of funeral homes and cemeteries.

Somehow, until he became a reporter, George had never realized that no one was buried in San Francisco. Well, that wasn't exactly true, although technically full, the National Cemetery at the Presidio occasionally accepted burials of veterans or their family members – if space became available. How did space become available in a cemetery?

Soon after starting at the Sentinel, someone mentioned that the subject of a story was on his way to Colma and then patiently explained to a stunned George that you can't be buried in San

Francisco. After some hysteria about diseases being spread from cemeteries on the westerly winds, the City outlawed burials in 1900. A new town was formed called Lawndale, and for decades, it contained only cemeteries, funeral homes, and florist shops. Later, Lawndale became Colma. And today, there is only one cemetery in the San Francisco City limits (the Presidio is officially Federal Land and not part of the city) – at Mission Dolores. The last burial there was in 1898.

"On her way to Colma?"

"Yes. It appeared to be natural causes, so no need for the Medical Examiner to get involved. Mike called them and they've sent out an investigator who will likely order an autopsy."

"Yep. There will be an autopsy," said Mike McKensey who entered Morris' office with Bob Simpson hanging back at the doorway.

"Let's grab a conference room," Morris suggested.

A few minutes later, looking out at the Bay Bridge and the East Bay from the 11th floor conference room, Morris kicked off the discussion.

"So what have you got?"

Mike and Bob looked at each other and Mike responded.

"Actually, not much more than I told you on the phone. Apparently Julia Lewis is quite the socialite. She was hosting a charity event for kangaroo awareness and she just collapsed. EMTs arrived and tried to resuscitate her on the ride to Community, but she was DOA. She had some heart issues, so everyone just assumed it was a heart attack. We'll see what the autopsy tells us. But I'm pretty sure your guy did it."

"Yeah," Bob chimed in. "We don't see your guy making a false claim here. And it was within 48 hours; and it was the wife of a technologist. He just lied to us about the MO."

"It kind of pisses me off," Mike continued obviously exasperated. "You can't trust murderers to tell you the truth these days."

"C'mon guys," George responded a bit irritated. "You've gotta stop calling him my guy. He's as much your guy as my guy, probably more so."

"It's okay, George," Morris jumped in. "They're just rattling your cage. So guys, if you don't have anything new, why are you here?"

"Well," Mike responded. "We were hoping to talk to you

about your coverage of the story. We'd like to keep it quiet for a while until we get a bit further along."

Morris laughed. "Remember 'in possession of material evidence in a murder investigation' from our last meeting? Well, just as you were doing your job then, we need to do ours now. This is news. We have multiple murders by the same perpetrator who's targeting very specific victims. And really, it's more than news. The public needs to know. I don't mean to be taking shots, but you weren't successful at preventing this murder. Maybe it's time we took a more active role in catching this guy."

Bob Simpson looked like he was about to explode.

"Let's step out into the hall for a couple of minutes," Mike suggested or ordered.

"Why don't you use my office."

Once they were out of sight, Morris turned to George.

"There's not much they can do to stop us from publishing this story but at the same time, we've developed a good relationship with Mike and Bob. They've given us information that they didn't have to. They've put us ahead of other outlets. I'd like to try to keep that going. Let me take the lead when they come back."

"Sure. What are you thinking?"

"Ah, I'm sure they're afraid we're going sensationalize this with a headline like 'Serial Killer Claims Second Technologist Widow'. We'll promise to be more circumspect. But, just as he pulled the trump card on us last time, I don't want to let them off the hook too easily."

Mike and a much calmer Bob returned a few minutes later.

After making them sweat a bit longer, Morris agreed to keep the story tame and investigative in exchange for Bob and Mike keeping them informed on the progress of the investigation.

They all shook hands and George got to work on the story about the non-serial killer serial killer.

6

Jack thanked the hostess as he and Sam were seated at a window table which looked out at the Bay. Green's offered one of the City's best dining views with the lights of the Golden Gate Bridge, Alcatraz, and Angel Island shimmering on the windswept Bay. Sailboats raced back into the nearby marina as the sun set to the west. With its subtle use of exotic spices and organic ingredients, even the most ardent meat-lover could revel in the gourmet vegetarian cuisine.

Jack has chosen Green's because it seemed to be just the right mix of elegant and casual. And with the views, it was the perfect spot for a romantic first date.

For the past few weeks, Sam and Jack had been getting together for lunches, several challenging hikes, and a few rowing sessions, but this was their first 'official' date.

True to her promise to herself and to Mary, Sam was taking the lead, and unexpectedly, Jack seemed to enjoy following. Sam was intrigued by Jack's commitment to fixing the internet. He almost seemed to take it personally that people had perverted what he thought of as a perfect egalitarian creation. And although Jack's feelings about social justice and politics seemed to match hers, he willingly admitted that his positions were his opinions and that different views could be valid.

As he went on about Balanced News and talked about the importance of tolerance of other, dissenting ideas and opinions, Sam found herself becoming less polarized in her own thinking. She realized that over the past few years, she had become quite convinced of the righteousness of her beliefs, often disdaining the more conservative among us, writing them off as uninformed and uneducated. She was beginning to believe that perhaps her narrow-mindedness was as bad as theirs; that as Jack argued, you needed to listen to both sides to really have an opinion. Even more important, if you wanted to change someone's mind you needed to understand where they were coming from. And, to truly win any argument, you had to grant points and allow the other to save face.

Yes. She really liked Jack. He was helping her expand her world view.

For his part, Jack was fascinated by Sam.

Not only was she beautiful and intelligent, she challenged him. He knew that she'd found their discussions on internet stories enlightening. But he was sure that she had no idea how much her discussions of psychiatry had opened his eyes. Somehow, until he saw what happened to Mark Johansen, he'd never thought about mental illness as something that afflicted normal people. Now, he realized that many of the 'normal' people around him might well be suffering from psychological problems; that psychological demons might very well lurk beneath what appeared to be a reasonable exterior.

"Lost in thought?" Sam asked, smiling at her charming dinner date.

"Ah, yeah. I was just thinking about how truly amazing you are and how happy I am to have met you."

Sam blushed. It had been a while since she'd felt so attracted to someone. Maybe tonight she'd take the next step. But for now, before she started babbling something stupid, she decided she needed to change the course of the conversation.

"And I'm really glad to have met you too, Jack."

Jack reached out and took her hand. Maybe it was the wine, but Sam suddenly felt warm all over. She gave him a smile full of promises and gently changed the subject.

"I know you do a lot of research on the news. Have you met this Sentinel reporter, George Gray?"

"No. I haven't had the pleasure. But I've found his work to be more than even-handed. I really appreciated the story he did on Michael James back when, and recently, he seems to be covering a lot of things that directly impact me and what I'm trying to accomplish. Like the one he just did on Boris Yanofski, a scumbag if ever there was one. I'm glad to see he's been taken down and I hope that soon, his conspiracy theories that turn people against each other will follow him. When they do, my life gets a lot easier.

"Were you thinking of that, or of the story he did a few weeks ago on Ryan Hamilton, the CEO of LotsofJobs.com. George pretty much single-handedly brought down his human trafficking ring. That's another internet bad guy now out of circulation."

Sam looked surprised. "I didn't know about Boris Yanofski and I guess I'm glad I haven't bumped into his conspiracy sites. I'm not sure how I didn't realize that it was George Gray who exposed the trafficking. I've been following the impact of the stories. It's impressive. A lot of women are coming forward and people are starting to look for signs of trafficking. Some of my patients are talking about it and I've had some calls about some rescued victims who need some help dealing with their experiences. I think awareness of the problem has finally come into the spotlight. Hopefully, it will stay there. Like the psychological problems we've discussed, trafficking lies just beneath the surface of what seems to be normality."

Jack nodded. "I hope that George Gray can continue to break these stories. There are more bad guys out there than I care to count and he's made a good start. But if you didn't know about his stories on my nemeses, why did you ask about George Gray?"

"Did you see the story about the murders of the two technologist's wives? Although he didn't use the words, it seems there's a serial killer out there who's targeting wives who've left their technologist husbands."

Sam paused before continuing. She was usually careful about making pronouncements about people with psychological problems, especially when she hadn't examined them, but this was social and this was Jack. It would stimulate the conversation. After all, he knew almost everyone in the Silicon Valley.

"From the story, it sounds like we have a psychopath out there who is unable to deal with the reality of our modern society. You can't go around killing women because they left their husbands."

Jack tensed. His face darkened and for the first time that evening, he took his eyes off Sam. He looked down at his plate, took a sip of wine, and then turned to gaze out at the Bay, obviously mulling something over. Was he about to tell her something? An awkward silence followed.

"Jack, are you okay?"

"Sure."

Alarm bells went off for Sam. Was she now seeing the real Jack, the hidden Jack that Mary had talked about? Did Jack have issues that would jeopardize any possibility of a long term relationship?

As much as she tried to cheer him up, Jack remained sullen for the rest of the dinner. Her skills as a therapist failed her as they always seemed to do when she tried to help people close to her. Help? Was she trying to help Jack? Maybe there was something wrong with her. Sam tried to change the subject, but the Jack she'd come to like so much refused to return.

He asked for the check, paid quickly, and drove Sam home in silence. Sam had originally planned to ask him to come up, perhaps to spend the night, but that wasn't going to happen. And maybe it was a good thing. Maybe, in spite of managing the pace, she just wasn't ready for a relationship. Then again, maybe Jack was the problem.

7

Richard Hatch looked over at Mark Johansen, his best friend and long-time business partner who was leading a design session in their all-glass-walled conference room. Mark was once again at the helm of Johatchen Software and the company seemed to be back where it was before Mark's breakdown. In fact, with Mark now at nearly one hundred percent of his old self, Johatchen was doing better than ever.

The team seemed to have regained faith in Mark and all of the insanity had been forgotten. And 'insanity' was the appropriate word.

As for Mark, he was working like a demon. It seemed like he had something to prove again. Richard thought back to their first startup. While still at the university, Mark had come up with an idea that he thought would change the industry.

At that time, there were quite a few operating systems for PCs, minicomputers, and larger mainframes, and they were all incompatible. A technology called Object-Oriented Programming (OOP), was just beginning to positively impact how engineers developed software. This technique and the programming languages that it employed dramatically increased the productivity of engineers and the reliability of their software. Companies began turning out software at a prodigious rate.

Mark wanted to go a step further. He created an object-oriented operating system. Richard was no slouch technically, but it was a real stretch for him to understand that this operating system was provably secure and could speed development even more. The cherry on the cake was that it could 'guest' other operating systems and make them and their applications secure at the same time, and it ran on any sized system, even very small microprocessors. Mark had named it the Great New Operating System in the Sky (GNOSIS).

With GNOSIS, not only would all systems be completely compatible with each other, they would be absolutely secure and completely immune to any attack from viruses, malware, or hackers.

Richard and Mark worked day and night to develop a prototype and then Richard began shopping it to see if they could raise enough money to hire a team to build the real thing.

The concept seemed to be beyond the venture capitalists

(VCs) at the time, but the Department of Defense (DOD) was fascinated and provided enough funding to get a basic multi-platform system running. Richard and Mark hired some of the smartest engineers in the industry who quickly got religion. The team worked ridiculous hours to get GNOSIS running in record time. As Mark had predicted, the object-oriented nature of the operating system itself allowed development and testing to go faster than anyone had imagined.

Richard made the rounds of the venture capitalist community again, but they all seemed convinced that it would be impossible to compete with the established companies, and that it wasn't operating systems that made money, it was the hardware they ran on and the applications that customers would buy.

Richard did manage to get a large Japanese mainframe company to invest, but they took over 50% of the company. And although the DOD successfully implemented the system in some top-secret facilities, apparently, funding dried up for that particular black operation and they didn't continue with GNOSIS. Worse, as the VCs predicted, there was no market for the product. Over the course of the next two years, they burned through all the cash they had and had to close down the company. The Japanese VCs took the technology as part of the dissolution.

Richard was devastated, but Mark just kept on going. They formed another company after convincing several of their top technical team members to work in exchange for equity. It was based on another of Mark's brilliant ideas, a way to both guarantee performance of video and audio data across the internet and ensure its absolute security. But, this too was years ahead of its time and that company failed as well.

After several weeks of serious discussions, Richard convinced Mark that they needed to look at market needs first rather than just coming up with technologies that were years ahead of their time. Mark sniffed at 'just', but given their two dramatic failures, he recognized the wisdom in Richard's approach. Richard and Mark gathered the team once again and they brainstormed several ideas based on what they perceived as needs in the now fast-growing internet.

Richard did market analysis on each and they finally settled on a system that borrowed a bit from the ideas of their previous efforts – a cross-platform system that would provide consistent security for all communications while preventing attacks. It relied on an underlying hook at the lowest level in each operating system that insulated applications from what was running underneath. The fact that it could run on a variety of different computers made it very attractive since a customer with different computer systems could run exactly the same software to protect all of them. And thus, Johatchen Software was born. And aside from Unbreakable Security Systems, Inc., they had little real competition.

Richard thought back to their teen years together. It seemed like Mark was always the smartest, always the fastest, and always the most adept at anything new while Richard inevitably took a close second. It had always been that way except during Mark's 'incident', as they like to call it now.

For several weeks, Richard got to feel what it was like to be the CEO. For once, the team had looked to him, not to Mark. They didn't question his decisions or run to Mark if there were a disagreement on something Richard had proposed. In fact, the company ran quite well without Mark; perhaps better than it had for most of the previous year when Mark was on his descent into schizophrenia. But now, Richard was playing second fiddle again.

How was it that a team of talented genius engineers couldn't recognize his contributions to the company? Realistically, the company wouldn't exist without him and they wouldn't have their impressive salaries or extensive benefits.

At least Mark appreciated him. Over the years, Mark had made it clear that he couldn't have done Richard's job and Richard knew that the company wouldn't survive without Mark. The company was growing and Mark's new ideas would drive it forward even faster.

Their friendship was back on track and Johatchen was back to normal. Mark had thanked him for stepping in during the incident, but Richard had to admit that he was now a bit jealous. He missed being in the driver's seat. Then again, maybe he was and always had been the one controlling the direction of the company. There was really no reason for jealousy. Unfortunately, like his team, Mark had no idea what Richard actually did for the company.

Business development, finance, marketing, and operations were critical to the success of a company, but all too often, it was the technology that captured the media's attention. And it was the technology that excited the team.

Somewhere along the way the team had forgotten that Richard was no slouch when it came to technology. Maybe he wasn't Mark, but he could hold his own against most of the engineers. After all, when they started Johatchen, he and Mark designed, coded, and tested everything together.

Yes. He was definitely underappreciated. He needed to think about how he could change that.

8

Sam looked out her window and watched Brittany Spangler drive away. Sometimes she hated her job. Usually she felt this way at the hospital where she saw indigent patients return again and again. They'd get treated, have their meds stabilized, and then be sent on their way after promising to check in regularly. But without a stable living environment, it wasn't long before they went off their meds, continued their risky behaviors, and were picked up and sent back to the hospital. It was frustrating.

At least in her own practice she'd never felt this way. She could see the progress her patients were making. Until now.

She should have known. She'd studied Borderline Personality Disorder and had seen several cases at the hospital, but she was never the primary psychiatrist on those cases. She'd consulted with Dr. Karmere about Brittany and he had warned her. BPD patients were the most difficult. They were intelligent, often too intelligent. They played games. They were masters of deception, selecting roles to play to best manipulate those around them. And Sam was pretty sure she was being manipulated. The progress that she'd thought they were making through the therapy appeared to be just a sham. It was almost like Brittany was setting up Sam for something. Sam couldn't imagine what, but she had a bad feeling about Brittany.

This session was, like the last few, unproductive. It was pretty clear that the Schema-focused Therapy, which appeared to be working at the beginning, wasn't working at all. Brittany just made it look that way. After today's session, Sam asked herself why Brittany kept returning. If anything, they seemed to be on the verge of fighting and Sam was struggling to maintain her objectivity. Brittany was constantly trying to turn the tables and find buttons that she could push. She'd hit close to home more than once. Clearly, she read people well, too well.

And in their 'innocuous' conversations, Sam had come to realize that like many BPD patients, Brittany was a sociopath. Her narcissism was all-consuming. Brittany didn't really care about anyone but herself.

As she thought about it, Sam realized that Brittany was never going to reveal what her feelings were about her mother. Sure, she gave the usual platitudes and made up adolescent complaints, but Sam sensed that there was something buried there. Actually, she didn't think it was buried at all. It was just that Brittany didn't want discuss it. She had something to hide.

Sam hated to go there, but a small part of her wondered if Brittany had killed her mother. Was Sam supposed to be a safety net for a possible insanity plea?

She was just finishing entering her notes when the phone rang.

"This is Dr. Lewis."

"Hi Sam," replied a voice she knew all too well. "I really want to apologize about the other night. The conversation turned in a direction that hit me really hard and I behaved horribly. I know this is when you usually take your lunch break. Can I buy you lunch and explain?"

Sam thought about it. She really didn't want to see Jack again. She wasn't ready to get lured into something just to have it fall apart. If the other night revealed the real Jack, he wasn't someone she wanted to be with.

Then again, she thought back to her conversations with Mary. Mary seemed to think that Jack was basically a good guy with a few problems. Well, who didn't have problems. Sam knew that she did. After all, her initial impulse was to just run away; to never see Jack again. And this was at the first sign of a problem in the relationship. Yes. She had her own set of issues.

She decided to give it one more chance. After all, what did she really have to lose. She could always run away later.

"You know, Jack, my gut tells me you and I aren't going to work out. So it might be better to just end it now."

"But —"

"But my rational side says that I'm probably just afraid of getting involved. So I tell you what. I was going to pick up a salad at the Rick's Deli down the street and have a quick lunch on the bench by the duck pond in the park. If you want to join me, I'll try to listen without putting on my psychiatrist's hat."

"Actually, I like it when you wear your psychiatrist's hat. I've learned so much about people and their motivations. And I can probably use some help myself — not that I'm ready for therapy, but I am ready to talk to a friend."

And before she could change her mind, Jack continued, "I'll see you in 15 minutes in the park."

There was a line at the deli and it was actually 25 minutes, but Jack was there, waiting patiently. His face lit up as soon as he spotted Sam. He started to move in for a hug, but sensed that Sam wasn't ready for that.

They sat together on the bench and gazed out at the ducks, which, one after the other, would dip their heads, rocking forward so that only their butts were above water, then rise and quickly swallow something. Bugs? Small fish?

It was one of those classic fall days in San Francisco. The interminable fogs of the summer were now gone and the rain and valley fogs of the winter had not yet arrived. These were rare days treasured by all who lived in the City.

"I love the fall," Jack began.

"Me too," Sam replied tentatively. "These are the days I love to play hooky and go for a hike in Land's End."

Sensing an opening, Jack gently proposed they do just that.

"No. I have a patient this afternoon. Sorry."

"Of course. You're seeing Mark. He mentioned it over lunch yesterday."

"Well, I know it's not the most professional of me, since I'm not supposed to have external involvement with my patients, but how do you think he's doing?"

Jack paused a moment to reflect on how to say this. Then he decided not to sugarcoat what he was about to say.

"I hate to say anything. But when you started seeing him, he was making great progress. Every day he seemed more confident and more his old self.

"But over the past few weeks he seems to be struggling. From what I can see, he's not drinking or using, but I can tell it's hard for him. Plus he's having mood swings and he mentioned memory lapses. Is he going to relapse?"

"I can't really say much other than we knew our current work would be challenging for him. Hmm, memory lapses?"

"Yeah. He says that he finds things on his computer – notes emails, and websites that have been visited, but he can't remember visiting those sites, sending the emails, or writing the notes.

"Should he be worried? Is this a side-effect of the medications?"

"Again, I really shouldn't say anything, and I feel guilty even having brought this up at all. But no. Memory lapses aren't usual side effects of his medications. I think we need to stop there."

After a moment of uncomfortable silence lost in their own

thoughts, Jack decided to dive in.

"Look Sam. I really like you. I think we have something special. I was a complete jerk the other evening and I'm really, really sorry. There's no excuse for my behavior, but maybe I should tell you why I reacted the way I did."

Seeing her nod somewhat hesitantly, Jack continued.

"I know it sounds strange, but the high tech world is my community. Most people think it's an old-boys club and in some areas, it is. Like venture capital. But if you go beyond that, there's something special. I guess you'd call it a connection. I mean, ah. We technologists, and I like to think I'm one of them, we share something. It's a vision that we can help the world become a better place. And in spite of what may appear to be competitive to those on the outside, our community loves to get together to invent new things. Most of us know that the big bucks are a matter of luck and timing – I guess they're the same thing – and while a few are in it for the money, most of us just want to see our technologies make a difference.

"I know. You're wondering what this has to do with the other night. Well, I knew both of these women but more importantly, I knew their husbands.

"Michael James and I used to have a lot of fun heckling each other at conferences and seminars. He'd show up at mine and give me the hardest time, then I'd do the same to him. Afterwards, we'd get together over dinner and late into the night to challenge each other's ideas. He was a great guy who really made a difference. When Ashima left him, and he committed suicide, I could have killed her."

Seeing Sam's shocked look, Jack jumped back in before she could interrupt.

"No. I didn't kill her. But there are times when I really wonder why people do what they do to each other. Ashima's actions were selfish and she didn't think about the rest of us when she left Michael.

"And it was even worse with Marshall Lewis. He was my mentor. I'm who I am because of Marshall. And I was there when Julia left him. She was fed up with his working hours, his lifestyle, and his overly generous nature. She took everything they had financially, as well as his kids. And he just couldn't handle it. In his mind, it was Julia who enabled him to think and create. It was Julia who made his non-working hours heaven on earth. He loved her. He relied on her. Her stability reassured him so that he could take intellectual risks. And when she was gone, he just couldn't do it anymore. He became depressed and basically drank himself to death.

"I tried to help. I encouraged him to seek counseling. But he refused. The always friendly Marshall, the patient guy who helped everyone he met, withdrew. And when he was gone, I hated Julia. I still do. I know it's wrong, but I can't help being glad that both Julia and Ashima are dead. Good riddance.

"I know. This sounds like some outdated men need wives to succeed story, but it's not that. It's about love and trust and what we need to be able to push ourselves to excellence. I'd feel exactly the same way if Steve left my friend Melissa Sanders. She's a genius but I know her life would be over if Steve left her. I don't know how to explain all this, but it's how I feel. And when you said the person who killed Julia and Ashima was a psychopath, I couldn't help thinking it could have been me. I could have killed them. And I don't think I'm a psychopath. I don't think you have to be a psychopath to kill people, especially evil people. I know it's rare, but I think sometimes it's justified. I wish I didn't feel that way, but I do. And I didn't want you to, ah, think less of me."

Sam looked over at Jack who was clearly drained. He was looking at his feet and shaking his head. Then, without looking up he said one more thing.

"Sam I know it's bad timing to say this, but I'm falling in love with you."

Sam wasn't sure whether she wanted to run away screaming or take Jack in her arms and comfort him. She decided to try something in the middle and hope that it didn't sound too professional. She put her hand on his. He looked up.

"Thank you for opening up to me. This is a lot for me to process right now and as terrible as it sounds, if I don't leave now, I'll be late for my next appointment. If you're available Saturday, why don't you pick me up about nine. I'd love to do a long hike in Marin."

She squeezed his hand and left a hopeful Jack on the bench watching her walk back towards her office.

9

Sam raced back to her office with her head spinning. Was murder justified? She'd never thought so. Could it be the act of a rational person? Maybe in a few exceptional circumstances. She remembered a question in one of her ethics classes. If you could go back in time and kill Hitler when he was a child, would you do it?

Almost everyone in the class agreed that they would. Sam had a problem with that. She felt that Hitler must have been damaged. She would have tried to change his life, to protect him from whatever made him a psychopath. The others were just lazy, seeking the most expeditious solution.

But as she'd gotten older and had seen people with problems that couldn't be fixed, her judgments had softened a bit – or maybe hardened. Sometimes it was too late. And she had to admit to herself that in the course of working in psych wards, there were a few patients – very few – who didn't seem to have any reason, genetic or behavioral, for what she really didn't want to label as being evil. That got into religion, and she didn't want to go there.

It still begged the question of whether a rational person could murder for a good reason. There was certainly self-defense. And if you allowed that, how far did self-defense go?

Courts had upheld mental cruelty as a justifiable reason in some cases. Physical abuse. What about a threat to society or a way of life? Isn't that the Hitler question in a nutshell? Were people who willfully caused others tremendous harm, even if just psychologically, exempt from any punishment?

Sam knew she wasn't going to resolve this question for herself, or the larger question of Jack and whether they had a future together before Mark Johansen came in for his appointment.

And indeed, her phone buzzed indicating that someone had opened the outside door to her waiting room office.

Sam welcomed Mark. Her waistline was grateful that she'd moved half of their sessions to the afternoon. They'd held onto the morning sessions because neither one was willing to forego the treasures from the bakery downstairs or the connection they reestablished while sharing them over a cup of tea.

Mark looked around the room nervously before taking a seat

opposite Sam. They exchanged a few pleasantries before getting down to business.

"So Mark, as usual, before we get into anything more substantial, how is it going with the meds? Any new or worsening side effects?"

"I don't know, Sam," Mark began, clearly agitated. "I'm much more nervous than before and I'm feeling paranoid. It's not as bad as it was before my incident, but it seems like a giant step backwards and it scares me. I've also been having more nightmares and I sometimes wake up screaming. My dreams are really vivid and they scare me too. I'm often afraid to go back to sleep.

"But what really has me scared is the memory lapses. I didn't mention it before because I wasn't sure about it, but now, I'm pretty sure I'm not remembering things that I've done."

"Tell me a bit more about these lapses. What makes you think you're not remembering?"

"Ah, well, it's just weird. Working from home, I sometimes find things on my computer that I don't remember putting there. I also see emails that have gone out that I don't remember sending, and when I've looked at the timestamps in my browsing histories, I see that I was home when I visited sites that I don't remember visiting. Same for the emails and files. I was home."

"Hmm. Have you noticed things like this elsewhere? When you're at work or out, have you noticed that you don't remember things that people might have said or things you might have done? I know you can't remember what you don't remember, but I would think that if this is occurring regularly, people around you would notice. Has anyone said anything?

"Not really. And, I've been very straight forward with my team at work. I've told them that if they see any unusual behavior, they need to tell me. So far no one has said anything."

Mark racked his brain.

"Actually, the other evening over dinner, Richard mentioned that we had just talked about the 49ers game and I didn't remember it. I thought maybe I'd just been distracted. That's happening a lot lately. I definitely find myself getting distracted easily. It's harder to concentrate. But maybe it's the same thing."

"Mark, I don't know where this would come from. I'm pretty sure it's not the medication. I suppose it could be a result of the work we're doing, but even that seems unlikely. Are you still keeping a journal?

"Absolutely!" Mark said proudly. "I'd never done anything like this before except for work – you know, keeping track of conversations with clients and even employees, but this is really cool. I can look back over my day or even look from day to day and see not only what happened, but how I was feeling about it. I've got to say though that if you read my journal, you'll see that these past few weeks have been pretty chaotic. I'm fine one minute, then crazy – sorry, probably the wrong term – the next."

Sam smiled. "Crazy is an okay word in this context. It's not pejorative. It's just a good catch-all word for unusual behavior.

"And do you see patterns of memory lapses in your journal? Are there things in it that you don't remember?"

"No. I guess that's a good point. But how can I explain these sites I don't remember visiting and the emails I don't remember sending?"

"I really don't know. Does anyone else have access to your computer?"

"No. And I've got our security software installed. No one should be able to break in or use it without me knowing about it."

"Well, if your computer is truly secure, you need to figure out if these memory lapses are real. Maybe you could document what you're seeing on your computer or be more detailed in your journal – like note the times you sit down with it and the times you stop. Maybe that will bring some clarity as to what's going on."

"That makes sense. Still, I think it's more likely my crazy mind is playing tricks on me than that someone is breaking into my system, getting past the best security system on the market, mine!"

"Well, let's move on for now. I'd like to hear about these bad dreams, but before we get there, tell me about this fear and anxiety you're feeling."

Mark paused a moment, closed his eyes, and took a deep breath.

"Sam, I think most of it is just that I'm really afraid I'm going to relapse, that I'll have another incident or that Janice will start appearing again. I know I'm getting paranoid. You remember my big episode when I was sure that Richard and Janice were plotting against me? I don't know what's going on, but sometimes I feel like Richard is plotting against me. It's not that he says or does anything, but sometimes, I'll walk out of a team meeting and he looks at me like I'm a specimen. Of course I say something friendly and we're best buddies again."

"Mark, as we discussed recently, the big difference between now and when you had your episode is that now you're aware that your perceptions are not always reality. Before, you believed in them completely and let your beliefs drive your actions. Now, you can try to evaluate your thoughts to see if they make sense, then act accordingly. I suspect you're doing just fine with Richard. Did you bring this up with him as we discussed? "

"No," Mark replied looking at his shoes. "Things are going so well at work that I really don't want to stir things up."

"And you think bringing this up with Richard will 'stir things up'?"

Mark looked up at Sam a bit sheepishly. "I guess that after all Richard has done for me, I don't want to question his loyalty."

"Okay. I can see that. How about I help you get off the hook. Sit down with Richard and tell him you have doctor's orders to discuss how he's feeling about you, the company, and your return. Hopefully that will open dialog between you two. After all, you've been best friends for years and I'm sure you've had some difficult conversations. Take a deep breath and go for it. If there is some resentment there, I can't think of anything better to resolve it than to have an honest discussion about your respective feelings. What do you think?"

"Yeah. You're right. I'll try."

Sam almost suggested he do more than try but she decided to move on. Mark understood what he had to do.

"So putting Richard aside for the moment, how are you dealing with the anxiety? You mentioned nightmares and paranoia. Is it manageable or should we be looking at upping your anti-anxiety meds to help out for a while?"

Mark thought carefully. Did he really want more meds? No. He could handle this. It was just tough.

"Sam, you warned me that it was going to be rough. It is. So far though, I think I'm handling it. Yeah, I'm frightened a lot of the time, but I'm holding it together. I'm not drinking or using coke again. When things get bad, I think about Johatchen, my team and the great work we're doing. You know, now that I'm clean and managing better, the company is growing faster than it was before. I'm focused on the fact that Johatchen is my baby and I'm going to do my best to nurture it."

Mark paused again before continuing.

"Before we dive into the scary stuff, there is one other thing I wanted to talk to you about. I know you saw George Gray's articles on the women who were murdered because I talked with Jack about it at lunch yesterday.

"Sorry. I know we can't go into the personal stuff. Anyway, I wanted you to know that I knew both of them and I knew their husbands. Michael James' and Marshall Lewis' deaths were tragedies. Michael and I were officially competitors, but in fact, we worked together more often than we competed. We did quite a few joint projects together. He was a genius.

"And Marshall. I'm sure Jack has talked about him, but Marshall was our mentor. We wouldn't be who we are without him. Both Michael and Marshall were bigger than life figures in my life and it makes me angry they're gone. And they're gone because of their wives.

"Janice and I were close friends with Michael and Ashima. I never really understood why she left him. Sure, we all discussed his step-daughter's issues, but they should have gotten counseling. Yeah, that Brittany. She's a piece of work.

"Instead, Ashima just walked out – no notice, no discussions. One day she was gone and never came back. Just like Julia and Janice. Sometimes I wonder if they didn't work together to get the courage to leave their husbands. Ashima ruined Michael's life; Julia ruined Marshall's life, and Janice ruined mine."

"Mark, we've discussed this. First, your life is not ruined. You, yourself, said that Johatchen is becoming more and more successful and you're enjoying working with your team. As for Janice, as we discussed, people leave for a lot of reasons, and I'm sorry to be a blunt, but as we've discovered, you've had issues for quite a while. They may have contributed to some of your problems as a couple. "

Sam kicked herself. That was totally inappropriate. Was it because of her discussion with Jack? She looked over at Mark and could see him withdraw. God! She was supposed to be building trust, not attacking Mark.

"Mark, I'm sorry. That was wrong of me to say. I don't know Janice. I don't know your marriage. Janice may well have been a horrible person. I truly apologize."

Then, before he could think about it too much, Sam asked, "So what about Janice? Is she still gone or has she returned with all the work you're doing?"

Mark paused. He stepped back mentally and did the exercises he'd practiced to separate what he thought and felt from what was rational. Sam was his only path back to himself. Okay. She'd made a mistake. She apologized. He needed to trust her. It made sense that as a woman, she'd feel defensive. After all, he probably came across as attacking all women, not just Janice. That's certainly what he felt during his lunch with Jack. Jack was really negative about wives of entrepreneurial technologists. He'd kind of gotten caught up in that.

"I'm sorry too, Sam. I think I went too far. I'm probably picking up on my conversation with Jack. He was pretty upset about all of this. I shouldn't have gone there."

Alarm bells went off again. Sam was walking too fine a line here. She was dating a friend of her patient. How stupid could she be? On the other hand, it sure seemed like everyone knew everyone in the tech industry. Maybe it was unavoidable. No. Probably not. She'd have to get some advice from Dr. Karmere. He'd certainly tell her to drop one or the other. She couldn't abandon Mark. They were so close to a breakthrough. She could feel it. And Jack? Jack was right. There was something there; something she'd never felt before. She couldn't walk away from either of them.

And then there was Brittany. Mark knew her too and she knew Jack, Marshall, Julia, and Janice. And now, there were these murders. Was this a macabre repeat of her experience with Liz? Could another of her patients be a serial killer? Could it be Jack? It was getting too complicated. She definitely needed to talk to Dr. Karmere. But for now, Mark had to be her focus.

"No, Mark. I'm the professional. But as you see, I'm human too and I make mistakes. I am sorry. Let's move on. So, what about Janice?"

"It's okay. I'm sorry too. Let's keep going. God knows I really need the help. No, Janice has not come back. But I have this ominous feeling that she or someone is lurking out there about to appear. It scares me. With all our discussions about my mother, I feel like my mother is watching me, not Janice. And my nightmares – they're all about my mother.

"I know she's dead, but I have this horrible feeling she's

coming to get me. You don't believe in ghosts, do you Sam?"

"No Mark, I don't. Let's hear about these nightmares. Maybe we can make some sense of them. In the worst case, in my experience, talking about nightmares reduces their power over us."

CHAPTER 4

"The media's the most powerful entity on earth. They have the power to make the innocent guilty and to make the guilty innocent, and that's power. Because they control the minds of the masses."

- Malcom X

1

George Gray settled into his chair and put his feet up on his desk. He grabbed the whiffle basketball and tossed a perfect swish shot into the small basket mounted on the top edge of his cubicle wall. Finally, a quiet day. He had no urgent stories to work on since he was winding down his work load in preparation for the vacation that he and Morris had discussed. It would be his first since starting at the Sentinel.

More than a month had passed since the last murder, and while what's-his-name promised more to come, George was happy for the respite. He and Janey were finally going to take a real honeymoon. In two days, they were off to Tahiti for sun, sand, snorkeling, kayaking, and whatever other water sports they could come up with.

It was the off-season in Tahiti and they'd gotten a great deal on their ten-day trip. They'd start with four days on Moorea, one of the main islands, then they'd catch a plane to a remote atoll in the Tuamotu islands called Tikehau. Although they'd be staying in a luxury resort with an over-the-water cabana and its private deck and ladder down into the water, they could kayak to one of the many nearby motus – small parts of the reef covered in sand and dotted with coconut palm trees.

Janey had done the research and explained to George what an atoll was. George had heard the term and knew about the nuclear testing that was done in the area decades before, but he hadn't realized that an atoll wasn't just another name for an island. No. An atoll was what remained after the island sank into the sea.

When Janey explained it to him, George almost thought she was making up a story of a Polynesian Atlantis. He wouldn't put it past her. Janey was constantly telling him fantastic stories with a perfectly straight face. Only about half were true and she took great pleasure in saying 'got ya!' when he fell for one of the false ones. He guessed she was working to help him sort fact from fiction – critical in his job. But she was definitely having a good time with these lessons.

Anyway, he'd learned that indeed, an atoll was the remnants

of a former volcanic island. Over time, the volcano created an island through its eruptions. Coral reefs formed around the island and built up to the point where they rose above the surface of the water. Millennia of pounding waves turned the tops of the reefs into sand and passing coconuts landed and took root. Over time, the island was surrounded by these reefs. Between the reefs and the island was a lagoon. Usually, there were breaks in the reefs called passes (named by sailors whose boats were able to access the islands through the otherwise impenetrable reefs).

The individual parts of the reef which were disconnected from each other (above water) were called motus. Apparently, the main islands of Tahiti, including Moorea and Bora Bora were volcanic islands with motus surrounding them. In time, they too, would likely become atolls – the volcanos that created the islands are now extinct and would eventually collapse into themselves leaving nothing but the surrounding motus. They'll become atolls – a group of motus surrounding the lagoon left by the collapsed volcanos.

Tikehau was one of thousands of atolls. One of its motus was big enough to include an airport and a small village. A few of the others had fishing, surfing, and diving resorts. And, there were some that were private refuges for the elite.

George couldn't wait to find one of the deserted motus where he and Janey could snorkel naked and stretch out in the shade of the coconut palms. George could even break open some coconuts so they could feast on the crunchy coconut meat and sip the sweet milk. He could just imagine licking Janey's lips. In just a few days, they'd be there.

Lost in reverie, George almost missed the sound of the incoming email. Some part of him knew that the vacation was just too good to be true. He looked as his screen. At first, the subject line made him think some spam had made it through the company's filters, But in the back of his mind, he knew from the sender's email address who it was. He double clicked and read the latest message.

From: fxt97ij5w8eqc<fxt97ij5w8eqc@fxt97ij5w8eqc.com>
Date: December 1, 20XX 07:01 AM PDT
To: George Gray <GeorgeGray@nysentinel.com>
Subject: She drives them crazy

George, George, George,

I hear you may be going on vacation. Sorry if my plans impact yours. Quite frankly, I think you should go whatever happens. You're doing great work and certainly have earned a break with that beautiful wife of yours. I'm sure you'll both love Moorea and Tikehau. I've been there and it truly is paradise.

Don't worry, I'm not targeting you or her (unless she does to you what the others have done to their husbands☺).

This time, the only clue I'll give you is that our victim literally drove her husband crazy. The world will be a better place without her.

Enjoy your trip!

fxt97ij5w8eqc

George couldn't believe it. The guy knew about his vacation and about Janey. This was scary.

George forwarded the email to Mike McKensey and Morris, and as he had done before, he headed over to Morris' office. Morris looked over his reading glasses as George approached. For the first time since they'd met, George looked angry. Morris invited him in and like the last time, Morris' phone rang almost immediately. Morris put it on speaker and Mike McKensey and Bob Simpson came on the line.

"I'm sure I know the answer," Morris began. "But have you guys made any progress on the other two murders?"

"Hold on. We don't have a third murder," Bob Simpson replied, clearly insulted.

"It's okay," Mike soothed. "We have to admit it, our track record on this one isn't too good. We'll dig in. We'll look for technologists who are in mental institutions or psych wards, or who went crazy and killed themselves, but it's really not much of a lead. I don't realistically think we'll stop this one. Maybe he'll make a mistake this time. They usually do eventually. He sounds pretty cocky. Plus, he may have overplayed his hand in bragging that he knows about George's vacation and his wife. And maybe he's telling us something in having visited Moorea and Tikehau. I don't know. It could be a red herring. Or maybe he just went to one of the islands. But if he went to both, it was likely a package. We'll get on that too. In the meantime, who knew about your vacation?"

"I hate to say it," George replied. "But in addition to our travel agent, pretty much everyone here at the Sentinel knows and I'm pretty sure all the folks at Janey's office know too. And by the way, it's only one island. The other is an atoll."

"What's the difference?" Bob asked.

"An atoll is just a reef encircling a lagoon with a collapsed volcanic island underneath," Mike replied tiredly. "But did you tell everyone that you were visiting both places, or just Tahiti generically?"

"Ah, as far as I know, I didn't tell anyone that we were visiting Moorea and Tikehau. I just said Tahiti. But as for Janey, she was pretty enthusiastic about the fact that Tikehau is an atoll. Don't feel bad Bob, I didn't know what an atoll was until last night when she explained it to me. Anyway, I suspect she's told everyone at her office about Tikehau and atolls."

"Okay. We'll look there and we'll talk to your travel agent. In the meantime, do you think it's possible that anyone could have had access to your computer or phone?"

"I really don't think so. I keep both with me all the time and our IT security guy, Miguel, does regular sweeps of our systems to make sure we don't have any viruses or malware on them."

Morris nodded. "We're pretty confident in our security here. Miguel is one of the best. But George, why don't you talk to Miguel and have him do a thorough exam of your system. You never know."

"Will do, Chief!"

"And don't call me –"

"Sure Chief!"

Mike and Bob chuckled. "I'm glad you guys can keep your sense of humor," Mike continued. "Keep us in the loop if you hear anything and we'll do the same. Quite frankly, though, it's getting depressing. We haven't had any success until now and I suspect these so-called leads are just red herrings. Last time he had us chasing our tails and we weren't even close to stopping him from murdering Julia Lewis. I just don't know.

"Ah George, each time he's contacted you, you've also had an email about internet bad guys, right? Did you get one this time?"

"I'll go check."

George made his way to his cubicle fully expecting to see an email about the next internet mogul target. Nada. He refreshed a few times but nothing came in. It actually felt a bit strange. Even though he tried to tell himself that he was dealing with two different people, he recognized that subconsciously, he'd associated the two. Now it felt like something was wrong. He couldn't put his finger on why, but his gut was telling him that this time, things would be different.

Returning to the conference room, George announced that so far, he hadn't received another email from the informant.

"Well," said Mike. "If you don't mind, let us know if you do get one. You don't need to tell us what it's about unless it affects the case at hand or if you need some help from our side, but I would like to know. I'm not sure why, but this feels a bit different to me."

George just smiled. Maybe he was developing a cop's instincts. Then again, it was just a change in the pattern. It didn't necessarily mean anything.

After Mike and Bob left, Morris turned to George. "So, what are you thinking with respect to your vacation?"

"Yeah. I was asking myself the same thing. It's paid for. It will be the first one since I started here. And Janey would kill me if we had to cancel."

"Look George. As you know, I've had a long career. In my early days I worked ridiculous hours with no vacations, and while I did get ahead faster than most, at some point, I was working longer and harder, but not as effectively. My boss at the time forced me to take a vacation. I didn't want to go. But once away, after three or four days of panicking and calling the office, I was finally able to step back and enjoy myself with Martine.

"She and I have always had an excellent connection and yet somehow I'd missed the fact that some walls were being built between us because of our crazy work schedules. The vacation make us both realize that while work may be critically important to our sense of ourselves and our places in the world, without stepping away once in a while, we could lose our perspective.

"And while I don't think you're quite at the point I was when my boss kicked me out for a few weeks, I can confidently tell you that if you don't go, your self-confidence will take a major hit when your productivity starts going to hell and you find yourself making more and more mistakes.

"So, just like my boss did for me, I'll make the decision for you. I don't want to hear from you until you get back. The paper will survive while you're away. Set up an out-of-office response on your email which copies me, and refer any callers to me on your voicemail. I guarantee the Sentinel will still be here when you get back and that you'll still have a job."

George was a bit skeptical. The story was heating up and something different was about to happen. He needed to be here for that. He paused in his thinking and realized that 'needed' was the wrong word. He just 'wanted' to be here. Morris was more than capable of handling anything that came up and George had nothing to fear from Morris, unlike some of his friendly but competitive colleagues. No. Morris had been his mentor and George had to trust his judgment on this. Janey would be happy.

2

Janice Livingston, formerly Janice Johansen, pulled her Mercedes SUV into the garage of one of the famous Painted Ladies. She still couldn't believe her luck in buying one. It had been decades since one of the historic Victorian houses next to Alamo Square Park in San Francisco had been on the market and when she saw it, she jumped. Not just to buy, but out of her tedious marriage with Mark.

Her house was world-renowned. As part of 'postcard row', it was seen in movies, television shows, and of course postcards depicting the most beautiful parts of San Francisco. From her Victorian, the views of the City were spectacular and now, all of her friends envied her.

She had the perfect life. Since the divorce, she'd become part of the rather exclusive elite social circle usually reserved for the old-money families in San Francisco.

With the settlement she'd received in the divorce, she had quit working. Actually, she had quit working before the divorce, and now, she was on the boards of several fund raising organizations, helping the less fortunate.

It was a shame about Julia Lewis. Janice had always appreciated Julia. Like Janice, Julia had left her technologist husband and had stepped into a very unique social circle. Both of them had the courage to get what they wanted out of life. Unlike many of the other technologists' wives, they had decided not to take a back seat to their husbands' obsessions, ridiculous working hours, and lack of social ambition. They had taken control and had created the lives they wanted.

And while she didn't know all the details in Julia's life, she knew that Julia had gotten out of her marriage at a good time while her husband and his company were worth something, and before he drank himself to death. Ironically, she was the only beneficiary of his multi-million dollar life insurance policy. Yes. Julia had done quite well. To some degree, Julia had inspired her to leave Mark. They had all known each other. Julia's husband Marshall acted as sort of a mentor for Mark, Richard, and their friend Jack. When Julia left, Janice knew she could one day do the same thing. And once Mark had become successful and started to give away their fortune, Janice knew it was time.

Mark had come from a lower-class family. For him, having

more money than they or their kids could spend in a lifetime was more than enough. He wanted to become a philanthropist and like many of the billionaires on the front pages, give away most of his fortune. He said they had enough money. More than enough. And no matter how much she encouraged, argued, and finally screamed, Mark was set on giving it all away. Janice couldn't convince him that you could never have enough money. Money was the key to the next level and more money to the level after that.

Ultimately, if you really wanted to make a difference in the world, as Mark and his cohorts claimed, you needed to move into the upper echelons where real money meant real power. Mark would never get there.

So before he could give it away, Janice took her half of their fortune (a bit more than half if truth be told), and left. This house was her first major purchase and her first major statement about who she was and where she was going. She had no regrets.

Janice stepped inside the renovated Victorian and made her way upstairs into her bedroom.

It was really too bad about Julia. At least she'd lived the life she wanted.

Janice stepped into the walk in closet off her luxurious bathroom and kicked off her shoes. Entering the bathroom, she turned on the water in the free-standing curved tub that she'd special ordered from England. Looking at herself in the mirror, she couldn't help but admit that she was getting older. Sure, she still looked good to the outside world, but makeup and clothes hid wrinkles and skin that was beginning to sag. You could only do so much with cosmetic surgery.

She was still attractive, and she'd used that to seduce several much-younger lovers soon after the divorce. But the more she thought about it, the more she realized it was probably time to marry again. She could certainly find someone older and wealthier who wouldn't impact her freedom, who could take her to the next level, and ultimately leave her his fortune. She started running through the list of potential targets from the attendees at that last fundraiser. She was sure they'd be sympathetic to the loss of her friend Julia.

Janice was suddenly startled by a dark movement behind her. She started to turn but was seized from behind. In the mirror, all she could see was a figure in black. She could now feel that he was wearing a wetsuit, complete with booties, gloves and a hood. It took a moment for her to recognize him. But she knew those eyes.

"What are you doing? Let me –"

But she never finished her demand. She felt steel against her wrist as he pulled her right hand towards her head. In an explosion of sound and light, the bullet pierced her brain and killed her instantly.

The killer placed the gun in her hand and closed her fingers around it. He double checked to make sure there was no blood dripping from his wetsuit, then verified that the note he'd put on the bed was still there. He drained the tub, left through the side door off the garage, walked casually to the Audi Allroad parked half a block away, and left the scene.

3

George was sound asleep next to Janey when his cell phone buzzed loudly enough to wake him.

"This is George," he answered sleepily.

"We've got him George," replied an excited Mike McKensey.

"Got who?"

"The killer. I can't believe he was this sloppy, but there's no doubt. We have a witness, evidence in his car and at his home, and his computer has emails that he sent to you. Come on down and I'll fill in the details."

George hung up and Janey asked. "Who have they got, George?"

"Well, I don't know how they did it, Mike says they have the killer. He sounded both happy and puzzled. He said something about the guy being sloppy in leaving evidence, but he was also convinced that they had the right guy."

"George, I've never asked this before but I know I'm not going back to sleep, so could I tag along?"

George thought about it for a second and couldn't see any reason why not.

"Sure. Can you be ready in five?"

"I'll be ready before you are!"

And indeed she was.

At four am there was no traffic as George and Janey raced up highway 101 to San Francisco. Driving at seventy-five miles an hour, they made it to the Hall of Justice in less than forty minutes. Mike McKensey came out to greet them at reception, clasped George's hand warmly and threw his arm around his shoulder.

"Thanks for coming up so early, George. I wanted to be sure you were the first with the story. I assume this is Mrs. Gray? Mike McKensey," Mike said offering his hand to Janey.

"Call me Janey, Mike!"

"George has told us a lot about you. He says you're quite the hacker."

"Actually, Mike, while I do know my way around the Net and most systems, I like to think of myself as a software engineer, not just a hacker. But let's not get into the difference now. I'm just here as George's ride. I hope you don't mind if I sit in."

"Not at all. I would, however, ask you to keep our

discussions confidential, aside from George, of course."

"Absolutely!"

"Okay. Let's get started. I can't give you all the details because the investigation is just starting. Forensics is going to take a while as is our examination of the suspect's computer. But here's what I can tell you officially for your story.

"Last night around eleven pm, Janice Livingston was murdered in her home – one of the Painted Ladies up on Steiner. It was set up to look like a suicide and the suspect did a pretty good job. There was gunshot residue on the victim's hand, and what appeared to be a hand-written suicide note. From the initial forensic collection, not much was found that wasn't the victim's.

"If it weren't for a neighbor who was walking her dog, we might well have concluded that it was a suicide. Or at least it would have taken us a while.

"She reported seeing a flash and hearing what sounded like a muffled gunshot inside an upstairs window of Janice Livingston's house, then seeing a man dressed head-to-toe in black - she seemed to think he was wearing a wetsuit – coming out of Ms. Livingston's property – the side door next to the garage. You've seen these houses, right? They appear to be butted up against each other, but actually have a small side yard separating them. There are doors leading into those yards and she saw him coming out of one. She saw him get into a dark Audi station wagon and actually got a plate number.

"Patrol officers knocked on the door and getting no response, popped open the side door, entered the unlocked garage and then the house and found the victim dead with a gunshot wound to the head."

"We traced the plate to the victim's ex-husband. His name is Mark Johansen. He's the CEO of Johatchen Software."

"I've met him," Janey interjected as Mike paused. "He's a brilliant guy. I wouldn't have taken him for a killer. Didn't he have some kind of mental breakdown a few months ago?" Then looking at Mike and a stunned George, Janey apologized, "Oh! Sorry about that. It's just that this case has been driving George crazy. I'll just listen. Sorry."

"No problem," Mike replied warmly. "I'm kind of excited about it myself. George is not the only one going crazy over this case.

"Anyway, we got a warrant, and woke the suspect up at about

one o'clock. He seemed genuinely surprised and said he'd been home and in bed since ten pm. He said his medication made it almost impossible to stay up any later. We arrested him and he called a lawyer. He's in custody and will be arraigned this morning.

"Forensics got to work, and as I said, this is only preliminary. One of our techs found what he called a secondary email account in a hidden folder and found emails that he sent to you. At the same time, they started a search of the premises and the surrounding area but so far, no wetsuit has been found.

"So while we don't have a complete case, it looks like this is going to be pretty solid. His mental health issues may be a complication, but that's for the courts to figure out. I did find out that the focus of his mental breakdown was rage at his ex-wife. So it's looking pretty good. He also knew both of the other victims."

"Why the wetsuit?" George asked.

'Yeah. That one bothers me a bit. We see this with pros – professional killers. It's a great way to stump our forensic teams as the perps don't leave any trace evidence. I was surprised to see it in a case like this."

"And you said something about a hand-written note?"

"Yeah, if we hadn't thought it was a murder, we probably wouldn't have looked more closely. According to our techs, there are now apps available where you can scan someone's handwriting and then you can write using that handwriting. They've even gone so far as to introduce normal irregularities since no one writes a character exactly the same each time. With close examination, our guys quickly determined that it was printed. Not sure how they did that so fast, but isn't technology wonderful?"

"Yeah, I guess so," George replied thoughtfully. "But what do you really think? Is this the guy?"

Mike took a deep breath and shook his head before responding.

"Officially, I have to say yes. He was the victim's ex. His car was spotted at the scene. He's had psychological problems and has had issues with his ex. Emails to you for this and the other murders were in his Sent Mail folder. It seems pretty open and shut."

"Off the record, I have to wonder why he would set himself

up like this. It seems like he was much smarter with the other murders. Plus, why try to hide it as a suicide? He didn't do that before."

"Officially, all I can say is that we have a suspect. We have evidence. I think the DA will be happy with what we have so far and I'm sure we'll have more soon. You can go with that for your story."

"And off the record?"

Mike looked hesitantly at Janey.

"My lips are sealed," she stated solemnly.

"Okay. Off the record. Ah. It doesn't feel right. All the evidence is there, but it feels like a set up. It's too easy, and you're right. From the emails and the previous murders, our perp was much smarter. And I've gotta tell you. When I confronted Mark Johansen, he really didn't have a clue. I may not be perfect at spotting liars, but with more than thirty years on the job, I'm pretty good at it. This guy was completely surprised by what had happened. So unless his psychological problems include some kind of multiple personality thing, I have my doubts. Officially, he's the one. Bob's convinced. The chief is happy. But me, I'm going to continue digging behind the scenes."

"I know I said I'd be quiet," Janey began tentatively. "But do you know if the emails or the folders were encrypted? Do you know if there was special encryption code on his systems?"

"Ah. No. I'll ask the techs. Is there something I should know about this?"

"Not yet," Janey replied enigmatically. "I've been chasing something for George regarding the emails from both the killer and from the Internet bad guy informant. I have a lead but I need to confirm it and unlike your guys, what I'm trying is going to take a while. If I find something interesting, George can get it to you."

"I definitely will," George responded nervously. "In the meantime, I'll get a preliminary story out based on the official facts as you've given them to me. I'll let you know if anything else turns up. But as you know, I'm leaving in a few days on vacation. "

Mike raised his overly bushy eyebrows. "Vacation at a time like this?"

"Boss' orders. Morris will be filling in for me."

"God! I haven't had a real vacation in years. Don't tell me.

It's Hawaii, right?"
   "Tahiti!"
   "You guys are killing me. Get out of here!"

4

Sharon Katell waited in the conference room on the second floor of the Hall of Justice in San Francisco. She'd just entered two pleas on behalf of Mark Johansen. The first was not-guilty and the second was not-guilty by reason of insanity.

In California, the State had to prove the accused was guilty, and if they succeeded, there would be a separate hearing to determine if the defendant were legally insane.

Sharon had only spent a few minutes with Mark before the arraignment and she felt this was the best strategy. It didn't admit guilt of the crime itself and put more pressure on the State to prove all of its case.

But then, just before entering the courtroom, she bumped into Marcia Burke, the Assistant DA who had been assigned the case. After hearing all the evidence against Mark and being told that in a few days, she'd be adding charges for the murders of Ashima James and Julia Lewis, Sharon wondered if she should have saved everyone time and money by skipping the not-guilty plea and just pleading insanity.

No. She'd have plenty of time to change the not-guilty plea if she needed to. For now, it was important she spend some time with Mark. The deputies had promised they would bring him right in, but she'd already been waiting nearly twenty minutes.

Sharon had been practicing law in San Francisco for over twenty years. Initially working for the DA's office, she had decided to leave to open up her own defense practice. Some of her coworkers thought she had left to escape the ridiculous pressure, work hours, and case-frustrating politics. Others were sure she wanted to capitalize on what she had learned to get rich off scumbag defendants. And almost all who remained believed she had gone over to the dark side.

But the truth was that it wasn't the hours, the low pay, or the politics. No. After successfully prosecuting dozens of criminal cases herself, and assisting in dozens more, Sharon saw that many defendants were just chewed up by the system. In spite of limited budgets, the DA's office had too much power. Add in the police, investigators, and a juror's initial belief that when a defendant's case actually went to trial, where there was smoke, there was fire. Innocent until proven guilty was a nice theory, but for average citizens and particularly for indigent defendants, the System was stacked against them. Once caught up in the juggernaut of police reports, forensic science that could baffle even the most educated, and the prestige of the State, these defendants were ill-equipped to get a truly fair trial.

After law school and years of practice, Sharon had begun to question the adversary system. It worked fine if the two adversaries entered the courtroom on equal footing. But that just wasn't the case in criminal courtrooms.

She met with her former professors and most of the judges she respected to discuss her concerns. And when challenged with what would work better than the current system, Sharon couldn't come up with the perfect system.

It was at that point she realized that the only real solution was to level the playing field by creating a stronger adversary on the defense side.

Sharon became a formidable defense attorney and over the years built one of the most successful firms in the City.

With that success, as her competent staff took on most of the caseload, Sharon decided to buy a vacation home in the spectacular coast-side town of Carmel, two hours to the south. Not surprisingly, the workaholic Sharon was unable to just relax with long walks on the beach, hikes in Big Sur, or luxurious dinners in the fine restaurants. The law was her first love and leisure just wasn't a part of her life. So, in her 'spare' time, she found herself sitting in as a spectator in criminal trials in the area.

Sharon soon discovered that because of major budget issues, the smaller surrounding counties could not afford their own in-house public defenders. Instead, they retained outside attorneys or small firms to provide criminal defense to the indigent. The problems she'd seen in the City were magnified ten-fold in the more rural parts of the state. The prosecutors steamrolled indigent clients and from what she could see, innocent people went to prison, and many who had relatively minor transgressions received unreasonable sentences. It was obvious that there was a real need for better defense attorneys and these small firms just weren't up to it.

So, much as she had done in San Francisco, Sharon opened small local law practices and began bidding for public defender contracts.

Ten years later, she had built a small empire of public

defender offices. Not only was this lucrative for her business, but because she could apply the best attorneys to each case, criminal matters were resolved much more quickly, offering significant cost savings to the counties.

Sharon now employed over two hundred top defense attorneys along with even more paralegals and interns. She kept her caseload light, usually just sitting in as second chair with newer attorneys or on cases that interested her.   Her administrative duties overseeing multiple offices took far too much of her time and as she thought about it, she had to admit, she missed fighting for the underdog.

And then, just she was thinking of making some sort of change in her career, she got a call from Mark Johansen.

She and Mark had been best buddies in high school and during their first few years of college. He had come to her high school in Cupertino during their sophomore year. His father had relocated to the Silicon Valley after retiring from the military. She quickly recognized Mark's exceptional intelligence in their shared advanced math and science classes, but was surprised that he more than held his own in literature and language classes – her areas of strength.

She invited him to a bridge party with several others of the school's intellectual clique and he fit right in. The diversity of his military brat life seemed to have prepared Mark to get along with almost anyone. He quickly became an integral part of their ongoing political and social debates. But somehow, he always seemed to hold back. For him, the discussions were intellectual exercises. Sharon pushed Mark to find some passion, but never really succeeded.

They had a brief fling in college, but realized that they really were better best friends than lovers. As grad school approached, they began to drift apart and later, with marriages and careers, their once-close friendship turned into regular social media contacts and postings where they could keep up on the superficial aspects of each other's lives.

Mark's postings had disappeared a few years before. Apparently this was during his divorce. Unlike many of her 'friends', Mark didn't share his pain with the world on the internet.

Sharon had tried to contact him several times outside of social media, but had no luck. She had heard through the grapevine that Mark had fallen on difficult times. Ultimately, her own time constraints prevented her from digging deeper.

And then, Mark called.

It was three in the morning when her phone buzzed. Usually she ignored these middle-of-the-night calls, but something told her to pick up. Mark had been arrested for the murder of his wife and possibly two other women. He briefly explained that he was being treated for schizophrenia and that it was going well enough for him to resume his duties as CEO of Johatchen Software.

Mark was a bit shaky on whether he had committed the crimes. As a rule of thumb, Sharon never asked a client about their guilt. But Mark volunteered that he'd been having memory lapses lately and that he couldn't say with certainty that he hadn't killed Janice.

With little more to go on, in the arraignment later that morning, Sharon didn't hesitate when the judge asked for a plea. Mark pleaded not guilty and he pleaded not guilty by reason of insanity. This was in response to a long list of charges that revolved around the murder of his ex-wife, Janice Livingston. The DA referred to the evidence found at Mark's home and at this point, there wasn't much to argue about. Sharon didn't bother to ask for bail, even as a formality since she knew it wasn't even a remote possibility.

She had to admit that she was excited by the prospect of representing Mark. She'd read about the series of murders and found it fascinating that Mark would be charged as a serial murderer. Could Mark have changed that much? Could he have gone so far off the deep end that he murdered three women and then didn't have any recollection of what he'd done?

Over the course of her career, she'd often been surprised by the actions of people she thought she knew. But Mark? No. He had been her best friend for years. She knew him better than anyone else. It just wasn't possible that he'd changed that much. Was it?

Her thoughts were interrupted as the deputies led Mark into the room. He was shackled hand and foot. In spite of what must have been a sleepless night, he looked alert and smiled warmly at Sharon.

"Could we take the shackles off?"

The two deputies looked at each other. One turned to Sharon

and asked, "Are you sure? This guy murdered three women."

"Yes. I'm sure."

Sharon watched as they removed the shackles and pressed Mark into a chair facing her.

"We'll be right outside if you need us."

Sharon nodded and the deputies left. Then she turned her attention to Mark.

"You know, I've missed you," she said warmly.

Mark burst into tears and shook his head woefully.

Sharon handed him a tissue from her purse and after a minute or two, Mark looked up and apologized.

"I'm sorry I didn't get back to you. After the divorce, things really went downhill for me. I started drinking heavily, doing drugs, and without even knowing it, I betrayed my team. Then I had a psychotic episode and spent time in a psych ward. Since then, I've been doing well, though the last few weeks have been particularly tough because of the new therapy I've started. As terrible as it sounds, I really haven't had time for anyone but myself and the company as I get myself together and repair the damage I did at Johatchen. I'm really sorry."

"No worries, Mark. We've had crazy busy lives and the hard work has paid off for both of us."

"I wonder about that sometimes. No actually, most of the time. It seems like Janice and I were happier when we were less successful. Once we got rich, things changed. It seemed like Janice changed.

"Then again, I know how much I worked and how often I was absent. She supported me through my failures, even while I put in ridiculous hours. I'm not sure what changed this time. After all, the hard work had finally paid off.

"I really miss what we had."

"It sounds like you really loved her."

"And I guess I still do – ah, did."

"Mark, I make a habit of not asking my clients if they're guilty. I present what the State has as evidence and I try to call it into question. However, even without having started discovery, the State has a compelling case. Your car was seen. You seem to have a motive.

"I know the Assistant DA pretty well, and she told me that she has evidence linking you to two other murders. You knew the victims, and there are emails on your computer which it appears you sent to a reporter claiming responsibility.

"At this point, other than the insanity plea, I'm not sure what else we have to argue."

"I don't know either. I took my meds which knocked me out, and the next thing I knew the police were there and I was under arrest. I certainly have no memory of hurting anyone. Not Janice or anyone else.

"On the other hand, I've been having memory lapses. So I really don't know. I just can't imagine I could do this. I still love Janice. And as for the others, why would I want to kill them?"

"Mark, today, you were charged with Janice's murder. I suspect charges for the other murders will be coming soon. I'm going to bring in my best investigator to see what she can find. In the meantime, I need you to sign this Authorization for Release of Medical Records so I can talk to your psychiatrist.

"Quite frankly, although my personal feelings are not supposed to enter into it, I can honestly say that I don't think you could have done this. But from where I'm sitting now, I'm not sure we're going to be able to get a not guilty verdict. We may have to rely on the insanity plea. I'm hoping it won't come to that, but I just want to set your expectations."

"You sound like Sam. She works hard to manage my expectations too."

"Is that your shrink?"

"Yeah. I have a feeling you two are going work well together."

5

After receiving assurances from Morris that everything was under control, George said goodbye to his office mates and begrudgingly cleared his desk and shut down his computer. With the arrest of Mark Johansen, from the Sentinel's point of view, things were going to move slowly while both sides prepared for trial. Perhaps it wasn't such a bad time to take a vacation after all.

George was supposed to meet Janey at 7 Hills, their last chance at real Italian food for ten days. After a romantic dinner, they'd make their way to the airport where they'd catch their redeye flight to Papeete, arriving just before sunrise.

George made his usual pit stop before leaving the office, and wouldn't you know it, his phone rang just as he was standing at the urinal. He took a quick look at the screen and seeing it was Janey, he decided to answer.

"George! I'm so excited. This is our first vacation. It's our honeymoon! I'm about fifteen minutes out. Are you almost ready?"

"Almost. I should be able to get to the restaurant about the same time you do."

"Where are you George? You sound like you're in a tunnel."

Thinking quickly, George offered a riddle, "If I weren't an American, but instead had been born in France, Germany, Italy, or Spain, what would I be?"

There was a brief pause as Janey thought about it and replied, "European? Eur-o-pe-an? Oh! You're peeing. I love you George! I can't wait to ravish you over and over for the next ten days."

For a moment, George forgot about the serial murders, about Internet Bad Guys, and about work. He pictured Janey naked in turquoise water on a pink coral sand beach. Yeah. He was ready.

"I won't tell you over the phone what I'm thinking about," he replied. "See you in a few minutes.

As it turned out, Janey beat him to the restaurant. The host led George to a quiet table in the back where Janey was waiting, clearly excited.

"Aren't you excited, George?" Janey asked after kissing George languorously.

"After a kiss like that, how could I not be. I'm glad we have a table in the back."

As he thought about it though, George realized that he really was excited. This would be the first stretch of more than a few days not working since he started high school. He'd always worked summers, vacations, and after school. And even in college, he held down multiple part-time jobs to pay his own way.

But now, not only were they going to take time off, they were going to Tahiti. George had never been to a tropical place. So yes.

"You know Janey, I really am getting excited."

"Me too! It's our honeymoon, George!"

"Sorry that it's so late. I started at the Sentinel just a couple days after we got married and haven't taken a break."

"Don't feel bad, George," Janey soothed. "I haven't exactly been Ms. Available with Uluru taking all my time. But this is really good timing. The past three years of hard work is about to pay off for Uluru and for us. I can finally take some time off, and we certainly have saved enough money with our conservative lifestyle to afford this trip.

"I know it's not a perfect time for you. But with a suspect arrested, it's not the worst time either, is it?"

George had to admit that it wasn't. Even if Mark Johansen wasn't the killer, the case was going to slow down for a while.

"No. It's probably not the worst time. But I do worry about missing something now that an arrest has been made. And, there is the other guy. Maybe he'll send me more bad guys."

"And if he does, Morris has promised to keep you updated. We'll have excellent phone service and internet the first five days, and if something really major comes up, we can cancel the last five."

"No," George replied, looking deep into Janey's startlingly green eyes. "Morris is right. The Sentinel can live without me for ten days, and I can certainly live without them, particularly if I have you by my side."

"Or on top?" Janey suggested lasciviously.

"Or on top!"

They finished a bottle of wine and were just tipsy enough to sleep during the entire overnight flight to Papeete.

It was first light when they got off the plane in Tahiti. After collecting their bags and going through immigration, they easily found the shuttle to the ferry to Moorea.

They stepped onto the boat and were whisked across the strikingly turquoise waters of the lagoon surrounding Tahiti into the deep blue inter-island waters. Thirty minutes later, George and Janey were stepping onto the hotel shuttle. The short ride to the hotel almost left them both with whiplash, not because of dangerous driving, but because they couldn't stop turning their heads from the turquoise ocean and motus beyond the lagoon on the right, to the rugged volcanic mountains to the left. Strikingly beautiful tropical flowers lined the surprisingly deserted road.

They checked into the hotel less than two hours from the time they landed. And as if destiny were blessing their trip, the very friendly Polynesian receptionist told them their room was ready. She explained that early December was their off season and they only had a few people staying in the overwater bungalows. She also invited them to partake of the breakfast buffet as soon as they were settled in.

"Vaea will take you to your room. Don't hesitate to let me know if you need anything. My name is Palila."

"Maeruuru roa, Palila," Janey replied to a pleasantly surprised Palila and a stunned George.

Vaea greeted them warmly and led them to their room.

Their 'room' was bigger than their apartment and far more luxurious than anything they had imagined. Except for the ceiling and roof made of palm fronds, the entire space was built from exotic woods and glass. Lush green plants with tropical flowers set off a decor that left them breathless. The bed with its hand-carved headboard could easily have slept four people and Janey and George smiled at each other knowingly before the valet led them into the 'bathroom'. This was a suite unto itself with a huge curved tub that would comfortably fit two, and a shower surrounded by glass windows that looked out over the lagoon.

As they returned to the living room, George couldn't believe that he'd missed the glass window in the floor. Walking over, he spotted dozens of fish along with several sharks.

"Janey, look!"

"This is amazing!"

"And, it opens. There is a ladder down into the water so you can access the lagoon without even going out onto the deck," Vaea explained. "The black-tipped sharks are very common here. They are completely harmless and you can swim with them comfortably, even the larger ones. There really aren't any dangerous sharks inside the lagoon, so you should feel free to venture out wherever you want. We have kayaks, paddleboards, and snorkeling equipment available for you whenever you like. You can even paddle to your bungalow and tie your kayak to the ladder below or to the deck," Vaea explained, leading them through the paneled French doors onto their private deck. No other bungalows were visible. It was truly private. Beyond the lagoon the surrounding motus offered dramatic white sands. A few were thick with coconut palms.

"You may see a few boats passing by or possibly one of the other guests in kayaks, but in general, people give a wide berth to the overwater bungalows to give you maximum privacy," Vaea continued.

The deck had two levels. There was a covered section shaded from the sun with a table and chairs on the upper level and two deck chairs laid out in the sun on the lower deck. They took the two steps down and walked to the edge where they spotted the ladder that led from there into the lagoon. Countless fish, many an intense blue, darted in and out of the underwater coral formations. It all was more than they could ever have imagined.

"If you don't have any questions, I'll leave you to settle in. Don't forget the breakfast buffet. Haere mai!

"Maeruuru roa, Vaea!" Janey repeated enthusiastically.

Seeing the look in George's eyes, Janey grinned. "George, I need a shower first."

"Shower?!" George answered sarcastically. "No shower!"

He undressed Janey, stripped off his clothes, pulled her naked body close and said, "Close your eyes woman of my dreams!" as he jumped off the deck into the crystalline waters with Janey wrapped in his embrace.

6

It was ten o'clock on Monday morning and Morris was at his desk thinking about George and Janey. He was proud of himself for chasing George out of the office. At the same time he felt a bit guilty about the fact that George hadn't had a vacation or more than a few consecutive days off since he'd started at the Sentinel two years before. Then again, it was the same story for most of the aggressive young reporters. With the print news industry suffering and blogs becoming more and more influential, full time positions in the 'newspaper' industry were hard to come by and even harder to keep. George had pretty much assured his tenure with the level of effort he'd put in since starting at the Sentinel. And this was a good time for a break and a recharge. Somehow, Morris suspected that George would be returning to some of the biggest challenges of his career.

His phone rang.

"This is Morris."

"Good morning, Morris," responded the unusually friendly voice of Mike McKensey. "I'm just calling to let you know that based on evidence found in his home and on his computer, the DA has charged Mark Johansen with the murders of Ashima James and Julia Lewis."

"Thanks, Mike. This wasn't totally unexpected. I already have the framework for the story."

"Will George be okay missing out on this?"

"George will be fine. While he's away, I'm bylining the stories as 'Morris Levinberg for George Gray'. Obviously we'll keep the story in the news during his absence, but I suspect the real meat will come after he gets back."

"God! Tahiti. A cop can only dream."

"You should take some time off and go. It's worth it."

"Yeah, right! The chances that two cops can both get extended time off for something like that are pretty slim."

"I'm sure the departments can spare you both."

"Yeah. That will happen when murders stop in the City."

"So Mike. Off the record. Did Johansen do it?"

"Off the record, right? Well, we've done some interrogations. Granted, his attorney was present so we're somewhat limited in how aggressive we can be. But like I suggested before, either this guy is one of the best actors I've ever seen, or he really doesn't remember doing it. Interestingly, he won't say he didn't do it, he just says he can't remember. I guess that's a good basis for an insanity plea given his history, but I'll tell you, my gut says we've got the wrong guy. But of course, it's about the evidence and right now, I think the DA has a solid case for guilty. As to insanity, who knows?"

Morris thought about some of the 'aggressive' interrogations he'd witnessed. Without lawyers present, the cops could lie, claiming evidence they didn't really have. They could promise clemency for a confession, using good cop, bad cop pressures that bordered on verbal abuse. And the interrogations could go on for hours. On one case, he'd witnessed the interrogation of a young immigrant accused of rape of his own daughter. The man was shackled to his chair for the duration of the ten-hour interview. The cops claimed they had DNA proving his guilt. They told him he could go home to his family if he just confessed. They lied and cajoled. Good cops used gentle Spanish while the bad cops berated the accused in rapid-fire English. Somehow, the man maintained his innocence. Morris knew that if he had been arrested, had passed an entire night without sleep, then been subjected to ten hours of non-stop interrogation, he would have confessed to anything. It was certain that cops were good at interrogations – much better than anything you could see on TV.

"And you say the lawyer is good?"

"It's Sharon Katell."

Morris had reported on several of Sharon Katell's cases. If he were accused of murder, Sharon Katell would have been his first choice for a lawyer.

"Without a doubt she's one of the best," Morris affirmed. What do you think her chances are?"

"I never predict what courts and juries will do. I suspect the insanity plea will stand up. But for now, not-guilty looks unlikely given the evidence. She's pressed me hard to look for other suspects, but the department isn't going to give me any official time for that, given what we have on Johansen. And that's what I told her. But just between us, I'm doing my best to look elsewhere. I'm looking forward to George's return so he and that brilliant wife of his can help me out."

"They'll be back in a week so hopefully nothing radical will happen in the meantime. But if you do need my help with anything, let me know."

"Well, since you suggested it, could you talk to Sharon Katell? Let her know that unofficially, I am looking for other suspects. And if she has anything she wants to pass on, any leads, maybe you could act as a go-between."

"Mike, I can't commit to working for you like this, but I'll do what I can, and I'll encourage George to pick up wherever I leave off."

They said their goodbyes and Morris fired off an email to George letting him know that Mark Johansen had been charged with the other murders and that Mike was looking for more suspects. Then he gave Sharon Katell a call.

7

Sharon Katell stopped at the bakery below Samantha Louis' office and bought a couple of pastries – religieuses – each with three stacked snowman-like cream-puff balls topped in dark chocolate and decorated with white Chantilly cream to make them look like nuns.

She hoped that food would help break what she assumed would be some very thick ice. In the course of her career, Sharon had tried to interview many psychiatrists. Even when presented with the patient release, the shrinks were reluctant to talk about their patients, let alone the treatments they were undergoing. Hopefully Samantha Louis would be different.

She climbed the stairs to Samantha Louis' office and entered a surprisingly cozy waiting room. Before she could take a seat, the door to the psychiatrist's private office opened and Samantha Louis greeted her guest warmly.

"Sharon, right? I see you've succumbed to the treats of our local French bakery downstairs."

"I couldn't resist. Plus, I thought these beautiful religieuses might be an ice breaker."

Samantha looked amused. "I'm Sam. Come on in."

And motioning to what appeared to be a comfortable over-stuffed sofa, she suggested that Sharon take a seat. "I've got coffee, iced tea and a few juices to go with those pastries."

"Ah, coffee, please. I must admit to living on its boost when I'm on a case."

"Cream and sugar?"

"Just black please. I don't want to dilute the caffeine."

Sam smiled, filled a porcelain mug shaped like a high-top button shoe with coffee and placed it on a small ornate tray, added two plates, cloth napkins, and her own fruit juice, then made her way over to Sharon. She placed the tray on the coffee table in front of the sofa and took a seat on the edge of the rocking recliner facing Sharon.

Doing her part, Sharon removed the pastries from the box and placed one on a plate which she handed to Sam before placing one on her own plate. She took a bite of the religieuse, wiped a smear of chocolate and Chantilly off her face, took a sip of coffee and sighed.

"That is exceptional. I haven't had a religieuse since my last trip to France."

"Do you go often?"

"As strange as it sounds, I'm sort of semi-retired. I manage several law offices, but have a great team that can offload most of the work. That way I can spend a few months a year in France. It's the one place in the world where I actually feel comfortable. I like the people, the politics, the language, and of course, the food."

Sam smiled. "I did a month abroad in France during high school and though I've promised myself to go back, I haven't found the time. I appreciated the sense of culture there."

"That's exactly it. It's not just the history, which is, in itself, interesting. It's this general respect for art, philosophy, literature, and all things that people create, even technology. Somehow, the French don't seem to have lost their souls to the frenetic pace of our American world. They seem to have a better life balance and they respect ideas. Not just their own, but any idea that might be interesting. One day, I might retire there – if I could ever really give up the law."

"So if you're semi-retired, how is it you're representing Mark?"

"Mark and I go back a long way. We were best friends for years but then with careers and his marriage, we kind of lost touch for a while. Actually we didn't really lose touch. We followed each other on social media, but haven't seen each other in probably at least fifteen years.

"But I know Mark. Or at least I knew Mark, probably better than anyone. And the Mark I knew could never have killed anyone, let alone three people."

Seeing that Sam had finished her pastry, Sharon reached into her briefcase and pulled out the Patient Release which she handed to Sam.

"I know you're reluctant to talk about patient information – "

Sam raised a hand to stop Sharon, carefully read the release, stood up and placed it on her desk, then returned to her chair.

"Actually, I'm more than happy to tell you everything I know about Mark Johansen. I only have an hour until my next appointment, so if we don't get through everything you need today, we can pick up our conversation again later. And if you knew Mark when he was younger, perhaps you can enlighten me a bit about his past. This is a bit irregular. I don't usually get involved with friends and family except in rare circumstances, but if there ever was one, I suspect this is an exceptional case."

"Great! So can you tell me about Mark's condition."

"Sure. Mark suffers from late-onset schizophrenia. Normally we see the onset of schizophrenia when patients are in their late teens or twenties. Most psychiatrists believe that schizophrenia is genetic and that there is no cure, just management through drugs and therapy. These therapies revolve around teaching the patient to recognize that what they think, and even what they think they see or hear, is not necessarily real.

"Late onset schizophrenia is somewhat rare. It tends to be more easily manageable, in my opinion, because older adults have a better ability to recognize when things don't make sense.

"With Mark, we took that approach. We used drugs to quiet his hallucinations, then used Cognitive Based Therapy – CBT, to teach him to manage his delusions and hallucinations. That went very well and he was able to return to work and he seemed to be fully productive."

"You said 'seemed'," Sharon queried, intrigued. "Is that past tense or was it not real?"

"No. It was real. I meant it in the past tense."

Sam took a deep breath and then continued.

"Okay. This is a bit rough, but Mark and I spoke about the fact that some recent research has shown that in a not-insignificant number of late-onset cases, cures are possible. There are several avant-garde psychiatrists who've had great success searching for non-physical, non-genetic causes, and they've found that trauma is a possible cause.

"Based on some of our therapy sessions, I suspect that Mark suffered damaging trauma as a child. We decided that although the new therapy would be rough on Mark, if there was a chance for a cure, we should pursue it."

"You say 'we'. Is that you and Mark?"

"Absolutely. I couldn't do this without Mark being fully on board. He knew it would be hard and that he might be taking a few steps backward, but if you know Mark, you know he'll do whatever it takes to succeed, and right now, success means a cure.

"I've also consulted with my mentor, and with two trauma specialists and they're reviewing each step we take."

"Thanks Sam. That helps. Mark tried to explain much of this to me, but right now, I think he's a bit confused and his explanation reflected that.

"At this point, Mark doesn't know if he's guilty or not. Unfortunately, all the evidence points to guilt, not only for the murder of his wife, but also for the murders of Ashima James and Julia Lewis. He says he's been having memory lapses so he can't rule out the possibility that he's guilty."

"Yeah. We discussed the memory lapses. Quite frankly, I'm not sure that he's actually having them. It's not a side effect from the drugs he's taking, and while it is common for schizophrenics to have memory loss, from the cognitive testing I've done on Mark, I just haven't seen it.

"Honestly, I don't think Mark is guilty. I just don't see murder as something Mark could do."

Sam hesitated. Thinking back to some of the violent patients she'd worked with, who outwardly seemed so normal, Sam knew she could be wrong on that count. Then again, none of those patients were schizophrenic, and schizophrenics were rarely violent in spite of their reputations to the contrary.

Seeing Sam apparently lost in thought, Sharon jumped in. "Mark and I go way back. I think I know – knew Mark better than anyone. I don't think he could have done this either. But the DA has the evidence and quite frankly, I can't even come up with another theory.

"The good news, if there is any, is that the lead detective on the case, a Mike McKensey, has a gut feel that something is wrong here – it's just too pat, and Mark doesn't fit what he thinks of as the profile of the killer.

"I hope he's right and I'm hoping that we can find some leads to the real killer.

"In the meantime, Mark is in jail. Because of his mental health history, they're allowing limited treatment. So far, they're permitting his medications –"

"Yeah. I got a call and confirmed his meds."

"And, they have some mental health professionals available. I've asked the court to grant you visits – if you're willing – to do some basic treatment. I don't know if you'll be able to continue your new therapy at this point, especially in the jail, but I suspect that meeting with Mark regularly would help him see things a bit more clearly. As I said, he thinks he might have done this. I need him to believe otherwise. And of course, we'll pay your fees."

"That's not an issue for me. I'll talk with Dr. Karmere – my mentor at Community. I know he's done quite of bit of work with prisoners with mental illnesses. He probably knows the staff over there and can help smooth thing along with my visits. I'll let you know how it's going."

Sam paused a moment before continuing. "You said you knew Mark years ago. When did you meet?"

"Mark started at my high school during the middle of tenth grade. He fit into our so-called intellectual crowd very easily, but was also good at sports. He was what used to be called a renaissance man – boy, ah. Anyway, we became absolute best friends."

"And did your relationship go beyond friendship?"

"We had a brief fling in college, but recognized quickly that neither of us was looking for a committed romantic relationship. We had a world to change. So we both agreed that continuing a romance could be dangerous for our friendship."

"That sounds like a very adult decision."

"Maybe, maybe not. As I think back on it, we were a pretty good fit. Our interests overlapped. After all these years, I've come to believe that a lasting relationship is based on a truly solid friendship and common interests. But I don't think we need to dwell on that right now."

"So, did you meet Mark's family? My therapy is digging into that, but so far, I'm not learning much."

"Yes. I often spent time at Mark's house. His dad was retired military and had just taken a job with Lockheed. God, I think about it now. He was in his early forties. I'm older than that. Anyway, my impression was that his dad was a pretty nice guy. I know he was absent a lot during Mark's childhood. He worked in military intelligence in some interesting places. But from what Mark told me, his dad was always supportive and encouraging and when he was around, they had fun together."

"And his mother?"

Sharon paused before answering. "Well, I never got to know her. Mark never talked about her and the few times I had dinner at their house, Mark's father seemed to be an almost bigger-than-life character. He made jokes and always had funny stories. I liked him a lot.

"But his mother? For me, I just couldn't imagine her with Mark's dad. They certainly didn't seem to be much of a couple."

"And how would you describe her?

"I guess if I were to use one word, it would be dark. She seemed reserved and maybe, a bit angry. I mean she didn't show her temper, never screamed or got violent, but it was like there was a seething anger under the surface.

"You know, Mark left home right after graduation and as far as I know, he never returned, except for his father's funeral during freshman year. I went with him. It was rough. But the thing that stands out for me as I think back about it is that Mark's mother was as cold as ice towards Mark and as we were leaving, Mark's mother told him that it was his fault."

"Did you guys talk about it afterwards?"

"No. Aside from telling me about activities he'd shared with his dad, Mark never talked about his family."

"Thanks Sharon. That fills in a few holes for me."

Sam glanced at her watch and Sharon stood up.

"You've really helped me too. Let's touch base after you talk to Mark."

Sam walked Sharon to the door and gave her a hug.

"I sure hope you can get Mark out of this."

"It's going to be a team effort. And on that note, there's one more thing. We appear to have an ally in Detective Mike McKensey. I know you're bound by confidentiality, but if he calls, and I'm pretty sure he will, try to help wherever you can. He may see something we don't."

"I'll do my best"

8

Mike McKensey gazed with wonder at May, his wife of just three years. Nearing fifty, she had the body of a twenty-year old athlete. Well, in fact, while not twenty, she certainly was an athlete. At times, having May for a wife was tough for Mike, who always considered himself to be in great shape. But most of the time, Mike couldn't keep up with May.

They'd met on a serial murder case. She was a detective with the Marin County Sheriff's department and a number of bodies had washed up on Bay Area beaches, some in Marin, some in San Francisco. They worked together well, chasing some promising leads that ultimately never panned out. It appeared the killer was a woman. Following a lead in the Tenderloin, the SFPD had almost caught her, but then she disappeared and the murders stopped altogether. Since then nothing new. For both of them, it was the most unsatisfying case they'd ever worked on. And truth be known, they continued to work on it in their spare time – what little there was of that for two homicide detectives.

Over the course of their professional relationship, they learned that each loved to run and that they often ran some of the same rugged trails. Mike had decided to do the Escape from Alcatraz Triathlon, which he was surprised to learn May had done the previous year. In fact, she did multiple triathlons every year and was training for her first Ironman. She agreed to help Mike with his training and on their first meeting kicked his butt on both the run and bike legs. And now, a few years later, she was doing multiple Ironmans each year and was in truly amazing shape. Quite frankly, Mike had no desire to keep up. And, in fact, even if he did, the demands of the SFPD homicide division didn't give him the kind of time required. But yeah, he was a bit intimidated by his amazingly fit wife.

"Rough day?" May asked as she served him what he thought of as an overly healthy meal.

"It really shouldn't have been. I mean this serial murder case is supposed to be wrapping up and now I just have a straight forward drug deal gone wrong, and an inter-spouse murder to investigate.

"But I gotta tell you. I'm struggling with this Mark Johansen case. All the evidence is there but I can't convince myself he did it. The hard part is I have no leads pointing to anyone else and nothing to exonerate Johansen."

"So you think he's being set up? If so, given how tight the evidence is, it's got to be someone pretty close to him, right?"

"Yeah. But at this point, he really doesn't have many close friends. In fact, I can only think of two."

"And?"

"Well, one is this guy Jack Trageser. They have known each other for years but I can't see any links that would provide a motive, other than the fact that they both knew the other victims and their husbands. But as big as the Silicon Valley is, I still see this particular group of tech gurus as pretty close-knit. I'm ninety-nine percent sure it couldn't be him."

"And the second?"

"That would be his business partner, Richard Hatch. They've been friends for decades and founded three companies together. From what I can see, Hatch has been incredibly supportive of Johansen and was there for him after the psychotic break that landed him in the psych ward. I'm not seeing a motive here either. The guy has plenty of money since the two were equal partners in the company, and as I said, they've been best friends for years."

"Maybe some internal rivalry? Control of the company?"

"I'll try to look into it, but I don't know…"

"Hey, something will pop up. It always does."

"You mean like in our serial murder case?"

"Come on. That was the first time in my career that we didn't find the perp. I can't imagine there have been too many of those for you either."

"Maybe I'm just losing it. Maybe I'm getting too old for this. Maybe my cop's nose is completely out of whack about Johansen."

May stood up, came around the table and plopped herself in Mike's lap, throwing her arms around him. She held him for a minute then took his hand and led him to the bedroom.

"Feel better?" she asked forty minutes later.

"Quite a bit!" Mike replied with a big grin.

"Okay. What's next then?"

"How about a pizza?"

May smacked Mike with a pillow.

"Okay. I'll agree to pizza if you can come up with one thing you'll follow up on."

Mike thought a minute, his mind cleared of the self-pity that had brought him to a dead end.

"All right. Here are two: I'll talk to Richard Hatch and will press him on who could want to frame Johansen. And, I'll see if I can get a waiver to talk to Johansen's psychiatrist. Maybe she knows something that will give me a lead.

"And I guess there's one more that I've kind of overlooked. Brittany Spangler, the first victim's daughter claims to be good with computers, knew the victims and knows Mark Johansen. I need to rule her out."

May kissed Mike, grabbed the phone, and called in an order for the deep dish pizza that Mike missed so much.

They fell asleep a few hours later on the sofa sated with pizza and beer just before the final scenes of Gaslight played out on the television.

9

It was their last full day in Tahiti. Moorea had exceeded all their expectations, but after several days in the somewhat populated tropical paradise, they had craved more solitude. Four days earlier, George and Janey had taken the one-hour flight to Tikehau, one of the Tuamotu atolls a few hundred miles north of the main islands of Tahiti. From the air, they got a real sense of what an atoll was. Tikehau had no island. It was just a giant, almost circular, ring of sandy motus with a huge lagoon in the middle. From the brochures, they knew the lagoon was eight miles across, but as they landed, it seemed much larger.

And the landing. A motu is just a spit of sand atop a coral reef. It seemed almost impossible that a plane could land on one. But all had gone smoothly. Twenty minutes later, the hotel shuttle had dropped them at a resort that was even more elegant than the one on Moorea. And this time, they learned that they were the only guests. They were given the largest over-water bungalow at the furthest reach of the walkway into the lagoon. The set up was almost identical, with private deck, luxurious appointments, and of course, the glass window in the floor.

George and Janey had spent three days paddling to nearby completely deserted motus. True to his promise, George scaled coconut trees and broke open the coconuts on sharp coral formations protruding from the pink sands. They swam and snorkeled naked in the crystal clear waters.

Most amazing were the oysters. Easily twelve inches across, these exotic multicolored shellfish bore no resemblance to anything either had seen before. And from underneath the dramatic blue, gold, red, and purple oysters, coral formations pushed up towards the surface. When snorkeling, George and Janey were surrounded by schools of fish that had Tahitian names longer than they were. And of course, they had become comfortable with the black-tipped sharks that seemed to be everywhere.

After returning from their final motu trip, George and Janey showered and got ready for dinner. Janey deftly wrapped herself in a Pareo – a single piece of sarong-like fabric – and teased George that she'd be wearing nothing underneath.

"Do we really have to go home tomorrow?" he lamented.

"It's been the best vacation ever, George. Will we come

back?"

"I can't imagine not coming back. Hey Janey, could you check email before we head over to the restaurant?"

"Sure."

Janey started her computer and went through the laborious process of getting an internet connection. The connection itself was so slow that it was hard to know if it was actually working. Many of the times they'd tried to access the Net from Tikehau, it actually wasn't working.

Janey downloaded George's email she didn't see anything urgent.

"It looks like just the daily update from Morris. Nothing terribly important."

George wasn't sure whether to be pleased that there was nothing to rush back to or disappointed.

He was just finishing shaving when Janey cried out, "George! Come see!"

George quickly applied a small piece of toilet paper to the nick on his chin and made his way over to Janey. Looking at her computer screen, all he could see was what to him looked like gobbledygook.

"And why did I cut myself to race over here to see this?"

"Oh George, I'm really sorry. I know this doesn't look like much, but my bot found a source of the names in the emails you got from both the killer and the informer."

"Are they both the same? Can you tell where they are?"

"Well sort of. Just a sec."

Janey typed furiously for a few seconds, waited what seemed like minutes, then typed more. A few minutes later, she turned to George.

"Okay. I can't tell if this is the informer or the killer. It's possible that there are more sources out there. I was able to track down the location of this one and it's in the SFPD. My guess is that this is Mark Johansen's computer. It looks like he has the program that generates these random email addresses. I can hack into the computer, but since it's with the police, it's probably not the best idea. Maybe when we get back, they'll let me have a look at it."

George was disappointed. This pointed further to Mark Johansen's guilt. It looked like Mike McKensey was wrong. Mark Johansen was guilty.

George decided to do his best to put this aside for their last evening in Tahiti.

"I love you Janey! Let's look at this after we get back."

"Ah, okay," Janey replied reluctantly. "I'm pretty excited that my bot actually works, but I guess I can wait. It would be too slow to do anything from here anyway."

Both disappointed but resolved to make the most of their last evening, George and Janey made their way to the restaurant where, as the only guests that evening, they were treated like royalty.

10

Mike McKensey swallowed the last bite of cream and pastry as he made his way up the stairs to Samantha Louis' office. Since he'd arrived a few minutes early, Mike had made the mistake of stopping in at the French bakery. The attractive young French owner patiently explained what each pastry was and Mike succumbed to the chou. With his recollection and limited knowledge of French, Mike asked her if a chou was a cabbage. And after confirming that it was, she explained that the pastry was a chou a la crème, similar to what Americans called a cream puff. But it was like no crème puff Mike had ever tasted. The pastry was light, delicate, and was dusted with a layer of a cinnamon-sugar mix. And the cream! The cream was more decadent than anything he'd eaten in years. May would kill him.

Mike climbed the stairs and entered Samantha Louis' waiting room. He'd just sat down and picked up a copy of Time Magazine when Samantha Louis stepped out of her office and greeted Mike, holding out her hand.

"Detective McKensey, I'm Samantha Louis. Call me Sam."

Mike noticed the confident handshake and was pleased that 'Sam' didn't seem intimidated meeting a police detective.

"I'm Mike," he replied, following her into her office.

"Have a seat Mike," Sam suggested. "Can I get you anything? Coffee, tea, juice? Something to wash down that pastry you just had downstairs?"

Mike was halfway seated and stood up suddenly.

"How'd you--?"

Sam pointed to her right cheek and her engaging smile brightened further. "Very few people can avoid the pastries downstairs."

"Well please don't tell my wife!"

"You look pretty fit. Do you have cholesterol problems or some other dietary issue?"

"No. May, my wife, is a triathlete. It's rare we deviate from a really healthy diet. She's incredibly disciplined. I tried to keep up for a while and realized that's just not me. Still, I try.

"As for something to drink, I think I'll pass. As you so astutely noted, I did just have a snack."

"Sorry," Sam replied. "I guess our fields aren't so different. I'm trained to notice details and most of my work is investigative."

Reaching into the folder he was carrying, Mike handed Sam the Authorization for Release of Medical Records.

"That's why I'm here. I'm hoping you can help me with this case."

Sam read the authorization then looked up surprised.

"It doesn't say anything about the SFPD here. If I'm reading this correctly, this is a request by you as an individual."

"Yeah. That's the complicated part. Officially, I'm not supposed to be investigating this. The Lieutenant and the DA, and even my partner think we have our perp and all the evidence we need. So yes. It's just me. I don't need records. I just want to be able to talk about Mark Johansen. I can give you my word that nothing you tell me will get back to the DA or the SFPD. I want to use it for my own – ah – private investigation."

"Aren't you putting yourself at risk?" Sam asked, concerned.

"Not so much. But I have to do this. There's something wrong about this case. It just doesn't feel right. My gut tells me that Mark Johansen is not our guy. The evidence all points to it, but sometimes the evidence doesn't tell the whole story. I'm hoping you can fill in some pieces.

"So please tell me about Mark. I've interviewed him and I don't think he's lying when he says he doesn't remember killing any of these women. He's also almost too cooperative. And he's confused. He did talk about memory lapses. Can you tell me about his condition, his medications, and possible side effects? Do you think he could have done this?"

Over the next twenty minutes, Sam took Mike through her treatment of Mark Johansen. And as she had explained to Sharon Katell, she said she didn't believe that Mark was having memory lapses.

"To sum it up, I just don't see any way that Mark could be a serial killer – in fact, no kind of killer at all. He's one of the gentlest people I've ever met."

Then, thinking about Liz, her former patient, she backtracked a bit, "Of course, as great a detective as I think I am, sometimes, people fool me. I don't think it's the case here, but I could be wrong. Still, Mark, serial killer. I just can't see it."

"Sam, this has been helpful. I think I understand Mark's condition and it just confirms my suspicions that he might have been framed. But to frame Mark, it would have to be someone close to him. Can you tell me about his friends or family? Any thoughts on someone who might want to do this to him?"

Thinking about Jack and also about Richard, Mark's closest friends, Sam answered hesitantly, "No. I don't think so." But her face gave her away.

"You have some whipped cream on your face," Mike replied seriously, touching his cheek.

It only took Sam a second to get Mike's subtle reference. He was a detective. He knew she was holding back.

"I'm really sorry. Ah. Okay. I really only know about two people who are close to Mark. He has talked about his coworkers, but even though they're like family to him, from what he's described, there's a healthy distance between him and his team. So the two people are – "

"Richard Hatch, his business partner, and Jack Trageser." Mike finished for her.

"Exactly. I met Richard early on. He's been incredibly supportive of Mark and has helped him stay on his meds, off alcohol and drugs, and has encouraged him to get back to work.

"I know Jack socially."

"So do you think either one of them could want to frame Mark for serial killings?"

Sam took a minute to think, then responded.

"Well, for Jack, I just can't see anything. As for Richard, he has been there for Mark. Still, in one of our recent sessions, Mark did mention that he was concerned that Richard was jealous of him and might be sabotaging him. But I have to tell you that while violence and memory lapses are unlikely for Mark, paranoia is a classic symptom. It's one of those things that we've been working on since day one."

"Still, sometimes, just because you're paranoid, doesn't mean that someone isn't out to get you," Mike joked sardonically.

"Of course. But I can't see Richard as a serial killer. But then again, I don't have much experience with serial killers. Do you?"

"Well, In spite of what the press may have you believe, there really aren't many serial killers. Most homicides are committed by someone close to the victims. If there weren't multiple victims, I probably would have had an easier time believing that Mark Johansen killed his wife.

"Serial killers are a different breed. All that I've encountered are detached sociopaths – I don't mean to use a technical term here. But yes. I've encountered a few in my long career. There are similarities and all have made mistakes that led to their capture. But not mistakes like Mark made. And then again, I have to admit that there was one case not long ago. You probably read about it. My wife May and I worked on it and quite honestly can't really let it go. It was a woman serial killer and she just disappeared. We never caught her – at least not yet.

Sam did her best to hold her composure. Hopefully, the ever-perspicacious Mike McKensey didn't see that he had touched a nerve.

Apparently, he didn't this time.

"I'll be looking into Richard Hatch and Jack Trageser. I really thank you for being so open with me."

Sam walked Mike to the door. They shook hands and agreed to keep each other up to date on any developments.

Closing the door behind Mike, Sam shuddered. She wasn't ever going to tell Mike McKensey about a particularly dangerous patient she'd treated. And, it wasn't just a question of patient confidentiality.

As she walked back to her desk, Sam asked herself if she should have mentioned Brittany Spangler. No. That would have been a real violation of patient confidentiality. What did she really know anyway? By law, she couldn't reveal information about a patient unless there was evidence of imminent danger to someone.

The killer certainly wasn't Mark. Richard seemed so supportive of Mark. He was doubtful as a suspect. Jack? There was something off there, but no. If she had to guess, of the three, it was Brittany who was the most dangerous. But Sam couldn't say anything.

Sometimes Sam wondered if she was really up to this job.

11

Morris Levinberg approached his star reporter's cubicle and found George staring dreamily at his monitor. Peeking around, Morris discovered a smiling Janey with a colorful drink in her hand and gorgeous turquoise water behind her.

"Are you back yet?"

George looked up, a bit surprised. "Ah, I guess not. Without a doubt, that was the best vacation of my life and it may take me a while to get back to reality."

"Yeah. You look more relaxed than I've ever seen you. It looks like the enforced vacation did you some good."

"Morris, I can't thank you enough for making me go. In addition to a much-needed break, I had a lot of long talks with Janey and I think I've gained some perspective.

"I don't know if you could see it, but I've been questioning what I do. I've been asking myself if I'm doing more harm than good, if my work isn't inspiring these crazies to hurt people."

"We all go through that, George, though I think you've been closer to some of these cases than most of us. So, where did you end up?

"As Janey has said countless times, all I can do is the best I can do. For some reason, on Tikehau, out in the middle of the Pacific Ocean, I realized that I can step back. I may not always be completely objective, nor will I be dispassionate, but I can accept that overall, my work will do more good than harm. And I will do the best I can."

"George, I'm glad to hear it. And I'm definitely glad to have you back. I actually haven't had to write stories with deadlines in years. It was fun for a while, but I'm ready to hand it back.

"I hope you're ready to hit the ground running because I've set up an interview with Mark Johansen for later this morning. Sorry to break your reverie, but we do have work to do!"

"Is there anything I should know beyond what's been in the press?"

"For the facts of the case, no. However, Mike McKensey has told me 'off-the-record' that he doesn't believe that Johansen did this. He's conducting his own unofficial investigation but so far has come up empty.

"Maybe you can find something. Maybe Mark Johansen knows something he's not conscious of. Then again, with his psychological problems, it may be tough to sort out reality from delusion."

George sat up in his chair.

"I hate to admit it, but I've missed this. I want to get into the heart of this case. I'm ready to dig in.

"And since I haven't seen any emails about new Internet Moguls, I assume there's nothing new. Did the police find any of those emails on Mark Johansen's computer?"

"No. If Johansen is guilty of the murders, it looks like our informant is a different person.

"Let me know how your interview with Johansen goes. I may be handing you the reins, but I admit to being hooked on this story."

As Morris walked away, George took one last longing look at his screen then picked up the phone and called Mike McKensey. Fifteen minutes later, he was on his way to see Mark Johansen.

12

Sam left Jack and raced back to her office. It had been a frustratingly unsatisfying lunch. It wasn't that the food was bad, but things with Jack hadn't gone as expected.

It all started out just fine. Jack was attentive and gentle. But then Sam decided to try to play detective. She brought up the arrest of Mark and Jack just lost it. He ranted. He raved about the incompetence of the police. Then stated flatly that Mark must have been framed.

But most disturbing was when Sam asked how Jack felt about Janice Livingston.

"Quite frankly, I think she got what she deserved. Look at what she did to poor Mark. He ended up in a mental institution for God's sake."

Ultimately, he calmed down. She told him she'd been able to visit Mark and to continue treatment. He seemed concerned. Jack couldn't have killed Janice and the others, right? Then again, there was something wrong here.

And now, she had an appointment with Brittany Spangler. She was going to try to play detective with a Borderline patient. Maybe she was the crazy one.

Sam made it to her office with time to spare. She poured herself a cup of hot water for tea and waited. As usual, Brittany was late. This was one of Brittany's ways of gaining control of her situation.

Twenty minutes later the subtle buzzer indicated someone in the waiting room. Rather than playing some sort of tit-for-tat and making Brittany wait, which never works for Borderline personality patients, she opened the door and greeted Brittany warmly.

Looking at Brittany, Sam wondered if she was about to make a major mistake. She probably should have consulted Dr. Karmere before trying what she was going to do. Then again, she knew what he would have advised: Don't get personally involved and Don't try to play a patient with Borderline Personality Disorder.

Brittany came in and took a seat in her usual spot. She turned down Sam's offer of tea or a soda.

"I'm sorry about last time. I know I can be a bitch sometimes, but I really do want to get better. I do need your help. This whole Schema Focused Therapy thing seems pretty solid. I'm struggling to stay with it, but in spite of what you saw at our last session, I really am trying."

"So what goals are you focused on?" Sam posed tentatively.

"Well, I thought I'd dig into my mom's murder, but that hasn't gone too well. The police won't tell me anything and the reporter following these murders is kind of leading me on, but I get it, he doesn't want me involved either. And honestly, if this is a serial killer, I'm not sure how much my mom had to do with all of this."

Sam almost smiled but thought better of it. Maybe this was going to be much easier than she thought. On the other hand, Sam didn't want to fall into the trap of most BPD family members and many therapists. It was too easy to believe that good, cooperative behavior was an indication of progress. The official term was 'variable intermittent reinforcement'. People tend to excuse bad behaviors or believe in progress because of periodic reinforcing positive experiences.

Unfortunately, many BPD patients have an innate sense of when they've just about gone too far and when they need to pull back and 'play nice' for a while. There was a good chance that this was what Brittany was doing. Nonetheless, Sam didn't want to miss an opportunity to get more information.

"Did your mom know the other victims? Maybe there's a link there."

"Yeah, my mom knew both Janice and Julia. In fact, more than once my mom bragged about her high-tech ex-wives club. I don't think it was an actual club, but I know that Janice, Julia and my mom got together pretty often after their divorces. Truth be told, they got together before the divorces too. I sometimes wonder if they plotted the timing of the exits from their marriages. Julia went first, then my mom, then Janice. And all of the husbands were destroyed. Marshall drank himself to death. Michael killed himself, and Mark went crazy.

"But as I think about it, there was one more member of the club. Mindy Hatch, the wife of Mark Johansen's partner Richard. She also plotted to leave her husband. I'm sure of it. However, Richard seems happy with her gone."

"I'm sorry for asking," Sam began cautiously. "But it sounds like you knew all of these people pretty well."

"Ah, sure. They were at our house all time, or we were at

theirs. We went camping together, skiing. It was a nice group until everything went south with the first divorce. Then everything changed. Our extended family came to an end. And with Michael's death and my problems, everything has gotten even worse. Three brilliant technologists are either gone or had their lives ruined. And as for my mom, Janice, and Julia, maybe they had it coming and got what they really deserved."

Not rising to the bait, Sam asked objectively, "And does talking about all of these people give you any ideas, any possible leads on who might have wanted to harm your mom and her friends?"

Brittany thought for a second. She looked up at Sam and realization passed over her face.

"You don't think? No! I've gotta go."

Brittany stood up and raced out of Sam's office.

What was it Brittany had suddenly realized? Did she have an idea who the murderer was? Or, and Sam hated to think she might have triggered this, but did Brittany think that Sam had concluded that she was the killer?

Sam double checked her clock and her calendar and saw that she had almost an hour before her next appointment. She poured some tea into a thermos and stopped by the bakery downstairs to buy one of their luscious eclairs.

Yes. In spite of what she tried to convince her patients (and herself), the bakery was a guilty pleasure that she couldn't resist when she needed an escape.

She walked down to the park and took her place in front of the duck pond. She bit into the éclair, wiped the excess cream from her lips and took a sip of tea.

What had she learned? They all knew each other. Brittany knew them all. Three technologists' wives. What about the fourth? What about Mindy Hatch? But then again, Richard was apparently happy with the divorce. Could he be the killer? He could have been angry at the wives for ruining their husbands' lives. Sure. Maybe he could have killed Janice as revenge for what she'd done to Mark. But if Mike McKensey was right, Mark was being framed. It didn't make sense that Richard would frame Mark. It just didn't make sense.

Sam asked herself if she had learned anything that could help Mike McKensey. Even if there weren't confidentiality issues, she was pretty sure she hadn't uncovered anything that the Detective didn't already know. All the victims were connected. He knew that.

13

George had to admit it. He was glad to be back. And this time, it was real investigative reporting. For now, his articles on the serial murders would follow the official party line. Mark Johansen had killed the three women. At the same time, George knew how to introduce subtle doubts in his copy. His readers would have a sense that all wasn't right with this particular case.

His meeting with Mark Johansen did not go quite as expected. In spite of Mike McKensey's prep, somehow George was expecting to encounter a tech titan with an ego to match. He'd met quite a few in his somewhat short career at the Sentinel, and all of the successful CEOs exuded disarming charm combined with a self-confidence that assured their credibility.

Mark Johansen seemed like a regular guy who was terribly confused. Maybe it was the medication. Maybe it was a superb act. But ultimately, George came away convinced that Mark Johansen was innocent and that he was being framed. Mark didn't have any resemblance to whoever sent the emails to George.

And this frame, if there was one, couldn't have come at a worse time for Mark, or a better time for the real killer. Mark was fragile.

After his psychotic episodes, Mark didn't trust his own perceptions. He explained to George that this was part of his therapy, that he had to question what was actually real. But George couldn't help but think that Mark was just too easy a target. Mark couldn't, in good conscience - and George believed that Mark was a man of conscience and principal - Mark couldn't claim innocence because he didn't know if his reality was reality. George couldn't imagine how you could get through the day if you couldn't believe what you saw, heard, or thought.

Now George had to figure out how he was going to help Mark.

During his debrief with Mike McKensey, George had offered to pursue things that might be difficult for Mike given the politics of the SFPD and the DA's office. Mike started to refuse, but by the end of the call, it was clear he was considering it. At this point, Mike was looking into Richard Hatch, Mark's partner, Jack Trageser, one of Mark's associates and friends, and he suggested to George that he couldn't completely rule out Brittany Spangler either.

Running through the possibilities, George almost didn't see the letter in his inbox. He picked it up and realized that there was more than paper inside. Feeling around, it was obviously a thumb drive.

While he didn't get a lot of mail – most things came in via email these days – some enterprising readers sent him thumb drives with pictures and documents for possible stories. This looked like one of them.

George opened the envelope carefully, holding it at arm's length, then sensing no danger, he poured the thumb drive onto his desk and removed the letter inside:

Hi George,

I'm sorry for any confusion or any concerns you might have had with this letter, but unfortunately there are some major security issues which we need to address. Read on and you'll understand.

Marcus Jameson is CEO of Unbreakable Security Systems. As you probably know, Unbreakable is the world's largest supplier of anti-virus, anti-spyware, and identity protection software. Millions of individuals and most companies use one or more of Unbreakable's products. Unbreakable has been ruthless with their competitors, killing off any technology or company that challenges theirs. While many of their tactics are unethical, they're unfortunately not illegal. But Jameson has gone beyond unethical practices.

Before founding the company, Jameson was a well-known white-hat hacker. These are the guys that break into systems to discover security vulnerabilities, then inform the companies of the problems so that they can be fixed, hopefully before attacks take place. He hired several of his cohort hackers, some not so 'white-hat', and together they have built a security empire. They're now all quite wealthy.

However, for Jameson, what he made off the IPO of Unbreakable wasn't enough. He wants wealth for wealth's sake and above all, he wants political power. What he's done to achieve his goals is shocking. He has hidden a Trojan in every copy of his software. He has gotten away with this because his security software embeds itself in the lowest layers of an operating system and thus his Trojan has visibility to everything running in that system: files, emails, web browsing, video and audio conferences, even encrypted files – he sees the content before and after they're encrypted.

This Trojan looks for specific activity and reports back to Jameson. When Jameson finds an interesting target, he can direct the Trojan to filter for specific information. Thus far, he has used that information for insider trading to make even more money, and for blackmailing adversaries and politicians.

The enclosed thumb drive includes three programs. These contain software that you can install and run on any computer. The first removes the Trojan. I suspect you will want to do this with your system and on those of anyone you work with on this. Your IT department should be able to help decrypt, install, and run it.

The second will watch the system it's installed on and will report when Jameson's Trojan goes live and transmits or receives information. I suggest you give this to your IT department and to the police and or FBI when you're ready. They can use it to not only verify what I've said, but perhaps also to set up a sting for Jameson.

The third gives you access to the logs that show what the Trojan has sent or received. These are kept in hidden encrypted system files that cannot be found through normal directories.

I've also attached a list of offshore accounts that Jameson is using as well as a list of surrogate traders that he employs to funnel other monies into those accounts. And finally, I've provided contact information for Larry Samuelsson, the former CEO of Zyzyx Technologies. Jameson blackmailed him and forced him to close his business. Larry will talk to you once you're sure you're ready to move ahead and are confident that you and the police can get Jameson.

I'd love to see a big story exposing Jameson. I suspect he'll find himself under indictment soon after.

Last and not least, be careful copying this letter. Just to show you how pervasively insidious Jameson can be, many copy machines include his software.

This is our biggest catch yet so enjoy. It may be a while before I get back to you with our next target.

George grabbed the letter and the thumb drive and raced to Morris' office. He didn't even knock.

"Morris, you've got to see this!"

Morris looked up over his reading glasses and smiled.

"I guess you're really back from vacation. Okay. Let's see what's got you so fired up."

Morris read the letter carefully and George observed wryly as his boss' face transformed from Morris' usual dispassionate interest to complete shock.

Picking up his phone and punching a button. Morris commanded, "Joyce, get Miguel in here stat! Tell him it's urgent!"

"George, I'm going to spend a few minutes with Miguel. Then I'll come by your cubicle and we can go for a walk. In the meantime, don't say a word about this to anyone."

"But…"

"No buts. Get out. I'll be there within thirty minutes."

George wandered back to his cubicle stopping along the way to spend a few minutes with his coworkers reminiscing about Tahiti. Several claimed they were making plans to take similar vacations. That killed about twenty minutes.

Arriving back at his desk, George just stared at his computer screen. If the informant was right, Marcus Jameson could be tracking everything George did, everything he wrote. His sources could be compromised.

George stared in awe at the image of Tahiti and a part of him wanted to go back and avoid this story. It seemed overwhelming.

"Let's go!"

Morris' command startled George from his reverie, or was it stupor?

They headed towards the elevators in silence and once outside started walking towards the Embarcadero. It appeared they were going to take their usual loop.

"I explained the situation to Miguel in utmost confidence and asked him to verify the claims in the letter and to test out the programs included. Given the solid track record of your informant, I don't have much reason to doubt what he or she said. So, I called Marsha Washington who immediately brought in Sterling Rockwell.:

Marsha Washington was head of legal for The Sentinel and with Sterling Rockwell involved, George hadn't underestimated the significance of this story.

"We'd like you to proceed, but we want you to be very, very careful. I've met Marcus Jameson many times. He's a sleazy son-of-a-bitch, all charm and always looking for an edge. I can now see how's he's become the political powerhouse he is today. You're going to need to proceed methodically and cautiously. Jameson is not afraid to sue, has a crack legal team that could even make life difficult and expensive for the Sentinel, and he's well-connected at all levels of California government and at the Federal level. He's a dangerous adversary."

Knowing Morris preferred George to think things through before responding, they continued in silence for a few minutes longer after they turned onto the Embarcadero. George started with an obvious question.

"Assuming we verify what our guy claims, when do we bring in the police?"

"Sterling, Marsha and I agreed that as soon as we verify the existence of the Trojan, we should contact the Fraud division of the SFPD. Most likely, they will bring in the FBI. The FBI is very thorough and their process of building a case often takes time, so we'll build our own case in parallel.

"You also need to keep this quiet. Don't talk to anyone in the office about it. If word leaks out that we're investigating, Jameson will cover his tracks. He's smart."

"I know this may seem like an inappropriate question, but can I talk to Janey about it? I suspect she may be able to help more than you might imagine."

They walked in silence for a few minutes. Easterly winds blowing off the Bay made this chilly morning quite cold.

"Okay. Sure. I know that Janey is a real genius when it comes to this stuff and from what Miguel told me after the holiday party, she helped him out with some of our stuff even then. Obviously, she'll have to keep this very quiet. But then again, she's a security guru, so I'm sure she can do better than we can."

Miguel and Janey had met at last year's holiday party and had hit it off immediately. They left the party for a while and spent time in Miguel's office doing whatever they do. Afterwards, Janey had told George that it was one of the most fun parties they'd attended. She had loved the change of scene. It was a far cry from her tech parties. Not only did she get to meet people from a different crowd, with Miguel, she got to see more of how her and other's tech products were used in the real world.

"I think we need to have a codename for your source and this investigation," Morris continued. "It should be something commonplace that wouldn't alert anyone if they heard it, but not so common that we would get confused if we heard a reference to it."

George thought for a moment and suggested, "How about 'Michael James'? We can talk about Michael James and everyone will think we're still looking into the serial killings. I have a feeling that case will take a while to resolve."

"Not a bad idea. If we really need to talk about the murders, we refer to them directly or to Mark Johansen. If not, we use Michael James. Okay. Let's do it. I'll pass this on to Legal too. That way if they need to refer to the case and Jameson is watching them, he won't get a red flag."

"So what about the Unbreakable security software on my system? Should I use the tool to remove it?"

"Ultimately, yes. Make sure you get together with Miguel before you leave this evening. Assuming the tools are real, he'll remove the Unbreakable software from your system before you get in tomorrow morning. I will work with him to decide which other systems we'll remove it from. Mine for sure, but there may be others."

"Why not remove it from everyone's systems. Couldn't we make it look like the Sentinel just changed security vendors?

"If it weren't for the fact that he installed a virus that remains even after his security products are uninstalled, I'd say yes. But if suddenly, everyone at the Sentinel stopped sending information to him, that would be a red flag. No, we'll just do a few critical systems. For now, the rest is business as usual. Plus at some point, we may decide to do our own sting or work with the FBI on a sting by supplying bogus information that will flush him out."

"Of course," George responded, somewhat embarrassed. "I should have thought of that."

"Look George, I'm going to set up a small circle of us to work together on this. Jameson is smart. He's a security guru and world-renowned hacker. We have to be careful, so we need a team to back each other up. We'll review each step before we proceed. That way we can minimize our mistakes and hopefully avoid overlooking something that can ruin our investigation."

"But do you think we will actually be able to publish a story here? That could be dangerous."

"You know George, there's always been this battle between the public's right to know and the harm information can cause. Many argue about shouting 'fire' in a crowded theatre and throughout my career, I've pretty much always come down on the public's right to know. But this time, I'm not sure. Sterling and Marsha were in the same boat. To keep this under control, we'll be trying to limit how much of the story we tell. This is a case where the greater good may win the day."

They made their way back to the office in silence.

"I suspect we'll be doing a lot more of these walks in the coming days."

"Looking forward to it Morris!"

George stopped at the café downstairs to grab a sandwich and a drink. Arriving at his cubicle forty minutes later, George was surprised to find Miguel hitting every basket he shot, even from a couple cubicles away.

"Do you play?"

"Yeah, I love basketball. I was a star in High School, but got crushed in college. I was just too short. But I'm in a league. You should join us."

"Well, I may be tall, and I'm pretty good here in the office with the mini-basket, but on the court, I'm just not that coordinated."

Miguel smiled. "Let's go to my office. We've got a lot to talk about.

On their way to Miguel's office, George couldn't help thinking how lucky Miguel was. He had a private office! Then he thought about the insane hours Miguel worked, and how often Miguel was called in the middle of the night, on weekends, or while on vacation, and decided that maybe he wasn't so envious after all. He'd never arrived at the office before Miguel, or left after him. Sometimes he wondered if Miguel lived here and if he had a life outside the office.

"Come on in. I have a lot to show you."

"Is my source right? Is Unbreakable really stealing information from all of their customers?"

"No question about it. It's an insidious and virtually undetectable Trojan. I've never seen anything like it. I've tried several anti-virus programs and none of them can spot it. I've also used some hacker tools. No luck there either. But your friend's software spots it. Part of its genius is that it's not always active. But it seems to know when to wake up and look at things and then it embeds the information it collects in other normal outgoing data which is split and untraceably rerouted once it hits the net. I'm pretty good at this stuff, but I can't figure out how it works. I'll tell you one thing though: your source is a genius and probably one of the best hackers I've encountered. I'm amazed anyone found this. Is it possible he worked for Unbreakable and knew about what they were doing? Could he be a whistleblower?"

"It could be, but he's the same guy who's been exposing these other Internet moguls. He gave me the leads for both Ryan Hamilton and Boris Yanofski. He claims he just wants to stop the perversion of the Internet. I'm beginning to believe he's a good guy."

George sat down in one of Miguel's guest chairs suddenly overwhelmed by the implications.

On the one hand, he had a great story. On the other, this was so big that it could shake up the entire industry, and not just high tech. These days every government, every company, and almost every user employed security software to protect themselves and their information. What would happen when they found out that their privacy and security were just shams?

"Are you okay, George?

"Yeah," George replied somberly. "It's just hit me that not only is this real, but that it affects the whole world: business, politics, personal privacy. That's a lot to take in."

"No one should have this level of access to information. I applaud availability of information on the Net, but there have to be limits. Privacy is an essential part of life. Unbreakable needs to be brought down to protect everyone. And while there may be some fallout, I suspect that between us and the FBI, we can avoid panic. At least as far as we know, the damage has been limited. If we stop it soon, it can be contained."

"You're probably right, Miguel. But now I wonder why my informant didn't go directly to the FBI. Why did he come to a news organization that could destroy any chance of containment?"

"Maybe he couldn't go to the FBI. Maybe he's wanted. Then again, perhaps he wanted to prove how good he is so that he'll have credibility for his next, bigger stories. 'Bigger' might just mean more important to him, and he may need the Sentinel's ability to reach the public to trap the others."

"Well, I guess we enjoy the ride for now. There's too much we still don't know about our source. Did you find anything about him?"

"Zip. I'm sure the FBI will do better. In the worst case, you could ask Janey. She's the smartest hacker I've met."

"I talked to Morris about it and he gave the okay. I guess you two will get to work together on something. I'm sure Janey is looking forward to that. She was really impressed by you. And I can tell you that's pretty rare."

Miguel blushed and brushed off the complement.

"I'm the one who was impressed. This is going to be fun!"

"So, what do we do next? Did you get a chance to update Morris?"

"Yes. Morris contacted the Fraud Division of the SFPD and they told him they will be bringing in the FBI. From what he said, we'll probably be spending a good part of the afternoon in a meeting with him, the FBI, Marcia Washington from legal, and Sterling Rockwell."

"In the meantime," Miguel continued. "I've used the tool to remove the Trojan from your system, my system, and Morris' system. We should be able to communicate freely about this without signaling Unbreakable. For now, I've left their software on all other systems to avoid setting off any red flags. I understand we'll be referring to this investigation as 'Michael James' and that this entire subject is confidential. Unless we have permission, this remains among a very small group. That's all I have on my side for now."

"Thanks Miguel. I'd better get going. The source sent me lists of offshore accounts, surrogate traders, and contact information for someone who was blackmailed by Jameson. I need to dive in so I'm prepared for the meeting. I guess I'll see you later."

"Enjoy it George. It's not every day that story like this comes around."

Maybe not every day, but George had two major stories on his plate right now with more promised for the weeks to come. Welcome back from Tahiti!

CHAPTER 5

"It's hard to determine where lies culpability."
- Roger Mahony

1

Brittany Spangler stormed into the offices of The Sentinel and demanded to see George Gray.

In spite of the obvious agitation of the visitor, Joyce responded calmly, "I'm sorry Ms. Spangler, but Mr. Gray is tied up at the moment. I don't think he's going to be available anytime soon. Perhaps you'd like to make an appointment?"

Slamming her first on the reception desk, Brittany screamed at the top of her lungs, "I don't need a fucking appointment. And I don't need a receptionist to tell me who I can see and when. Get George Gray out here or I'll be suing this paper."

Joyce eyed Brittany Spangler. Over the course of her many years at The Sentinel, she'd had to deal with her share of crazies and Brittany was certainly one of them. Now the question was whether she should call security. Watching her pace and fume, Joyce decided that Brittany wasn't dangerous. This was a performance designed to intimidate.

"Ms. Spangler, Mr. Gray is involved in meetings with Morris Levinberg and our security staff. There's no way I can interrupt that meeting and I don't see it ending any time soon. As you might imagine, if security is involved, the issue is quite serious. You're welcome to wait, or as I suggested, you can make an appointment."

Brittany glared at Joyce who waited patiently and calmly for a decision.

"Okay. I'll wait. No. I'll be back in an hour. If he comes out, tell George I'll see him then.

"Thank you Ms. Spangler. We'll see you in an hour, but as I said, the meeting may go longer."

"Thank you Ms. Spangler," Brittany echoed sarcastically. She turned on her heels and left.

Joyce typed a quick message to George so he could be prepared and got back to work.

Forty-five minutes later, Brittany returned.

"Well?"

"Ms. Spangler, I messaged George to let him know you wanted to see him but have had no response. He's still in the meeting. You're welcome to wait or - "

"Yeah, I know. OR I can make an appointment. I'll wait."

Nearly an hour later, George Gray came into reception.

"Brittany, I understand you need to see me?"

"Yes, George, I do. Where can we talk?"

George glanced at Joyce who proposed, "Mr. Gray, Alcatraz is available."

Brittany glared at Joyce, thinking she was being sarcastic. George touched her shoulder. Brittany turned and George could see the anger turn to charm.

"Joyce means that the Alcatraz conference room is available. Don't worry. We're not planning to lock you up in Alcatraz. You haven't committed any murders, right?"

Brittany's face transformed instantly from an overly confident young woman to that of a frightened little girl.

"Not you too?"

And she turned and ran out the door.

'George," Joyce joked. "That was brilliant. I couldn't figure how to get rid of her!"

"Yeah, I guess I just have to accuse her of murder. I certainly hope she's okay. That woman has some serious psychological problems."

George headed back to his office to continue his research into Marcus Jameson's illegal activities. He wanted to be prepared for his meeting with the FBI.

At 1:30, Morris came by George's cubicle with Miguel in tow. Miguel looked a bit disappointed.

"Let's head over to the conference room."

Closing the door, Morris continued.

"George, as I told Miguel, Sterling Rockwell, Marcia Washington and I spent the morning working with the FBI. They'll be taking over and our role will be supportive until the investigation is nearly complete.

"I know, this is right out of every police TV series you've ever seen. The FBI comes in and everyone else backs off. But you know, in this case, I think that's for the best. They're the pros and Marcus Jameson could be dangerous. Miguel, you're clearly going to be the most affected by this but I suspect the FBI techs will be working very closely with you over the coming weeks. George, you'll be hearing from them as well.

"Thus far, we haven't given them Larry Samuelsson's name. We've simply explained that once they are convinced they have a solid case, we have an informant who will come forward with additional evidence. They've agreed to keep us in the loop so you can contact Samuelsson and get his story at the right time. The meeting this afternoon will be short. Sterling, Marcia, and the FBI want to make sure we're all on the same page. They should be back from lunch any minute."

George wasn't sure if he was annoyed or relieved. He'd spent the morning digesting and verifying all the information he'd been sent on Marcus Jameson thinking he'd be briefing the FBI. Now it looked like he had just wasted his time. His tenure as an investigative reporter on this case seemed to have come to an end before it began. Then again, it was his story and he would be working with Larry Samuelsson to put the final nail in the coffin. And, he still had the inside track on the murders.

His thoughts were interrupted with the entrance of Sterling Rockwell, Marcia Washington, and the two FBI agents.

Sterling Rockwell kicked it off.

"Miguel and George, I'd like you to meet Special Agents Barbara Fox and Clint Winston. They'll be heading up the investigation. We spent the morning together going over what you and Miguel have found and laying out the ground rules. I know both of you will be disappointed, but the Sentinel will be taking a back seat on the investigation into Marcus Jameson and Unbreakable Security. When the FBI has enough to arrest Jameson, they'll let us know and the Sentinel will break the story. George, this may be challenging since we have agreed that we don't want to create a panic. Nonetheless, it will be a big story. And if we have to leave out some details, you can take solace from the fact that you helped stop a power-hungry blackmailer who has been corrupting our political process.

"The FBI will also be working with you to identify your informant. As you get more emails from him, you need to turn them over. However, the informant is not the most critical part of the investigation, so their focus will be on the information he or she provided."

"Mr. Rockwell, I'm sorry to interrupt, but I do have a question. My informant has already given us two significant stories, Ryan Hamilton and his human trafficking, and Boris Yanofski and the murder of his wife. He or she has promised to identify other so-called unscrupulous individuals who have perverted use of the internet for their own personal gains. I can't imagine that these investigations would have anything to do with Marcus Jameson and Unbreakable. So far, all the investigations and targeted individuals have been completely unrelated. Do I really need to turn over all correspondence from him or her?"

Agents Fox and Winston stepped to the back of the conference room and had a brief hushed discussion, then returned and took their seats.

"Mr. Gray," agent Fox began, "My colleague and I disagree on this point, but it's my call. It is not a priority to identify your informant though that could be helpful in the investigation. Clearly if any correspondence pertains to Jameson or Unbreakable, we need to see it. On the other hand, we don't want to step on your toes in these other investigations and quite frankly don't need the distractions, particularly if what he or she is trying to expose is out of our jurisdiction. So for now, we'll leave it to your judgement. Clint?"

"Okay. I agree. But getting back to the main topic of this meeting, as Mr. Rockwell indicated, Jameson is our investigation. If you learn anything that can help us you must let us know as soon as possible. Also, it may sound cold, but we won't tolerate any interference in our work. Poking around on your own could jeopardize our case and could put people in physical danger. I know it's hard, but you really need to let us do our job. And Mr. Flores, I know it will be tempting to take some initiative on the network security side, but you really need to leave it to our techs. Please follow their lead. We don't want anyone to inadvertently flag the fact that we know what Jameson is up to."

"And," said Agent Fox, picking up the momentum and looking at each of the Sentinel employees individually. "As we've discussed, this is absolutely confidential. We can't afford any leaks. Are we in agreement?"

George, Morris, and Miguel nodded.

"Yes we are," Sterling Rockwell confirmed. "We look forward to helping you nail this scumbag."

2

Sam was pleased. Leaving San Francisco County Jail #2, she couldn't help but think how far the system had come since her early days as a student and in residency. She had done a rotation in a psych ward at a prison and the San Francisco County facility was a world apart from the dangerous environment she had found herself in then.

The San Francisco County Jail seemed more like a staging area than a prison, which she had learned it often was. Suspects awaiting trial were housed here but so were those close to release from prison. The County had determined that for low-risk prisoners, it was better to confine them in what they called pods. These were two-level circular dormitory areas which housed inmates, and which also offered large communal areas. Some of the other County jails had adopted this pod philosophy and it seemed to present more creative opportunities for real rehabilitation rather than hard punishment.

At intake, the County used a classification system to determine a prisoner's risk to him/herself and to the rest of the jail population. Based on the results of a complex evaluation process, prisoners were placed in high-risk facilities, medium risk pods, general pods, low-risk pods, medical and psych pods, and reentry pods. Some were even co-ed.

As Sharon had explained to Sam, in spite of the severity of the accusations against him, Mark had been classified as low-risk. He had no criminal history, did not appear violent, had no gang connections, and had held a high powered tech job until his arrest.

As for the psychiatric evaluation, while it was clear he had issues, the staff decided that Mark was not a risk to himself or others so he was not placed in the psychiatric pod. On the other hand, recognizing his history, and with a bit of pressure from Sharon, they had agreed to allow Sam to continue her treatments. The only real issue was confidentiality. Sam had some doubts about the privacy of the psych pod. She'd been promised that nothing said there was recorded, but since the room contained cameras, she wasn't completely convinced. Nonetheless, it all seemed quite civilized for a jail.

Her first few sessions with Mark were rough. They focused on getting him re-stabilized after his arrest. Mark had been lost.

He couldn't say he hadn't committed the murders. He didn't trust his memory. And, he saw clearly that the evidence against him was convincing.

The worst was his computer. During his interrogations, the police had showed him what they'd found. And he just couldn't remember the emails, the visit to the bomb-making sites, poison sites, or the surveillance notes and videos that he had apparently taken when stalking the three women.

Over the course of those first few sessions, Sam tried to show Mark that he might have been framed. But he remained unconvinced. He had the best security software on his computer. It would have flagged any intrusion.

But in their previous session, Sam had told Mark about her meeting with Mike McKensey. She told him Mike believed him to be innocent. Completely surprised, Mark started to listen and to think. Now he too had to wonder who could have framed him. Who would have technology sophisticated enough to get into his system without him knowing about it?

With relative stability achieved, Sam decided that instead of trying to have Mark figure out who could have framed him, she'd get back on track with the therapy they'd started before all this happened. She'd leave it to Mike McKensey and Sharon to chase new suspects. Her recent attempts had probably caused more harm than good.

When she got back to her office, she poured herself a hot cup of English Breakfast, added cream and sugar and sat down in her recliner with her notes and her laptop.

Yes. Today had gone well.

She had started the session carefully. "So Mark, Sharon tells me that you two have been friends for years."

Mark thought about it, obviously reliving a memory, smiled and replied. "Yes. I guess you could say Sharon is my oldest friend.

"We met when my family moved to the area. She and a few others welcomed me into their intellectual crowd in high school, and she helped me fit right in."

"What kind of things did you do together?"

"Well, most of the time we all got together as a group. It sounds pretty nerdy as I think about it now, but every week we had duplicate bridge parties."

'Duplicate bridge? I played a bit of bridge myself in college, but what's duplicate bridge?"

"In contract bridge, you shuffle the cards, play the game, then reshuffle the cards and play until someone wins."

"Yeah, just like any other card game. So?"

"With duplicate bridge, the cards are placed in boards, each of which holds four hands. There are many boards, depending on the number of people playing.

"The basic idea is that you team up with a partner and over the course of the evening you play all or most of the different boards. What this does is it takes all the luck out of the game. Instead of the pair (or couple) with the most wins, each pair is scored on how they did on a particular board. The winner of the tournament is the pair who did the best overall on the most boards.

"To give you a weird example, Sharon and I once had a great win. We were pretty good players but on one board, every pair that played the opponent's hand completed a Grand Slam – the highest possible score in bridge. But on this hand, Sharon opened with five hearts. This is unheard of but completely legal. The opponents really had no way to bid beyond that to communicate what they needed to get to the Grand Slam, and I understood Sharon's signal. We ended up at 6 hearts and failed to make it by one trick doubled – meaning we got negative 100 points. But on every other table, the opponents had scored over 1200 points, so we effectively beat every other team playing our hand by 1100 points. It's silly, but I'll never forget that game."

"It sounds like you two were quite a team."

"You know, we really were," Mark replied, clearly nostalgic.

"So where did these bridge tournaments take place?"

"We moved from house to house, changing pretty much every week."

"And did you play at your house?"

Mark's face darkened. "Ah, no. We never did."

"Did Sharon ever come over to your house?"

Mark thought briefly, then smiled. "Yeah. She came over quite a bit."

'Did she get along with your parents."

"Absolutely! My Dad loved her."

"And your mom?"

Mark withdrew.

"Mark, I know this is difficult, but did your mom like any of your friends?"

Mark sat in silent reflection for a moment.

"Mark?"

"I'm sorry, Sam. I've never really thought about this. My mother was just my mother. My dad was outgoing and friendly. My mother, not so much. But lots of families are like that, right? I mean one parent is upbeat and friendly, and the other more withdrawn, right?"

"Was she withdrawn, Mark?"

You could almost see the wheels turning in Mark's mind. After a minute or two, he seemed reluctant to admit, "I guess withdrawn is the wrong word."

"Do you have a better word to describe your mother?"

After a moment, Mark responded solemnly, "Angry."

"Angry? And what do you think she was angry at?"

"I don't know Sam. I don't know."

"Mark, we're running out of time – others are waiting for the pod. But I want to give you something to think about in preparation for our next session. I noticed that you refer to your father as 'Dad' and to your mother as 'mother'. When I see you next time, could you talk to me about that?"

Hearing the knock on the door. Sam stood up and gave Mark a quick hug.

"Hang in there, Mark. You're making great progress! I'll see you in a few days."

A guard came in and led Mark out of the psych pod. Sam had signed out and left smiling. She was a good detective, though maybe just for psychiatry, and she was hot on the trail now.

3

Morris gestured George and Miguel into his office.

"Guys, I know this isn't what you wanted, but I think this is how it has to be."

"No. That's not it," George began. "We're in complete agreement that the FBI needs to take the lead on this. It's ah –"

"Janey," Miguel interrupted.

"What about Janey?" Morris asked, intrigued.

"Well, we previously agreed that Janey should take a look at this, but now the FBI is saying we should stay away and shouldn't get involved in any way. Should we hold off telling Janey?"

Morris frowned.

"Miguel, how good is Janey?"

Without hesitating, Miguel stated seriously, "Janey is the best I've ever met. She's light-years beyond me, and I suspect the best the FBI has couldn't begin to keep up with her."

Morris looked at Miguel and George, then reviewed his notes from the meeting with the FBI.

"Okay, guys. I have to trust the FBI, but I also have to look out for the interests of the Sentinel. Talk to Janey, but be very, very careful. We don't want to be charged with interfering with a Federal investigation, and we certainly don't want to get in their way. Miguel, since the FBI is looking at you as our point person, I want you to keep an eye on Janey. Anything you two come up with you need to bring to me. I'll decide if and how it goes back to the FBI. George, you've got to be a spectator on this one. I don't want you involved in bypassing the FBI. Is that clear?"

George was tempted to reply, 'absolutely, Chief', but knew this wasn't the moment for a joke. He looked at Morris and agreed solemnly, "I understand, Morris."

"Good. Guys, be very careful. This could not only alert Jameson, it could put lives at risk. Jameson is dangerous."

That evening, after their standard arrival ritual, George helped Janey prepare dinner. As Janey took her first bite, George took a deep breath and told Janey about his day.

"The informant contacted me and this one is the biggest yet."

"That's great, George. Can you tell me about it? You look a little nervous."

"Well, the FBI has asked us not to tell anyone, absolutely no one about it, but after discussions with Morris and Miguel, we've decided to bring you in, if you're interested."

"Of course I'm interested, Silly."

Crossing her heart, Janey continued, "And I won't tell anyone anything about it until you all agree it's okay."

"Ah, well," George stammered. "It's more than confidential. The information is dangerous. I'm not sure we should get you involved."

Janey's look turned somber.

"George, if it's dangerous and I can help, I want in. Tell me what's going on."

"Actually, if you decide you want to do this, it will be Miguel who brings you in. You'll be working with him and I need to stand aside – Morris' orders."

"Hmm. If I find something, I can't tell you about it? I'm not sure I can do that. We always tell each other everything. Maybe you should just keep it confidential."

They continued eating in silence as George thought about it. Morris said George needed to remain on the sidelines. But sidelines didn't mean you couldn't watch the game. You just didn't get to play.

"Okay. I think you can keep me informed. I'll just have to not act on anything without consulting Morris."

George took a deep breath.

"The informant says that Marcus Jameson, CEO of Unbreakable Security has embedded a Trojan in his software. Apparently it collects confidential information and sends it to Jameson, completely undetected. Anti-virus software can't see it. He's used the information he's gathered to force competitors out of business, to blackmail politicians, and to get inside information for securities trading.

"The informant sent me software that spots this activity along with a tool to remove it. He also sent me list of offshore accounts, and people that Jameson uses for insider trading. And, he gave me contact information for Larry Samuelsson, the former CEO of Zyzyx Technologies, that hot startup that folded a few months ago. Apparently he was blackmailed into closing the company.

"From the look on your face, I can see that you get the impact of this."

"George, this is terrible. Most companies, government agencies, and countless individuals use Unbreakable's software.

My company uses it. It's on my laptop and on yours. If this gets out, our whole industry could be compromised. In fact, our government and the entire world as we know it will be impacted. George, it's a disaster!"

"Yeah. I know. Right now though, it's critical that no one make any dramatic changes. You can't alert your company yet. That could tip off Jameson. I brought the tools from the informant so you can take a look but –"

"George, I want to see them right now!" Janey ordered, jumping up from the table, her dinner unfinished.

George went to the bedroom and returned to an anxious Janey already sitting at her computer. George handed her the thumb drive. Janey plugged it into her laptop and waited. She opened a couple of files, quickly read the contents, and her fingers flew across the keyboard so fast that George could hardly see them. He watched transfixed as Janey ran through the tools, then opened up other software to examine the source code of the tools themselves, looking for some kind of developer's signature. Clearly, the code had been scrupulously scrubbed before it was digitally signed. She wasn't going to find out who had developed the tools.

She did something to isolate the tools to prevent them from accessing her system and then watched them run through her own custom debugger. After nearly an hour of non-stop typing with hundreds of screens that made no sense to George, Janey pushed back her chair.

"Okay. I understand what it does and how it works. Most intriguing to me is the tool that watches what Jameson's Trojan sends out. Jameson was very clever in hiding that information. Very clever. I wonder how your informant figured it out so that he or she could develop this tool. Maybe he or she is an insider.

"So, what do you want me to do with this? I know I can't alert my team at Uluru, at least not yet. But how can I help?"

"Janey, I really don't know. The technical side of this is way over my head. Why don't you contact Miguel and figure out how you guys can work together?"

Janey dove back into the code for a few minutes then responded very distractedly, "Okay, George. I'll work with Miguel. But in the meantime, what are you planning to do?"

"I'm not sure. The Sentinel is waiting on the FBI and we're following their lead. But somehow, just like saying that serial murders weren't done by a serial killer, I'll have to balance anything we do write so we don't create some crazy panic. As I think about it, maybe we shouldn't publish anything at all. Then again..."

George's eyes glazed for a moment.

"George! Don't even think about doing anything stupid. You have to be careful. You're potentially putting a billionaire at risk. I don't want to lose you."

"I won't tell you not to worry, but I will do my absolute best to be careful. I'll be working with Morris to decide when to publish and what we're going to publish. I'm not going to do anything until the FBI has arrested Jameson."

"George, even after the arrest, you could be at risk. You won't be safe until Jameson is in prison. And even then."

George lifted Janey out of her chair and pulled her close.

"I promise. I will be cautious. I never want to put us and what we have at risk."

They held each other for a moment. Then suddenly, Janey pushed George away from her.

"George!" she shouted, clearly excited. "Who is Jameson's biggest competitor?"

"Sorry Janey, I don't keep up with this stuff."

"George, it's Johatchen Software!"

"Johatchen as in Mark Johansen's company?"

"Yes. Didn't you say that Mark Johansen couldn't figure out how someone could have gotten into his system? Maybe Jameson is trying to frame Mark Johansen to disrupt Johatchen."

"But why would Mark Johansen have Jameson's software on his system. Unbreakable is a competitor. Wouldn't he use his own software for security?"

"Of course he would. But at some point, Mark Johansen might have downloaded the Unbreakable software to look at its features. Then again. I could be on the wrong track here. At Uluru, we have a separate lab that looks at competitor's products so that we, the engineers don't inadvertently get contaminated by looking at our competitor's features. Still, if Johatchen does the same thing, there's nothing that would prevent Jameson's Trojan from finding its way into other systems. Given what we know, what better way to keep an eye on his competitors?"

"And what better way to frame the CEO of his biggest competitor," George concluded.

4

Mike McKensey arrived at the Sentinel intrigued by Morris' call. He told Joyce he had an appointment with Morris and she said that Morris would be right out.

Mike didn't even make it to the reception area sofa before a clearly excited Morris greeted him.

"Mike! Thanks for coming so soon. Let's head to my office."

Arriving at Morris' office, Morris motioned to a seat next to an equally excited George Gray and closed the door behind them.

"Something to drink?" Morris asked, trying to calm down.

"You guys obviously have something important to tell me, so let's get to it. What's up?"

"George, why don't you explain it, keeping in mind our discussion about confidentiality?"

"Okay. Mike, our informant gave us a lead on another internet mogul who he says has perverted use of the Internet. Unlike the others, this one could have a dangerous impact if revealed. The FBI has put a lid on it and we're not to divulge anything about it to anyone. Not only could it jeopardize the case, it could cause irreparable harm, as ridiculous as it may sound, globally."

"So. Why am I here if you're not supposed to tell anyone about it?

"Well. Ah. We had a long discussion with the FBI this morning and told them that it's possible that Mark Johansen is being framed by the internet mogul. Our use of the word 'possible' didn't convince them, but Morris knows how to apply pressure when needed."

"George, just get on with it," Morris replied, a bit miffed.

"Anyway. It's possible that the subject of this investigation has put software on Mark Jameson's computer that is completely undetectable, even by a security expert like Mark. It's possible that this person, who works for a competitor, could be trying to frame Mark Johansen to gain an edge. He could even aggravate Mark's condition by –"

"Gaslighting him?"

"Gaslighting? George asked, a bit confused.

"Sorry George," Morris interrupted. "It's another film you need to see. Charles Boyer marries an innocent Ingrid Bergman and subtly makes her question her sanity. There's even a common term for that – Gaslighting. Great film."

"So yeah," George continued. It's possible he's gaslighting Mark.

"We convinced the FBI to let Miguel check out Mark's computer just to see if the software is there. They said it must be Miguel and that the detection tool can never leave his possession. Do you think that you could get him access?"

"Guys, I don't know. First, I'm not supposed to be pursuing other suspects. Second, we have issues with chain of custody for evidence. If someone else touches Johansen's computer, the defense could say it was contaminated. Worse, even if we did figure out a way to do it, and even if it did turn out positive, it does not prove that your 'subject' actually used the software to frame Johansen. And, even if somehow we could prove that, I suspect the FBI would never tell me who it was – at least until their investigation was complete. I don't know. I just don't know."

Morris and George looked at each other, their enthusiasm clearly dissipated.

"Sorry to pop your bubble, guys."

Mike got up to leave.

"One second, Mike," Morris suggested.

He picked up the phone, dialed and said, "Miguel, could you come in here?"

A minute later, Miguel came into Morris' office and closed the door.

"Miguel, it's possible that Michael James' software is on Mark Johansen's computer and that Michael James framed Johansen. Mike here tells us that because of chain of evidence issues, the police wouldn't allow you to look at Johansen's computer."

"Michael James?" Mike interrupted.

"Not to worry," Morris replied, smiling. It's a code name we're using for the investigation."

"So Miguel, you're familiar with police chain of evidence procedures for computers, right?"

"Absolutely. We follow the same rules here when we're involved in investigations. Number 1 rule is NEVER work on the original. Always make a copy and do your testing on the copy."

"But would the Michael James software propagate to the copy? Couldn't it be smart enough to defeat that?"

"It would definitely propagate. First, I'm sure Michael James would want his software on as many computers as possible, so if someone changed computers, he'd want it to follow. But the real reason is that we do what's called a hash of the system. That is, we use a sophisticated algorithm to verify that every byte of data is exactly the same between the original and the copy, right down to the firmware."

"So, as far as chain of evidence is concerned," Morris continued. "You could use the tools on the copy to see if Michael James' software is there, right?"

"Yes. I could."

"And could you find out if the software were used to plant evidence?"

"Absolutely! One of the tools the informant gave us dumps the log of everything that has come in or gone out via the software."

"Mike?"

"Okay. Sure. You've answered the chain of custody issues. Now I just have to figure out how to convince the team to let us get a look at the system. That won't be easy."

"What about Sharon Katell?" George suggested cautiously.

"Sharon Katell?" Morris asked, momentarily confused.

"Yeah. That could work," Mike replied. "As the defense attorney, Sharon could request a copy of the computer to help prepare her defense. Miguel could work on that copy."

Morris looked worried.

"But then we'd have to tell Sharon about our theory. The circle is widening. I can't see the FBI letting us do that. And Sharon is a shark. If she smells blood, she's going after it and could blow open the whole case against Michael James."

Morris paused for a moment deep in thought.

"Maybe not. I have an idea. I'll talk to Sharon and will convince her that we need to look at a copy of Johansen's system. I'll find a way to get her to back off until we know more."

"But don't we still have a problem with the FBI?" George asked. "If we do find something, they'll know we brought Sharon in."

"Don't worry George. I can get around that. And if for some reason I don't, it'll be on me.

"If it does pan out, we can hand it to Mike who can pursue it independently of Sharon. And he can talk to the FBI to negotiate learning the identity of Michael James. Then again. It may not pan out. Guys, thanks. I've got work to do."

5

Mike McKensey left the Sentinel shaking his head. Was it really possible that a competitor had decided to torpedo Johatchen Software by framing their CEO, capitalizing on his recent bout with mental illness? It just didn't fit. Why three murders? Why not just one? And would eliminating the CEO bring down the company? Not likely. No. George and Morris were on the wrong track.

From the emails to George, the killer hated wives of technologists who had left their husbands and wanted to cleanse the world of them. This wasn't just corporate greed. Then again, maybe the competitor wanted to cleanse the world too.

No. It didn't fit.

Mike was tempted to look at Johatchen's competitors to see if he could come up with some leads. But thinking about it, he'd probably just stir things up, piss off the FBI, and get Morris and George in trouble. And, it was probably a dead end anyway.

For the moment it was best to let things play out a bit. If it turned out that Johansen's computer was being used to set him up, he could look further. In the meantime, he needed to meet with Mark's friends, Jack Trageser and Richard Hatch. He'd contacted both and had set up meetings.

The first was with Richard Hatch, Johansen's business partner.

Mike entered the lavish offices of Johatchen Software and told the receptionist that he had an appointment with Richard Hatch. He took a seat in the lobby and thumbed through a magazine dedicated to Internet Security. While much of it was over his head, one article in particular caught his attention. It was targeted at non-techie readers and was called 'How can a hacker break into my computer?'.

Apparently there were quite a few hackers who did this for fun. Just for the challenge. Others wanted to turn your system into a zombie, which Mike learned was a system they could use to carry out their bidding in the background without you ever knowing they were there. Most used zombie systems to send spam – thousands of emails could be sent from your computer instead of the hacker's. Or it could be harassing emails – they'd be traced back to you instead of the hacker. Some hackers tried to look for credit card information or financial information for identity theft. But apparently these hackers were a very small minority. And, Mike supposed, some could hack your system to frame you for murder.

Mike's thoughts were interrupted by a tall, slightly balding, very fit man, probably late 40s, stylishly dressed in chinos and a logoed polo shirt. Holding out his hand, he introduced himself.

"Detective Mike McKensey, I'm Richard Hatch."

Mike stood up and shook Richard's hand, noticing the solid grip. He glanced briefly at the clock above the receptionist's head. He'd been waiting twenty minutes.

"Sorry about the wait," Richard stated frankly. "I got a bit tied up. Would you like something to drink?"

"Water would be nice."

"Sparkling or flat?"

"If you've got it, I'll go for sparkling. I'm in an effervescent mood."

Richard smiled and turned to the receptionist. "Mary-Ann, could you bring two sparkling waters into my office?"

Richard led Mike through a large high-ceilinged space with groups of what appeared to be engineers actively debating things Mike couldn't understand in front of gigantic white boards. It looked dynamic and creative. Not at all like his office

In the center of the room were two large glass-walled offices, each with a desk, a small conference table, and a large whiteboard. Richard led Mike into the office on the right and took a seat at the conference table, motioning Mike to join him. Mary-Ann delivered the sparkling water along with two glasses and a small ice bucket.

Richard smiled and thanked Mary-Ann who made a discreet exit closing the door behind her.

"No corner office with a view?" Mike asked, surprised and curious.

"This was Mark's idea. We do need private offices, but he wanted to make the team feel like we were working with them, not like we were the bosses with elite privileges and spectacular city views just for ourselves. With the glass walls, the team can see us working and we can see them working.

"Often, Mark will see something pop up on one of the white boards that he finds intriguing, and he'll join that team in their discussions. Although he's their boss, the engineers see him as a team member – one that has a different job. His is double-checking ideas, and at times, when there's no consensus, making the final call. Surprisingly, this works better then you could ever imagine."

"No. It makes sense to me. So in general, how does the team feel about Mark and about his recent problems?"

"They admire and respect Mark. He has enabled them to work in the most creative ways possible and it shows in what they produce. He's been an inspiration. As far as his recent problems are concerned, everyone saw the decline after his divorce. With the conference room incident, they knew he'd lost it. Most think he just needed a break. He's worked ridiculous hours ever since we started the company. I haven't shared the schizophrenia diagnosis with the team, though both Mark and I have asked them to alert us to any weird behavior to avoid a recurrence. They're all glad to have him back.

"As far as the murder charges are concerned, quite frankly, no one believes it. That's just not Mark. Maybe if it had just been Janice, it might have been credible, but with three? No. It doesn't make sense."

"It sounds like these are your conclusions as well?"

"Absolutely. Mark didn't really have anything against Ashima James or Julia Lewis. And even for Janice, he might not have understood it, but I don't think he really blamed her for leaving him. Mark is the kind of guy who blames himself when something goes wrong. You probably know the type. It works well for an engineer."

"And what about a CEO? Does it work for a CEO?"

"I think in general, it wouldn't. But here at Johatchen, it has worked just fine. I think that's because I can be the aggressive bad guy watching out for the business side while Mark leads the creative side. To run a business, to get products out, that's perspiration. And as Edison is quoted as saying, 'genius is one percent inspiration and ninety-nine percent perspiration.'

"So are you saying that Mark and the engineers are the inspiration and you're the perspiration?"

Richard laughed. "Not at all. Mark and his team are the creative side, but they also do a tremendous part of the implementation. The company couldn't exist without them, and that one percent? No company can sustain growth without new ideas, new inspiration. If you're thinking of me as a suspect, trust me, I wouldn't possibly kill the goose. And besides, Mark and I have been best friends for years. We've been through a lot together. And right now, I'm doing my best to help him manage his illness, and get past these false accusations."

Mike examined Richard. Despite his confident manner, there was something more there, a bit of nervousness.

"So from what you've said, it sounds like you think Mark is innocent."

"Absolutely. Mark would never intentionally hurt anyone except possibly himself."

"And you don't think his mental illness could drive him to seek revenge?"

Richard thought for a moment.

"I suppose it could be possible. Mark clearly has psychological issues, and from what I've seen he has had memory lapses. I guess it's remotely possible that he could be guilty. But then again after talking with Sam, Mark's psychiatrist, I think it's very unlikely. It has to be someone else."

"Do you have any thoughts on who might want to kill these three women and frame Mark for the murders?"

"Kill these women? Well, I suspect quite a few people might subscribe to the idea that these women needed to be eliminated to allow geniuses to fight the good fight with technological innovation. But as for framing Mark? Maybe a competitor?"

"A competitor," Mike mused. "Could a competitor break into Mark's system, plant incriminating evidence, and send emails? Aren't you guys the security gurus?"

"Detective Mckensey – "

"Mike."

"Mike, security is an interesting business. For the most part, it's a game of catch up. Somebody breaks into a system, we figure out how to block it. Someone creates an attack, we figure out how to stop future attacks. The reality is that no matter how good security is, there's always someone trying to get past it, and they will eventually succeed. Quite frankly, our business revolves around stopping others from doing what's already been done by a hacker. So, to answer your question, it is quite feasible that someone could have broken into Mark's system in spite of our best of brand security software. But I can't imagine who."

Mike looked through his notes and thought about Richard's responses. Everything looked right. Richard didn't seem to be a good suspect. Then again, something Richard had said during their conversation set off some faint alarm bells. There was something he'd heard before. Getting old and losing your memory sucked. Too bad he hadn't recorded the conversation. Maybe that was something he should do in the future.

Mike stood up and handed Richard his card.

"Thanks for taking the time to meet with me. If you have any ideas, anything at all, don't hesitate to call me."

They shook hands and Richard walked him out. One down. Now he needed to prepare for his meeting with Jack Trageser.

6

Jack Trageser walked Sam to her office and kissed her briefly before heading back to his own. He didn't get it. No matter how hard he tried, how charming he was, he couldn't break through. Sam had erected a wall. It seemed like she wanted the relationship to continue, but at this point it was more like a high school courtship than a passionate romance.

They spent lots of time together, hikes, movies, concerts, plays, and even snuggling in front of the TV, but their intimacy hadn't gone beyond that. It wasn't just that they hadn't had sex, it was that she was holding back emotionally. At times it felt like she didn't trust him.

And maybe that was it. Ever since that dinner. Or maybe it was the discussion about the murders where he implied that maybe these women deserved what they got. Whatever it was, their relationship was not growing. It had stalled.

Jack climbed the stairs and opened the door to his startup, Balanced News. At least here he was loved and admired. At least here, he was in control.

Sitting in the lobby was a middle-aged man who looked like a cop. He'd completely forgotten that he had a meeting with Detective Mike McKensey.

"Detective McKensey," he began holding out his hand. "I'm sorry if I'm late. I lost track of time."

"No worries. You're actually right on time. You do seem a bit distracted. Is this a bad time?"

Jack smiled. "No. It's perfect. Our discussions will help take my mind off my personal issues."

"A woman?"

"Yep. Ah, would you like something to drink?"

"Sure. Sparkling water would be nice if you have it."

"Absolutely." Then turning to the receptionist, "Nancy, could you bring two sparkling waters to the conference room?"

While not as big or lavish as Johatchen Software, the engineers at Balanced News seemed to be working in much the same way. There were large open areas with frenetic engineers debating in front of whiteboards.

Nancy caught up to them as the entered the conference room.

"Have a seat," Jack suggested.

Mike took pulled out one of the chairs in the middle of the

table and Jack took a seat facing him.

"So what can I do for you, Detective McKensey?"

"Mike."

"Mike."

"I'm investigating the murders of Ashima James, Julia Lewis, and Janice Johansen."

"Aren't you guys convinced Mark is guilty?"

"First, my job is not to decide who is guilty. That's for the courts. I find suspects. Right now, Mark Johansen is our best suspect, but I want to make sure there aren't other possibilities."

"Okay. So how can I help?" Jack asked, a bit nervously – something that was not lost on Mike McKensey.

"Well, can you think of anyone who might want to frame Mark Johansen for these murders? A competitor? Someone who might hold a grudge?"

Jack thought for a moment.

"No. I really can't think of anyone. Mark is one of the good guys in our industry. He's done some great things and has built a solid team. Everyone at Johatchen has done quite well both financially and career-wise."

"What about Richard Hatch? You guys all know each other pretty well, right? Would Richard have any reason to frame Mark for murder?"

"No. I don't see it. Richard and Mark have been a team for years. They've had numerous failures together and now some success. It's a symbiotic thing. Mark could never have built Johatchen without Richard, and Richard could never have done it without Mark. Nah. Not likely."

"And what about you? How did you feel about Ashima James, Julia Lewis, and Janice Johansen?"

"Ah. Ah. Am I a suspect?"

Attempting to lighten the moment a bit, Mike replied, "As Inspector Clouseau once said, 'I suspect everyone and I suspect no one'."

Jack appeared very nervous now.

"I'm sorry Mr. Trageser, but it looks like I upset you."

"It's Jack. And I'm sorry, Mike. This is a sensitive subject and it brings me back to the personal issue I was hoping to escape from."

"Does it have anything to do with the murders or with Mark Johansen?"

"Only indirectly. My girlfriend – at least I'd like to think she's my girlfriend – got really upset with me when I admitted that I thought these three women may have gotten what they deserved. Quite frankly, our relationship has been going downhill ever since. And I really like this girl, ah woman. The whole thing has me pretty shook up, and I'm usually immune to these kinds of emotional issues."

"What did you mean, they deserved what they got?"

"If I tell you, it won't make me more of a suspect, will it?"

"Hard to say until I hear it, but look, it might give me an idea what logic would be behind these murders."

"Okay. You may have heard this before or maybe you've know enough of us, but technologists are a close-knit group. We may compete; we may argue, but at the end of the day, we all try to support each other as we fight the good fight. We believe in something larger than ourselves – that technology can make the world a better place. Most of us recognize that success isn't the main goal. And often, some of the absolute best ideas – world-changing ideas – never see the light of day. But they're recognized for their value and appreciated.

"A lot of technologists like Michael James, Marshall Lewis, and Mark Johansen work ridiculously hard to create new products and services. They rely on a stable home life as a strong base to launch from and to come back to when things get rough. And in spite of what might look like easy success and money, believe me, things always get rough.

"Anyway, what I hated to see was how these three women ruined the lives of some of the best technologists the world has ever seen. I knew all three and I can tell you, it wasn't because they had terrible married lives or were horribly unhappy. They just decided that they could take half or more of what their husbands had made and run. They didn't care if they broke their husbands' hearts or destroyed their work. They just didn't care. I see that as morally wrong, and I suspect there are a lot of people like me that feel the same way. These women didn't deserve to benefit from the disasters they created. So for me, yeah. I think they deserved what they got."

"But Jack, a woman leaves her husband. Whatever the reason, do you really think she deserves to die because of it?"

"Mike. I hear you and the logical side of me agrees. But if you're in the middle of this and you see misery that these women have caused, let alone destroying a vision of something larger, while I personally wouldn't kill someone over it, I can imagine that others might."

"Jack, have you ever been married?"

"No. I've escaped marriage so far. It's let me dive into technology without torturing a family with long work hours, missed birthdays and anniversaries, and financial failures. But you know, if Sam could just put aside what I said, she could be the one."

"Maybe she suspects you're the killer."

Jack paused for a minute then smiled. "That's it! Mike, thanks! I think you've given me the answer I've been searching for."

And as Jack walked Mike to the door, Mike responded in kind, "Jack, I want to thank you, too. You may have given me the answer I've been searching for too."

7

As Sam made her way to the jail for her next session with Mark, she tried to put Jack out of her mind. It was all her fault. She could see it. She could feel it. Jack was charming, kind, patient. He let her take the lead even though she didn't know where they were going. It was clear he was in love with her and just as clear that her feelings for him were getting stronger every day. And yet, she kept him at arm's length. If truth be told, she pushed him away. Hard, but not quite hard enough for him to actually give up.

What was wrong with her? Did she really think Jack was guilty of these murders and had framed Mark? He certainly had the technical savvy to do so. And he had said that those women got what they deserved. He talked about it being justified to rid the world of evil people. Maybe that was it. Maybe she was afraid Jack was the killer. On the other hand, maybe she was just afraid, period.

Forcing herself to think about Mark, Sam was excited. While she had thought she was hot on the trail, now she knew for certain that she was on to something solid.

In recent sessions, they'd delved further into Mark's relationship with his mother. He was beginning to remember events from his childhood that he'd buried for self-preservation. Sam could feel that a breakthrough was imminent.

As she entered the jail and was cleared through security, Sam wondered if being incarcerated had helped. Here, there were few distractions. Mark had plenty of time to think and reflect on their sessions. The progress was far more rapid than she could have ever hoped.

A pair of guards led Mark into the psych pod and stepped out after letting Sam know that she had forty-five minutes. Mark appeared calm, much more relaxed than usual as he took a seat across from Sam.

"Mark! How are you doing?"

"Good and bad," he replied, smiling warmly.

"Okay. Tell me about the good."

"Well, ah, Sharon came by earlier and she says they may have found out that someone hacked my computer system to frame me. They have a lot of work to do to prove it, and then they have to find out who did it, but there's a good chance I was framed.

"And if that weren't good enough, I had another visit from that Detective, Mike McKensey, and he told me that he has some leads. He's pretty convinced I didn't do this and while he said it's unfortunate we have to prove my innocence, he had very little doubt that we would. That's the good news. I'm actually feeling hopeful for a change and I'm looking forward to my life after I get out of here. And deep inside, I know I'm going to get past this."

"Mark, that's great news. You look more relaxed than I've ever seen you. So, I almost hate to ask. What's the bad?"

Mark's face darkened. His brow furrowed and he responded soberly.

"Sam, I've been having a lot of dreams, nightmares, really. They're all about my mother. But what's really weird is that during the daytime, I not only remember the dreams, but they seem to be turning into real memories. Do you think they're real or just dreams that I'm beginning to think are real?"

"I don't know, Mark. Sometimes dreams are messages from our subconscious that are metaphors for things we need to know or learn. Sometimes, they're memories that are cast a bit differently.

"Why don't you tell me about some of these dreams, how they make you feel, and which ones seem to be triggering memories. As you've seen in some of our sessions, talking about dreams often takes away their impact and may help you get some clarity on what your subconscious is trying to tell you.

"Start with the scariest one and let's go from there."

Mark took a deep breath, closed his eyes, and started describing a dream.

"In my dream, I'm just a little kid, maybe three or four years old. My mother is screaming at me, calling me names, blaming me for ruining her life. Then she grabs me by my hair and the back of my pants and shakes me, continuing to scream. She tucks me under her arm, opens a closet and throws me inside head first. My head hits the back wall of the closet. I'm crying. I'm saying over and over, 'Sorry momma, sorry momma. Please let me out. Please let me out.' But she doesn't. I spend what seems like an eternity in the darkness. Eventually I stop crying and try to fall asleep. I guess I do because when I wake up I really have to pee. 'Momma, let me out. I have to go pee-pee'.

But she doesn't let me out. I try to hold it but I wet myself. I don't know how long I'm in the closet. My mother finally comes and when she sees that I've wet myself, she starts screaming at me, saying I'm disgusting. Disgusting. She drags me to the bathroom and puts me in a cold shower, telling me to take off my clothes and clean myself up. She comes back, pulls me out of the shower and brings my face close. If you ever tell your father about this, I will kill you. I promise. I will KILL you. Then she throws me on the floor and I wake up."

Sam took a deep breath. She suspected something like this.

"So Mark, is this one of the dreams that's becoming a memory?"

"Mark shook his head back and forth. For a moment, Sam thought he was going to say no. But instead he started nodding.

"Yes. But now as I think back, I have vague memories of other times. I think this continued for several years, probably until I was too big for her to pick up and throw around.

"But what's worse is that other parts of the memories are coming back. I remember – or maybe I just think I remember – that when she started screaming at me, she chased me with a metal coat hanger."

"A metal coat hanger!?"

"Yes! I'd try to run away but she'd catch me. She'd pull down my pants, bend me over a chair and start hitting me with the hanger. After she was tired or I started to bleed, she'd tell me to pull up my pants and then it would be the closet again.

"Sam, all of my dreams include the closet. I'm locked in the dark for hours. I cry. I plead. And I usually wet myself. When my mother comes, she says I should be ashamed of myself. Ashamed. You know, Janice used to say the same thing in my hallucinations. She said I was disgusting. She said I should be ashamed of myself. She called me worthless."

And Mark broke into tears.

Handing Mark a box of tissues, Sam waited patiently. Progress. Great progress, indeed!

8

Sharon Katell welcomed Miguel and Janey into her office. They were both carrying loaded backpacks along with what appeared to be large document cases.

"You must be Janey Gray,' she said warmly. "I've heard a lot about you. And it's good to see you again, Miguel."

"Yeah, you too," Miguel responded. "It's been a while. Where can we set up?"

Not in the least put off by Miguel's lack of pleasantries, Sharon was equally direct, "I have a conference room all set up for you. We moved in a small fridge and a coffeemaker as well as plenty of healthy and unhealthy snacks. Follow me."

On the table of the conference room was what appeared to be Mark Johansen's computer.

Miguel and Janey gave each other knowing smiles.

"Ms. Katell, I've read a lot about you. You've had a very impressive career," Janey began. "Sometime I'd like to hear more about it if you have time, but right now it appears that we need to get moving on this quickly."

"Unfortunately, you're right. The preliminary hearing is coming up next week and unless you guys find something exculpatory, I've got the fight of my life, and Mark Johansen's life, on my hands.

"I'll let you get to it."

Miguel opened one of the cases and pulled out what appeared to be a duplicate of Mark's computer. Then the two engineers set to work replicating Mark's system, so that they could preserve the police copy in case they needed to start over. Almost two hours later, they were ready to start.

Miguel loaded the software provided by the informant and they ran the test to see if Unbreakable's Trojan was on the system. And, it turned out that it was.

Next it was Janey's turn. She loaded the tool that accessed the logs from the system. But it didn't work.

They created a virtual connection to the internet, attempting to fool the Unbreakable Trojan into waking up and capturing data, and then to send it out, but this proved more complicated than expected. They had to scaffold several other pieces of software and it was several hours before they actually fooled the code into attempting to send something.

"Aha!" Janey shouted enthusiastically. "Gotcha!"

Unlike other systems they'd looked at, this Unbreakable code was logging data to a different hidden location on the system. Janey decided to take a closer look at the code through her debugger and discovered that there were substantial differences between this code and the Unbreakable Trojan that had been found on all the other systems. Still, the informant's tool had spotted the code so clearly they were related. As she dug deeper, Janey discovered that it wasn't just the logging. The mechanisms for encoding the outgoing messages were different as was the destination.

She and Miguel decided to try to track the destination. Given that the messages were piggybacked and that they were split and sent through multiple zombie servers this was a daunting task. They divided up the work and didn't look up until there was a knock at the conference room door and Sharon Katell came in.

"Good Morning!"

"Morning?" Janey and Miguel said simultaneously.

"I guess you guys have been working all night. Do you have anything for me?

"Go ahead," Miguel suggested to Janey.

"Well, first of all, we don't have a final answer. Obviously we lost track of time. The adrenaline just wore off for me and I realize that I'm tired. I suspect I'm not doing my best work right now."

Looking over at her partner, she saw that Miguel was exhausted.

"Anyway, we have some news. It's incomplete and I'm not sure how much it will help, but we did find the code we were looking for on the system."

"That's great!" Sharon replied enthusiastically. "That means someone could have hacked Mark's system. Did you find out if they did? Is it this suspect you can't tell me about?"

"From the logs, I can see that someone did hack the system. They did visit sites from another system and they sent emails from this system. So, there's a chance that Mark is being framed."

"What do you mean, 'a chance'? Doesn't this prove that Mark has been framed?"

"I don't know. We have a problem. Until we dove into the code, we thought that if we found the Trojan on this system it would belong to that suspect we can't tell you about. That would be pretty definitive proof – no one else has the code. Hence, he or she is guilty of framing Mark. Unfortunately, it's not the same code. It's very similar, but it's not the same. And, where it sends and receives information is different. That means someone else put the code on Mark's system, not the person we've been looking at so far. That means it's even possible that Mark put the code on the system himself."

"Oh shit!" Sharon exclaimed, disappointed. "So where do we go from here?"

"We need to track down where the data was sent and where it came from. That's what we've been doing for several hours. So far no luck. Miguel?"

"Me neither. I'm running out of things to chase. Maybe I'm just too tired."

Sharon looked at the exhausted pair.

"Guys, go home. Get some rest. Sleep and take a shower. Sometimes the best ideas arrive under steaming water. You can pick this up tonight or tomorrow. I'll give you both the security code so you can get in anytime you need to.

"You've done a great job so far. We do know that someone likely hacked Mark's computer and framed him. It's something we can show the police. Granted the DA may argue that Mark could have planted it, but I can use it to at least plant a little doubt and even if you don't come up with anything more, it should be enough to get the police to finally look at other suspects.

"Of course, if you find the source, and the real guilty party, you'll have saved an innocent man. No pressure."

Seeing that her joke fell flat, Sharon changed course.

"Sorry about that. My attempt at humor was misplaced. You guys are wasted. Go home, rest, know that you've helped tremendously, and that I really appreciate all the work you've done. Because of you, we finally have a chance!"

9

Janey had taken two days off work so she could focus on working with Miguel to find the person who framed Mark Johansen. Two days of non-stop work and they'd come up empty. The paths through the Net were just too complex to follow. Janey and Miguel were trying to brainstorm different strategies when Janey's phone rang.

"Hi George," Janey answered. "What's up?"

"Janey!" George responded excitedly. "Mike McKensey wants to meet with us as soon as possible. Can you and Miguel be here by 11?"

"Sure. Do you know what it's about?"

"No. He wouldn't say anything over the phone, but I think he has a lead."

"We'll be there."

At 11am, Joyce led Mike McKensey into the Alcatraz conference room where Morris, George, Miguel, Sharon Katell, and Janey were anxiously waiting.

Seeing anticipation on all their faces, Mike decided to lower their expectations a bit.

"Guys, first of all good morning. Miguel and Janey, Sharon has kept me up to date on your progress and on the fact that you're kind of stuck.

"I don't have anything solid, but after my interviews of Jack Trageser, Richard Hatch, Brittany Spangler, and a few others, I may have a lead. It will be up to you to see if you can prove that my suspicions are correct."

Just then, Janey's phone played an unusual sound.

"Sorry everyone. I hate to interrupt, but I need to look at something."

She opened her computer and typed furiously for a few moments.

"Again, I'm really sorry about this, but George could you check your email to see if you've received a message from the informant and whether he used y3pnzw5mp7uz as his name and email address?"

George looked puzzled. He excused himself and returned with his laptop.

"You're right. There's an email here from the informant and

he did identify himself as y3pn whatever. How did you know?"

"My bot got a hit."

Everyone turned towards Janey.

"Your bot got a hit?" Miguel queried, wide-eyed.

"Ah, yeah. A few months ago, I developed a bot to try to spot usage of the name generation, routing, and encryption software used by the killer and by the informant that was sending the messages to George. I just got a hit and I suspected he or she was emailing George."

George opened the email and read it.

From: y3pnzw5mp7uz <y3pnzw5mp7uz@y3pnzw5mp7uz.com>
Date: January 29, 20XX 05:31 AM PDT
To: George Gray <GeorgeGray@nysentinel.com>
Subject: Another Bad Guy for you

Greetings George,

I haven't seen any articles about Marcus Jameson or Unbreakable so I suspect between the Sentinel and the FBI, you either aren't going to publish anything or the FBI has a lid on you until they wrap up their case. That makes sense to me.

So, in the meantime, just so you're not lacking for an interesting story to write, I thought I'd give you one more. You should be able to publish this one as soon as you verify my information.

Mary Canter runs playcardswithyourfriends.com. It looks innocuous enough. People sign up and can connect to other members to play a variety of card games online – Cribbage, Hearts, Bridge, and many more, even Go Fish. The site appears to make its money through advertising and Mary Canter has done quite well with it. But as you probably expect based on our history, there's a darker side.

Based on profiles and playing patterns, the site targets specific individuals who appear to be addicted to risk. Selected players are contacted through the dark web through many layers of security to invite them into illegal illicit gambling activities. Many of these people have lost their life savings just from the gambling alone.

But what's worse is that Mary Canter has connections into organized crime. The wealthier victims who pursue some of the more morally questionable games, including bets on life or death games, violent sexual games, and outcomes of criminal activities are blackmailed. And they pay.

Attached are files showing how one of my fictitious personas started on her legitimate site, was then recruited onto the dark web, and was finally blackmailed after it pursued some very nasty gambling activities. I have also attached contact information for one of the victims who was ruined.

Once again, this person would like to remain anonymous until Mary Canter and her associates are under arrest, but he will come forward with his story.

Have fun with this one George. I'll be in touch.

y3pnzw5mp7uz

After reading it, George turned to Morris and asked, "Can I show this to everyone? I know you wanted to keep Sharon out of the loop on the previous mogul the informant gave me, but since Janey and Miguel have cleared him of framing Mark, it shouldn't matter, right?"

"Sorry George. The FBI has asked that no one know about that investigation. You understand the potential repercussions. Can you make a copy of the email and delete those unacceptable references?"

"Sure."

When he was finished, George connected to the projector in the room and everyone read the redacted email. Then they all turned towards Janey who was so excited she could hardly stay in her seat.

"So Janey," George began. "It's great that you have a lead on the informant, but what does that have to do with Mark Johansen?"

"Miguel, could you look over my shoulder?"

Miguel positioned himself next to Janey as everyone else tried to stand behind her.

It wouldn't have mattered. Janey's fingers flew across the keyboard as window after window appeared and disappeared. No one, except Miguel, had the faintest idea what was going on.

When she finally stopped, she moved the current window to the side and set another next to it. Miguel whistled.

"Wow!" he exclaimed, clearly excited. "Janey, you've done it. Your bot's info traversed exactly the same path as the one on Mark Jameson's computer. It's the same person. Whoever sent George this latest email framed Mark Johansen. Now we just have to find him or her and – oh. There's still one problem. How did that person get the software that looks almost identical to the others we've seen?"

"I have an idea about that too," Janey replied enigmatically.

"And, as I started to say when I walked in," Mike McKensey interrupted. I have a pretty good idea who did it and quite frankly, this confirms it for me."

10

Sharon Katell waited impatiently in the conference room reserved for attorney-client conversations. The guards led Mark into the room and left. Mark looked more relaxed and confident that he ever had, at least since his arrest.

"Mark!" Sharon exclaimed, pulling him close for a hug. "You look, well, great."

"I feel good," Mark replied. "Sam and I have had what I call breakthroughs but which she conservatively calls excellent progress. As rare as it is and as surprising as it sounds, I may be one of those rare lucky late-onset schizophrenia patients who can actually be cured."

"I always thought of you as a rare person, Mark," Sharon joked.

"Well, it looks like I'm not the only one who seems remarkably happy. Good news I hope?"

"I think so. But first I have to ask you a couple of questions about Johatchen, particularly the early days."

"Sure. What do you want to know?"

"First, keep in mind that my techie skills are limited to email and navigating browsers. I've seen VPNs and run anti-virus software on my computers, but I've left the details to my IT staff. So be gentle.

"Did Johatchen ever develop a Trojan that would snoop on a system and return confidential information via an untraceable path?"

"Ah, Sharon, how would you know about that?"

"Just tell me about it."

"Well, as you know, Johatchen provides a suite of security software. Its job is to scan incoming information and protect outgoing information. We are also constantly scanning the system for viruses, Trojans, and malware.

"Most security software identifies and blocks existing, known attacks. Ours does too. But what differentiates us from most of our competitors is that our software looks for anomalies in the system. Not just background programs or zombies, but things that just aren't right.

"Because we were hoping our software would spot new, unknown attacks, but had no real way to test it, since obviously, those attacks hadn't happened yet, we split into two teams. I, along with a small part of our team, developed our own very nasty, virtually untraceable Trojan. We challenged our main development team to find it and remove it. It took quite a while, and quite frankly I had to give some hints, but eventually, they nailed it. It exists in our product today, which, all modesty aside, I think is the best security product suite on the market."

Sharon nodded, deep in thought.

"Did you guys have any significant financial problems when you first started?"

"Of course. All startups have financial problems. Fortunately, I had Richard. He took care of making sure we had enough operating capital. And he did a great job. We wouldn't be where we are today if it weren't for Richard's astute financial management.

"That confirms my suspicions."

"Okay. You've got me. Spill!"

11

"Mike! To what do I owe the pleasure? Did you finally figure out that Mark isn't a serial killer? Did you find the real culprit?

"Yes. I think we have. What I don't understand is how you could have done this to your best friend and business partner. You guys have been together for years."

"What do you mean, how could I have done this? Aren't you arresting Marcus Jameson for the murders?"

"Marcus Jameson is under indictment for a number of other crimes. But you should have been aware of that. After all, you're the one who told George Gray about Jameson's Trojan."

"Okay. I admit it. I'm George Gray's source. We've done some great work together. We've helped rid the Internet of a hate-mongering conspiracy theorist, a massive human trafficking organization, and a power-hungry corrupt blackmailer who was prepared to manipulate our financial and political system to his own ends. George is also starting to chase down a woman who ensnares people into sordid gambling ventures and then blackmails them. We've made the world a much better place. Wouldn't you agree?"

"Yes. There's no doubt about it. You've done some great things. You've had a major impact. If I look at your career, you built a company that helps protect people and their information. You've been a huge success by any standard. And, you've paid back by going after these scumbags.

"What I don't get is why you murdered these women and why you tried to frame Mark."

"What makes you think I'm the murderer?

Mike handed Richard Hatch the search warrant he'd brought with him. Two officers came into the room and handcuffed Richard. Mike read him his rights.

"But no. It wasn't me. It was Marcus Jameson. He hacked into Mark's computer and tried to frame him. I'm the good guy in this story!"

Steve Jackowski

EPILOGUE

"You write your life story by the choices you make. You never
know if they have been a mistake."
- Helen Mirren

1

The FBI raided the offices of Unbreakable Security Systems and Marcus Jameson was arrested and charged with extortion, money laundering, and securities fraud.

Because the Trojan was embedded in all of Unbreakable's software, the company was enjoined from selling their products. The engineers scrambled to find a way to remove the Trojan from the software, but by the time they succeeded, the company was suffering. As news of their CEO's arrest spread, and as customer support faltered, customers worldwide began to move to other security products. Within a year, Unbreakable was broken.

George Gray broke the story of Marcus Jameson's arrest but made no mention of the Trojan. Instead, this story became one more example of corruption by some of the biggest names in high tech. With the subsequent arrest of Mary Canter and FBI seizure of playcardswithyourfriends.com, George became known as a crusader against Internet corruption. That, along with his continuing series on human trafficking made George one of the most well-known and respected journalists in the country. George wasn't quite prepared to deal with his new-found notoriety.

He dropped by Morris' office just before lunch as Morris had requested. They took the elevator to the lobby and began what George thought would be one of their standard walks. But when they turned south onto Kearney Street, George knew something was up.

They continued in silence until Morris directed them onto Claude Lane, home to one of San Francisco's best French restaurants, Café Claude. Morris had brought George here on his first day at the Sentinel and he and Janey had joined Morris and his French wife Martine here for dinner once about a year before.

"*Bonjour Monsieur Levinberg!*"

"*Bonjour Pierre, vous allez bien?*" replied Morris in what to George sounded like perfect French.

"*Oui. Tres bien, merci. Et vous, ça va?*"

"*Pas mal. Pas mal du tout.*"

"*Suivez-moi. Votre table est prête.*"

Once seated, Pierre turned to George and, in perfect accent-less English, asked if he'd like anything to drink. George ordered sparkling water and Morris nodded. Pierre suggested a bottle which they gladly accepted. He returned moments later and poured each a glass of crystal clear bubbling liquid.

"I'll be back shortly to take your orders."

Morris turned to George.

"Your work the last several months has been remarkable, George. You've had more earth-shaking stories in this short period than most reporters see in their entire careers. Not only have you helped identify individuals who were using the Internet for criminal purposes, you're largely responsible for the arrest of two murderers. And to top it off, your series on human trafficking has brought us more readers and has saved countless people trapped in slavery. It really is quite remarkable."

George couldn't help blushing at the over-the-top praise.

"I couldn't have done it without a lot of help. There was the informant, Mike McKensey, Miguel, Janey, and of course you and the staff who helped me with my research."

"George, I appreciate the modesty, but realistically, none of this would have happened without you. You deserve the credit. And you need to know that upper management, including Sterling Rockwell, has commended you and recommended you for a promotion."

"A promotion? What kind of promotion?"

"Well George, that's kind of up to you. The first question I have to ask is do you have any interest in management? If not, do you have any interest in running a desk – having a group of reporters submitting their stories to you which you review, and then decide which get published?"

"Ah, I don't know Morris. I had a few people working with me on the trafficking series, but a desk? That sounds like a lot of responsibility. Let me think about it."

With a pause in the conversation, Morris nodded at Pierre who approached to take their order.

They decided to share the Moules a la Provencal, steamed mussels in a hard cider, olive, tomato, saffron stew as an appetizer. George ordered the Casserole de Champignon, which consisted of Farro, trumpet mushroom, kale and broccolini, while Morris chose the Confit de Canard, crispy duck with lentils.

The Moules arrived and Morris decided to change the subject.

"So how's Janey doing? I understand she and Miguel put in some crazy hours solving the murder case. I mean, Miguel gets paid for this but Janey?"

"Don't worry Morris. She said it was the most fun she'd had in years. She's completely enthralled that she applied her skills to catch a serial murderer. She says it's much more exciting than developing software."

"Do you think she'd give up developing software?"

"Not likely. It looks like her company is about to go public. I'm sure she'll be there for a while, but she might have a lot more time to pursue things like this."

"Well, she's certainly good at it."

"She's good at everything. How's Martine?"

"Actually, she's in France right now visiting family. I was hoping to go, but things got a bit crazy. She's due back this weekend."

They chatted for a few more minutes, finishing their appetizer. Pierre arrived with their main courses and wished them, "*Bon continuation!*"

Before taking a bite, George looked up at Morris.

"Morris, I really didn't need to think about it. I love what I do and I just don't see myself managing people or even leading a team at this point in my career. I hope you're not too disappointed."

"Not at all, George. Management was pushing me to make that offer. I want you to keep doing the magic that you do. Plus, I seem to be getting your wife in the bargain. The Sentinel couldn't do better.

"So, given your decision, I can offer you a promotion to Senior Correspondent. Effective today, you've got a pretty substantial raise, and here. This is from Sterling Rockwell in appreciation of the work you've done."

Morris handed George an envelope. George opened it and couldn't believe his eyes. The check was huge.

"Morris, I don't know what to say. Thanks!"

"George, you're more than welcome. But now we should talk about your career a bit."

"But I thought we'd agreed that I'd be continuing with what I've been doing."

"Of course you will. At least here at the Sentinel. I'm talking about your novels."

"Morris, you know very well that I'm not working on any novels."

"George, you should be. I know you struggled with the Michael James story, but with all that's happened, you have more than enough material for several novels. Don't you?"

George thought about it briefly, reflecting on the past months. "I guess I do. I guess I do."

2

Samantha Louis looked out her second story office window above Haight Street in San Francisco and watched Mark Johansen drive away in his brand new galaxy blue metallic Audi etron. As he turned the corner, sunlight seemed to change the color of the car as reflections of dark teal shimmered on the surface of the exotic vehicle.

Mark had spent their last session evangelizing electric cars and even convinced Sam to drive his new EV. He loved the fact that he could drive wherever he wanted without adding to the world's climate problems. He was so convinced that electric was the answer that he had installed charging stations at his offices and was encouraging his employees to give up their gas guzzling polluting ICE vehicles with a thousand dollar bonus if they bought an electric car. He'd explained to Sam that ICE stood for Internal Combustion Engine and that in his opinion, this was now obsolete technology.

Sam had to admit, the silence and power of the Audi was impressive. And when she asked about charging on longer trips, Mark patiently explained that the Audi could add nearly two hundred miles in twenty minutes of charging. If the technology had come that far, Sam would seriously consider replacing her ten-year-old Subaru with an EV.

But as far as Mark's case was concerned, their work together was done. They'd just had their final session together. Sam knew it was coming. Mark had made fantastic progress and now seemed to be 'normal'. By any standard, he was cured of his mental illness – a condition that had threatened his career and his relationships. It had aggravated the murder case brought against him.

As much as she tried to convince herself to be proud of her success, Sam couldn't help but feel a sense of loss. This was the case of a lifetime. Weirdly, it was her second case of a lifetime. Much like the previous one, her mentor, Dr. Ken Karmere, hadn't seen another schizophrenic patient cured in his entire thirty-plus year career.

What were the chances Sam would ever see a case like this again?

So here she was, thirty-eight years old, almost three years into her private practice, still not quite making enough money to quit her part-time job at the inpatient facility of San Francisco Community Hospital. But she had to admit, she was happy with her career choice.

Sam stepped into the small shared bathroom outside her office and examined herself in the mirror. There were a few more strands of gray starting to show, but she was not at all unhappy with her appearance. If anything, she seemed less stressed than she had been several months before. She looked – content.

Her buzzer sounded and she opened her office door to find a smiling Jack Trageser obviously excited about their evening out.

"Come in while I shut down my system and put away a couple of files."

Jack took a seat in the recliner and watched as Sam worked. She was smart, beautiful, and it finally seemed like she was ready for a real relationship.

As they stepped outside into the chilly winter evening, Jack put his arm around Sam and she moved in close, reveling in the warmth. Jack drove sedately through the busy San Francisco streets and pulled into Fort Mason. Green's was on the agenda again. Jack had called it a restart.

They were seated next to a floor-to-ceiling glass window that looked out on the Bay towards Alcatraz and the Golden Gate Bridge. If possible, the night was even more beautiful than the previous one.

"So, Mark is cured? Isn't that kind of unheard of for a patient suffering from schizophrenia?"

"Unheard of, no. Rare? Absolutely. Mark's case was unusual, and he did some major work. I feel very lucky."

"I suspect it was a bit more than luck. You're good at what you do. Are you a bit sad to see him go? I mean, when I finish a project, particularly when a new product goes out the door, I feel like I've lost something. Is it similar with patients?"

"Yes. I guess it is. It's weird. I've had two cases of a lifetime, the kinds of cases my mentor, Doctor Ken Karmere, has never seen in his entire thirty-plus-year career.

"Part of it is seeing the patients I've come to know so well move on. But the other part is thinking how exciting these cases have been and how unlikely it is I'll have anything like it again."

"Well, Brittany Spangler has told me you're treating her for Borderline Personality Disorder. Maybe this will be your next big case."

"You know I can't talk about my patients, but I can tell you that unlike schizophrenia, where there are rare examples of cures, as far as I know, with BPD, there's never been a cure."

"And you don't think you could be the first?"

"No. Not a chance."

"You should be proud of yourself. Mark has his life back and if you want my opinion, he's better than ever. Plus, I think he and Sharon may have something more going."

"I guess I am proud of myself with respect to Mark – at least as far as his schizophrenia is concerned. Not so much with the murders. Don't get me wrong. I was convinced he wasn't a murderer. But I thought I could play police detective and that was a big mistake. I'm truly sorry."

"You really suspected me, didn't you?"

"I don't know if 'suspected' is the right word. I was scared. Not about being murdered, but afraid of getting into a relationship. I think I was looking for any excuse to try to avoid losing control of my life."

"And you've changed your mind?"

Sam reached across the table and took Jack's hand. "Absolutely!"

They looked out at the shimmering lights on the Bay and Sam broke the silence.

"Jack, I know that Mark was proven not guilty and that it was Richard who broke into Mark's computer to frame him, but I don't think I understand the whole story. Can you explain it to me?"

"Yeah. It took me a while to fully understand it. As you know, Richard and Mark's company sells security software. Back when they were just starting out, Mark decided that he wanted to do more than create standard anti-virus software that blocked known attacks. He wanted to recognize attacks that had never been seen before. He created a Trojan, software that hides in your system and does nefarious things. He then challenged his team to find it. It took them a while, but they got their software to work and within a few years became the number two supplier of security software. Mark put the Trojan on the shelf and forgot about it.

"But like most startups, well before they saw success, they had financial issues. Richard, who had followed the team's work and was no slouch as an engineer, raised a big chunk of change by selling the Trojan to Unbreakable, the largest player in the security market. Richard is a shrewd businessman who knew he could raise a lot of money and at the same time keep an eye on his biggest competitor.

"When I found out that Richard was the murderer, I couldn't understand how he could frame his best friend. I mean I've known these guys for years and they've been more like brothers than business partners. It just didn't make sense.

"After talking to the detective on the case and to George Gray, I realized that this was a big competitive play. Richard was going to bring down his biggest competitor by ruining his company and by framing him for murder. He knew that Marcus Jameson, CEO of Unbreakable was using the Trojan to gather information so that he could blackmail people to gain financial and political influence.

"He put the Trojan on Mark's system and framed Mark, but then he revealed the existence of Jameson's Trojan to George Gray. He knew that eventually, the Trojan would be found on Mark's system and it would be clear that Jameson had framed Mark.

"Unfortunately, George Gray's wife Janey is one of the world's best hackers. She figured out that the data entering and leaving Mark's system was not going to Jameson. She didn't know where, but Jameson was in the clear on that count, and so was Mark. Between some additional work that's too technical to explain, and the work by Detective McKensey, they found Richard."

"But did he need to murder these women? I have to say that I don't understand why he did it."

"Richard is an interesting guy. From what George Gray told me, Richard gave him the stories about Boris Yanofski and his conspiracy theories, Ryan Hamilton and the human trafficking, and perhaps the worst of all, Marcus Jameson. He was a real force for finding criminals who have corrupted the Internet and bringing them to justice.

"But, and I hate to bring this topic up again since it caused us some problems, Richard hated women. You know that Mark, Richard, and I were very tight with Michael James and Marshall Lewis. When Richard saw what Ashima and Julia did, and then what Janice did to Mark, well, he felt that they were criminals much like the others but who couldn't be stopped by law enforcement. In his mind, it was morally right to rid the world of these evil women. And although he would never admit it, his own wife leaving him was probably a big trigger."

"Okay, I hear what you're saying about him hating women. And I guess I understand the technical side of how he framed Mark and how he thought he had set up Marcus Jameson. But what I don't get is how he could have sent his best friend to jail."

"That bothered me too. So, I actually visited Richard yesterday and asked him. The answer goes a bit deeper into Richard and his motivation in killing Janice Johansen. After what she did to Mark, even more so than the others, Richard believed that he needed to rid the world of Janice. In his warped sense of duty, he felt that not only was killing her revenge for what she'd done to Mark, it would help Mark get better if Janice were no longer on the planet. As for the sending him to jail, he knew that if Janice were murdered, Mark would be arrested. He was too obvious a suspect. So, as strange as it might sound, he orchestrated it so that Mark could be completely exonerated. Somehow, he got the impression that a month or two in jail wouldn't hurt Mark or his recovery.

"I'll never believe that murder is the right answer, but I can certainly understand where Richard was coming from. In his mind he had the best intentions in all that he did, exposing bad guys and eliminating those that go unpunished. He's a good man, and a bad one."

After sharing a decadent dessert and sipping glasses of port, Jack drove Sam home.

"We're still on for rowing on the Bay tomorrow morning, right?' Jack asked, hoping he hadn't gone in the wrong direction again. "What time should I pick you up?"

Sam turned her face up to Jack, pulled him close and gave him what Jack thought was a languorous kiss good night. Then, taking his hand, she said, "You can just nudge me in the morning."

ABOUT THE AUTHOR

Writer, extreme sports enthusiast, serial entrepreneur, technologist.

Born into a military family, Steve traveled extensively throughout the US and overseas, attending fifteen schools before graduating from High School. After studying mathematics, computer science, comparative literature and French at the University of California, Steve began his career with IBM as a software engineer. He later founded three successful high-tech startups.

A former competition hang glider pilot, Steve continues to surf, ski, kayak whitewater, play disc golf, and dance Salsa with his wife Karen whenever possible.

Steve divides his time between Santa Cruz, California and the Basque Region of France.

Find out more about Steve, his extreme sports, his interests, and his other novels at:

http://www.stevejackowski.com

And check out his blog on entrepreneurship, technology, electric cars, and travel in Europe (especially France and Spain) at:

http://www.stevejackowski.com/blog

CPSIA information can be obtained
at www.ICGtesting.com
Printed in the USA
LVHW042150111019
633942LV00003B/337